BREAKING FREE

A Colorado High Country/I-Team Crossover
Novel

PAMELA CLARE

BREAKING
FREE

PAMELA
CLARE

Breaking Free
A Colorado High Country/I-Team Crossover Novel

Published by Pamela Clare, 2021

Cover Design by © Jaycee DeLorenzo/Sweet 'N Spicy Designs
Image: fotorince74

Copyright © 2021 by Pamela Clare

This book is dedicated to my younger son Benjamin Alexander and his fiancée Courtney Peterson in the year of their wedding. May the years ahead be filled with joy, and may your love grow ever stronger. I love you both.

Acknlowledgements

Many thanks to Michelle White, Benjamin Alexander, Jackie Turner, and Shell Ryan during the writing of this book. Heading into this story after a long recovery from a difficult surgery was hard. I couldn't have done this without you.

This story is for the fans of my I-Team and Scarlet Springs series. I hope you love Win and Jason together as much as I do.

Chapter 1

West of Genesee, Colo.
Sept. 17

JASON CHIAGO PULLED his Ford F-450 to the side of the highway, climbed out into the cool September evening, and took in the stunning beauty around him. White-capped peaks stretched as far as he could see, disappearing in an orange-pink haze to the west, the valley below him golden with aspen.

It was enough to put a hitch in his chest.

He'd never been to Colorado. He'd grown up in the Sonoran Desert in Sells, Arizona, the heart of the Tohono O'odham Nation. After high school, he'd gone to college in Phoenix to study criminal justice, working construction jobs in the heat of the summer. Apart from his training at the US Customs and Border Patrol Academy in Artesia, New Mexico, he'd never left Arizona.

He loved the beauty of his desert homeland with its sacred peaks, springs, and giant saguaros. Some people thought the desert was a wasteland. But they didn't see what he saw—the explosion of life after a spring rain, prickly pear and cholla ripe with fruit, hummingbirds drinking from saguaro blossoms, the first rosy rays of sunlight hitting Baboquivari Peak.

But this...

This blew his mind.

Whose homeland was this? The Cheyenne? The Arapaho? The Ute? He ought to know, but he didn't.

An SUV with Texas plates pulled up, and a family of tourists climbed out and began snapping selfies with the mountains and sunset in the background. Another vehicle drew to a stop behind them, this one from Arkansas.

Jason didn't take photos but inhaled the scents of aspen, fir, and pine, doing his best to breathe in the view, to imprint every detail in his mind. Then a teenager from one of the vehicles loosed a drone into the sky, its buzzing an unwelcome disruption. Jason climbed back into his truck, started the engine, and headed down the highway.

He was on his way to the home of a friend, Zach McBride, the chief deputy US marshal for the Colorado Territory. He'd met McBride when the man was assigned to the US-Mexico border about ten years ago. Jason had taught him as much as he could about cutting sign in one short week. When McBride had heard Jason was knee-deep in shit, he'd invited him to come camp with him above a small mountain town called Scarlet Springs and join him and other volunteers in rebuilding a summer camp for Native kids that had burned to the ground this past July.

You've got nothing else going on, buddy.

That was the truth.

A year ago, he'd been about to marry Elena and had

2

just gotten a promotion. Now, Elena was in prison, and he was on the brink of losing his job.

It's the choices we make and the twists and turns on our journey through life's maze that make us who we are.

Jason could almost hear his grandmother's voice. But this didn't feel like a twist in the road. It felt like the loss of everything he'd worked for, as if the past sixteen years of his life were coming to a dead end.

One month's administrative leave without pay.

He'd gone too far. He knew it. Still, he couldn't bring himself to regret it, not when it meant a drug-runner wouldn't kill again. He *was* sorry that the fallout of his actions had left his fellow Shadow Wolves shorthanded.

The Wolves, an all-Native Border Patrol unit, were his brothers. A team of only fifteen, they didn't have the number of agents they needed to patrol the line—the 76-mile stretch of border that divided sovereign O'odham lands in the States from those in Mexico. With him on leave and Ren still recovering from that round to the belly, their job would be even more difficult and dangerous.

You should have stayed on the US side of the line.

Yeah, he should have. But the bastard who'd shot Ren would have gotten away if he hadn't crossed over and gone after him. And, hey, land on *both* sides of the line belonged to Jason's people. He had a greater right to be there than either US or Mexican authorities.

Tell that to the brass at your hearing.

A herd of mountain goats grazed beside the highway, one of them stepping toward the road before changing its mind and turning back.

Jason slowed. "Good choice, little brother."

The GPS told Jason to take the next exit and follow a winding, paved road south for another three miles. He had expected a city neighborhood. Instead, he found himself passing big, luxurious homes that were set back from the road and surrounded by forest with lots of space between. The house ahead on his left had glass walls, while the one on the right had a row of columns along the porch like a Greek temple.

No, that wasn't ostentatious at all.

McBride had clearly done well for himself if he lived in this neighborhood. Then again, his old man had once been a US senator and was loaded.

As a teenager, Jason would have been bitter, envious. He'd caught glimpses of the world beyond the reservation, and he'd felt ashamed of his family's circumstances. It was his grandparents who'd taught him O'odham history. After his parents' deaths, they'd taken him in. They'd shown him the riches to be found in their culture and traditions, straightening him out, putting his feet on a sure path.

Hell, he might not even be here if not for them.

"The destination is on your right."

Jason turned onto a paved driveway and found himself outside a sprawling, one-story house made of native flagstone with lots of floor-to-ceiling windows. He knew the house also had a pool and a Jacuzzi because McBride had told him to bring a suit.

He parked, climbed out, and grabbed his duffel bag from the back just as McBride stepped outside, his wife Natalie standing in the doorway, their little boy, Aiden, beside her. Jason bit back a grin. The first time he'd seen McBride and Natalie together, they'd been on O'odham land, naked and having sex.

No, he'd never told McBride.

"Hey, man, what's up?" McBride clasped Jason's hand in a homie handshake and clapped him on the shoulder.

"Good to see you, man. Hey, Natalie. Hey, little buddy."

"You hungry? Let's get some steaks on the grill. I'll grab you a beer."

"Sounds good to me." Jason followed him inside.

———

Scarlet Springs

WINONA BELCOURT WOKE WITH A START, heart hammering, a scream trapped in her throat. She threw back her covers, sat up, and looked around her, her blood like ice. She was safe in her bedroom, safe in her own home.

It was just a bad dream.

She drew a deep breath, did her best to let go of the nightmare, terrifying images of John Charles Ready sharp in her mind. It had been five years ago this past summer, but in her dreams, it always felt like it was happening again.

He's dead. It's over. You're safe.

She repeated the words in her mind until her heartbeat slowed.

It wasn't quite six o'clock, the sun not yet up. She'd set her alarm for six anyway, so she got up, walked into the kitchen, and lit the sage bundle she kept in the middle of the table. Wafting the smoke over herself, she thanked Creator for another day, the sage purifying her, cleansing her of the nightmare.

She took a hot shower, the water reviving her, washing the dregs of her nightmare away. She put her towel-dried hair into a French braid, her gaze on her reflection. There were dark circles beneath her eyes, but she'd never worn makeup and had no idea what to do about it. With her hair braided, she slipped into her bathrobe and made herself a cup of coffee, sipping while looking out her kitchen window.

She'd bought this house not long after her older brother, Chaska, had married Naomi, moving out of the home she and Chaska had once shared. Grandpa Belcourt now slept in her old bedroom when he was visiting from Pine Ridge, while she lived around the corner next door to her clinic. While there were good things about living in her own space—like having a bathroom and all the hot water to herself—she found it hard to be alone at night. That's when the fear and the nightmares crept up on her.

If Shota had still been here, nothing would have scared her. But Shota's enclosure stood empty, its tall fence just visible beyond her back gate. It had broken Winona's heart to let him go. Still, it had been best for him, and that's what mattered. He was now where he was meant to be, running wild at a sanctuary with other wolves.

She finished her coffee and dressed in jeans, a T-shirt, and a button-down denim shirt she'd borrowed from her brother a few years ago. She packed for the day, grabbed her keys, and was out the door.

There was frost on the grass as she made her way out her back gate to the clinic's rear entrance, the aspens on the mountainsides above town shimmering gold in the dawn light. Because she was a wildlife vet, summer was her busiest time of year. Things had begun to slow now, but she still had a few winged and four-legged patients, among them a beaver, a red fox, a raccoon, and a golden eagle recovering from a broken wing.

It gave a cry when she entered the aviary and flew from one perch to another.

She smiled, happy to see it in the air again. When the game warden had first brought it in, she hadn't been sure she could help it. Birds' wings were part of their respiratory systems. That was especially true in soaring birds, like eagles. She'd had to operate, carefully pinning the fragile hollow bone back together.

She tossed in its breakfast—raw deer hearts donated by local hunters—and locked the aviary once more. "You're almost ready to leave us, aren't you?"

It swooped down, talons out, and tore into its meal with its powerful beak.

She left it to feed in peace, tended the other animals, and locked up the clinic.

Around the corner, she found Chaska loading a box of egg crates into the back of his SUV. "How many eggs is that?"

"Seven dozen." Chaska settled the box inside. "We've also got eight pounds of bacon, three pounds of ground coffee, and five half-gallons of orange juice, flour, lard, cut fruit, cream—and a bunch of other stuff for lunch and supper."

It had been a long time since Winona had cooked for a large number of people. At least twenty volunteers were camping up there, and Naomi felt the least she could do was feed them. "Are we sure that's enough?"

"Naomi went over it with Joe."

"Joe ought to know." He was the owner of Knockers, the local brewpub and the center of Scarlet's social scene. "Can I help?"

"This is the last box." Chaska glanced at her, frowned. "Hey, what's wrong?"

"I'm just tired. I didn't sleep very well." She left it at that.

But Chaska knew her too well. "You're having night-mares again. You need to tell Old Man, let him help."

"I don't want to worry him. It's been five years. I should be over this by now."

Chaska rested his hands on her shoulders. "That's not how it works."

The front door opened, and Grandpa stepped outside, his long white hair pulled back in a braid, his new cowboy boots on his feet. He glanced up at the sky, smiled. "*Le hinhanni ki wasté!*" *This morning is good!*

At ninety-three, he seemed to have more energy than Winona did at thirty.

Chaska lowered his voice. "Talk to him."

Naomi stepped out of the house, wearing a maternity T-shirt that read *Growing My Tribe* and had an arrow pointing to her bulging belly. She was only three weeks away from her due date and wanted to get as much done at the camp as she could before the baby was born.

She locked the door behind her. "Chaska, did you remember the salt and pepper? And what about the salsa?"

"Relax." Chaska opened the vehicle's front passenger door for her. "I packed everything on your list."

They piled into the SUV, Chaska at the wheel, Naomi up front where there was more room, and Winona and Grandpa in the back.

"Will there be a lot of young Native men there?" Grandpa tried to sound casual, but Winona knew where he was going with this.

Naomi glanced back at Winona, a knowing smile on her face. "I think so. Kat's Tohono O'odham friend from the Shadow Wolves is coming."

Grandpa was clearly pleased with this news. "Maybe my granddaughter will meet a good, strong man today."

Winona was torn between amusement and annoyance.

"Grandpa, I'm sitting *right here*. You can talk to me. Just because there will be Native men around doesn't mean I'm going to bump into Mr. Right. Most of them are probably already married. Besides, most of them come from out of state, and I won't leave Scarlet."

Grandpa said nothing, an impassive expression on his face.

It wasn't that Winona didn't want to meet her half-side —her perfect, matching male half. She would love to meet the right man and have what Chaska and Naomi had. But so far, fate hadn't intervened on her behalf the way it had for them. The guys she'd dated in college had proved disappointing. The only men in Scarlet who interested her were on the Team or married, and those were lines she wouldn't cross.

Chaska met Winona's gaze in the rearview mirror, an amused grin on his face. "It's best not to meddle, Old Man."

But Grandpa was serious. "I want my granddaughter to be happy. I want to see her with a good man before I make the journey."

"What if I like women instead?"

Grandpa turned his face toward her, likely trying to decide whether she was coming out or just being contrary. "If you were a *winkte*, a Two-Spirit person, I would honor that, too and would want to see you settled with the right Two-Spirit woman. I just want you to be safe and happy."

"I know." Winona squeezed his hand, unable to stay annoyed with him for long. Two months ago, she'd come close to losing both him and Chaska.

―――

JASON DROVE while McBride sat in the passenger seat,

tools and camping gear in the back. Jason had known McBride would ask eventually. They were both federal agents who had worked the line. If anyone besides his fellow Wolves would understand what Jason had done, it was McBride.

"They had tried to brush out the vehicle's tracks, but I caught it."

"Of course, you did."

"I called the others, and we moved in to surround them." The Wolves functioned as a pack, hunting together to bring down criminals who trafficked in drugs and human beings. "We didn't want them to hit the hardball— the highway—and escape again."

Once traffickers reached the highway, it was much harder to stop them. An SUV loaded with coke was a lot easier to spot in the desert than in traffic.

Jason passed a car with Illinois plates. "Ren flanked them. I came up in front. Ellio and Dale cut them off at the rear. We moved in, but no one was there. We thought they had abandoned the vehicle."

Traffickers often chose to dump their cargo rather than risk capture.

"What were they carrying?"

"Thirty kilos of uncut cocaine."

Zach gave a low whistle. "That's what—five million on the street?"

"Something like that. Ren and I went after them, following boot prints, but they hadn't gone far. They ambushed us, opened fire, hitting Ren in the belly. I took one out, but the other rabbited, heading south again."

"You pursued."

Jason nodded. "Once I saw that Ellio and Dale were taking care of Ren, I pursued on foot. His trail was easy to follow, but he knew the landscape as well as I did. When we got close to the line, he started to run. He thought he was home free."

"You followed him to the other side, crossed the border."

"Hell, yes, I did. I'm TO and a dual citizen. That land belongs to our people, even if it is in Mexico. The bastard had just shot a federal agent on TO land. I wasn't going to let him get away."

"I get it. I do. I've worked black bag jobs on the other side of the line, bringing high-value suspects across the border in secret. I called it 'unofficial extradition.' If you don't get caught, you're a hero. If you do, you're fucked."

"Yeah." Jason was definitely the latter. "He was out in the open. The area there is pretty flat, so he had nowhere to hide. He turned and raised his rifle. I fired before he did and killed him. I didn't know there was a group of Mexican agents nearby."

"Oh, shit. That's when the real fun began."

Jason nodded. "They came in hot, weapons out. They frisked me, cuffed me, took my firearms, my badge, my personal ID. I thought they might be working for the cartel and have instructions to blow my head off right there. I was lying face down in the dirt with a pistol to my head when the rest of the Wolves showed up."

"The pack had your six."

"They were careful to stay on the other side, but there was a lot of shouting. The Mexican agents finally released me. They escorted me back to the border and filed a complaint with DC the next morning."

"I heard that part of it—the complaint, the unpaid leave—but I didn't know what had happened. I feel for you, man."

"I've got a hearing next month. The board will expect me to grovel, but I don't regret it. The bastard was still on

TO land, man, *our* land. He'd just shot one of my brothers."

"How is Ren?"

"He's going to be okay, but he won't be back on the job for a while."

For a moment, neither of them spoke. McBride didn't bring up Elena, which was a relief. All Jason had told him in his email was that he'd broken off their engagement. He hadn't told him why.

He changed the subject. "Tell me about this camp."

"Naomi Belcourt, a Lakota friend, bought it and opened it last summer. She named it Camp Mato Sapa— Camp Black Bear. The idea was to bring in Lakota kids who live in poverty on reservations here and give them a space where they can build their confidence and feel pride in their heritage. They do fun things like art classes, jewelry-making, a ropes course, Lakota language classes, story-telling—stuff like that."

"That sounds fun." Jason could see the value of that— provided the experience didn't encourage children to leave the reservation when they grew up.

The Nations needed young people to stick around to help build a better future.

McBride told him how a wildfire had threatened to burn the camp and Scarlet Springs to the ground just two months ago. The phone lines to the camp had been brought down by a fallen tree branch, and there was no cell service in the canyon. "No one at the camp had any idea that a fire was heading toward them until a sheriff's deputy drove up to make sure they had evacuated. By then, it was almost too late."

"Good God."

"There were more than forty people still there, most of them children. They didn't have enough room in the available vehicles to evacuate everyone. Volunteers stayed behind knowing they would probably die—some of the camp counselors, a kid who'd hidden in a tipi, Naomi's husband, Chaska, Chaska's grandfather, and Gabe Rossiter."

"Kat James' husband?" Jason knew him.

The man had lost a leg saving Kat's life, but it hadn't slowed him down.

"Yeah." McBride took a swig of his coffee. "I was in Scarlet that day, helping to evacuate people. Members of the Rocky Mountain Search and Rescue Team tried to get to the camp but came close to being entrapped themselves. Rossiter and Belcourt are both Team members, so it was personal for them. Then we got word via radio that the rescue attempt had failed and the camp had burned over. There were a few awful hours when we believed they had all burned to death."

That wasn't how Jason would choose to die. "That must have been hell."

"Naomi and Winona, Chaska's younger sister, were in shock. The whole town was grieving. When the fire was under control, members of the Team went out with a search dog to recover their friends' remains and found them alive. I almost couldn't believe it when I got the message."

"Thank God." Jason had been raised with a mix of O'odham beliefs and Catholicism and was tempted to cross himself. "How did they escape?"

"They spotted a cave in a cliff wall above the camp. Rossiter free soloed up to it, ropes on his shoulder, then pulled the rest of them to safety."

"I should have known." Jason chuckled, but his relief was genuine. "That guy has a gift, some kind of superpower."

"Tell me about it." McBride grinned. "The camp itself was obliterated. We'll be camping on-site and helping to build new cabins. They hope to have the place up and running again by next summer."

Jason was more than happy to help with this cause. "Let's do it."

Chapter 2

WINONA POURED two cups of coffee grounds into steaming water and set the big, old enamel coffee pot on top of the grate above the cookfire to boil. Breakfast was over, but she wanted to make sure there was plenty of caffeine to keep everyone going. She glanced around to see what else they might need.

Cups. Creamer.

Around the nearest picnic table, Naomi and Chaska handed out hard hats to those who didn't own one and went over the day's strategy with the volunteers. Fortunately, some of them had construction experience.

"The floor systems are finished, and the utility runs are in place." Naomi spread out the architectural plans for the cabins so everyone could see them. "The goal this weekend is to complete the rough-framing on all ten cabins."

Heads nodded.

"We can do that."

"No problem."

Well, that was a relief.

This camp had been Naomi's dream, her way of giving Lakota kids a positive outlook about their heritage and reinforcing their sense of self-worth. In the aftermath of the fire, Naomi had just been grateful that no lives had been lost. Now, she wanted to rebuild the camp better than it had been so it could reopen next June. Winona would do all she could to support that goal.

She walked back to the Mess Hall and made her way through the dining area to the kitchen, where Kat was cleaning a cast-iron skillet with a paper towel. "The coffee is on. I'll start on the dishes."

"There's really not that much to wash." Kat set the skillet down, picked up another, wiped it clean.

"Thank goodness for compostable plates and utensils." Winona filled one of the big, stainless steel sinks, put on a pair of rubber gloves, and settled the big stainless serving pans in the hot, sudsy water.

Winona hadn't known Kat well until this past summer when they'd all believed that Chaska, Grandpa, and Kat's husband Gabe had died in the fire. She'd watched Kat muster the emotional strength to comfort Naomi despite her own grief. Winona had the highest respect for her.

They fell into a relaxed conversation while they worked, talking about their families, their jobs, the news from Pine Ridge and Navajoland, Kat's home.

Then Winona remembered.

She slipped off the rubber gloves. "I forgot to take out more cups and creamer. I'll be right back."

She grabbed two more plastic-wrapped packages of cups and a container of powdered creamer and hurried out the door—only to run headlong into a black T-shirt and a very hard body. "Oh! Sorry."

"No problem." The man looked down at her through

intense brown eyes, his hands on her arms to steady her. "I'm looking for Winona."

Winona stood there, staring up at him, temporarily speechless.

Aiii.

He was so … *hot.*

He spoke with a rez accent and stood at least as tall as Chaska, his dark hair cut short. His black T-shirt stretched over a muscular torso, a tattoo of a maze peeking out from beneath his sleeve on his left shoulder. And his face...

Piercing brown eyes. High, angular cheekbones. A strong jaw. Full lips.

Say something!

"I'm … uh… I'm Winona."

He stepped back, let his hands fall to his sides. "Naomi said you'd have coffee cups. I can see she was right."

"Oh. Yes." Winona tried to open the plastic to give him a single cup but somehow dropped both packages onto the porch.

He bent down, picked them up. "I can take them from here. You can go back to whatever you were doing."

"Thanks." She handed him the creamer, too.

"I'm Jason Chiago." He tucked the cups under one arm, held out his free hand, a hint of amusement in his eyes.

She shook his hand, his fingers warm, his touch seeming to ignite sparks on her skin. "Winona Belcourt. I'm Naomi's sister-in-law."

"Jason!" Kat came up behind Winona, stepped outside. "It's good to see you."

"Hey, Kat. It's been a while."

That's when it clicked.

Heat rose into Winona's cheeks.

This was *that* friend. Kat's Tohono O'odham friend. The Shadow Wolf.

The Shadow Wolves were legendary among Native people and were widely acknowledged as the best trackers in the world.

Great.

She'd certainly made a good first impression.

Fighting the impulse to slink away and crawl under the nearest rock, she stood politely while Kat and Jason spoke. She couldn't help but notice his broad shoulders. Or the bulge of his biceps. Or the way his jeans rode low on his narrow hips.

No, of course, she wasn't staring at him. Okay, so maybe she was, but he was standing right in front of her. What else was she supposed to do?

"How long are you staying?" Kat asked.

"I'm not sure—a week or two maybe. I thought I'd lend a hand here and then maybe see some sights." He glanced over at the group of volunteers, who were dividing into teams. "I should probably get to work."

"Chiago, you slacker!" Zach McBride called, a grin on his face. "Quit talking to the pretty women and pick up a hammer."

"You go on. We'll talk soon." Kat waved. "Hey, Zach!"

"Nice to meet you, Winona." Jason walked down the stairs and rejoined the others, leaving Winona to gawk … at his butt.

Holy smokes.

Back in the kitchen, Kat grabbed a dishtowel. "There's something you should know about Jason. I know he's good-looking, but, last I heard, he was engaged."

Given that Winona had just made a fool of herself, the news almost came as a relief. "The good ones always are."

—

"THAT'S IT." Jason held fast to one side of the wall frame, McBride the other, as they raised it and set it in place. "Perfect. Hold it there."

Grandpa Belcourt took Jason's end. "I've got it."

Jason dropped to one knee, grabbed his hammer and the framing nails, and fixed the wall frame into position, starting with the ends and then moving toward the center. "One wall frame in place, three more to go."

Given that the fourth member of their team, a young Cherokee named Adam, was sick from the altitude and resting in his tent, Jason was proud of their progress.

It felt good to do something physical, the sun on his face, fresh air in his lungs, sweat on his skin. More than that, the work got him out of his head, giving him something to focus on besides his screwed-up life—or Winona Belcourt.

Damn.

Okay, so maybe she was still on his mind.

She *was* beautiful, with long, dark hair, delicate features, and sweet curves that her oversized denim shirt couldn't conceal. She'd gotten flustered when she'd bumped into him, her embarrassment adorable. He'd felt a strange pull between them when he'd shaken her hand, and he'd seen the flush in her cheeks. She'd felt it, too.

Mutual attraction.

Yeah, well, he needed to shut that down now. He no longer did casual hookups, and he had no interest in starting a relationship. His fellow Wolves told him he'd get over what Elena had done and learn to trust again. Maybe that was true, but he wasn't there yet. Besides, he had no intention of moving away from Sells and abandoning his people or the O'odham *himdag*—their way of life.

He knew where he was meant to be.

Jason tested the wall frame with a shake. "Let's level this, square it, and brace it."

Grandpa Belcourt pulled a bandana from the pocket of his jeans and wiped the sweat off his forehead. "It looks like my granddaughter has food for us."

Jason saw Winona setting bread and rolls on the table. He willed himself to look away. "Let's finish this and wash up."

By the time they were done and Jason had washed his hands—he always carried paper soap to use with water from his water bottle—lunch was waiting for them. Volunteers drifted toward the picnic tables, joking and laughing with one another.

Winona explained to the group how it worked, the breeze teasing tendrils of dark hair that had come loose from her braid. "It's a do-it-yourself sandwich smorgasbord. Start on this end with the plates and forks. There's turkey, roast beef, salami, baloney, bread, and rolls, with all the fixings. We've got cookies and fruit for dessert."

Naomi pointed to a large cooler at the end of the table, fingers massaging one temple. "We've got soft drinks and bottled water on ice if you're thirsty."

Jason motioned Grandpa Belcourt forward. "You first, Grandfather."

It was an almost universal Indigenous custom to refer to all elders as Grandfather or Grandmother—or Uncle or Auntie—out of respect.

The old man gave a nod of thanks and picked up a paper plate.

Winona stood across from him, hands on her hips. "Are you working hard, Grandpa?"

"I'm hardly workin'." The old man tossed two pieces of white bread onto his plate, chuckling at his own joke.

"That's not true." Jason found himself wanting to draw her gaze. "He's keeping the rest of us in line."

But Winona's attention seemed to be reserved for her grandfather, concern on her pretty face. "Promise me you won't overdo it, okay?"

Grandpa Belcourt slathered mayonnaise on his bread then piled on the roast beef. "Have you met my granddaughter, Winona? She fusses over me like an old hen."

"She and I bumped into each other this morning." Jason put mustard, turkey, and Swiss on wheat bread. "Thanks for the meal, Winona."

At last, she looked up at him. "Thanks for your help today."

The moment her gaze met his, Jason felt it—a bone-deep sense of awareness. He found himself searching for words and finding none.

Grandpa Belcourt spoke, giving Jason time to pull himself together. "Winona is a wildlife vet. She helps our furry and feathered relatives."

Jason stupidly repeated what the old man had just said. "A wildlife vet."

So, she was smart, too.

She nodded. "I rehabilitate sick and injured animals."

A hand came down on Jason's shoulder. "Hey, Chiago. Kat said you'd be here."

Jason turned, found Gabe Rossiter standing behind him, a broad grin on his face. Jason shook his friend's hand. "Good to see you. I hear you were a hero this summer."

Gabe laughed. "Is McBride telling stories about me again? I'll grab some food, and we can sit down somewhere and catch up."

"No cutting in line," Jason teased. "You have to go to the back."

"Ah, man!" Rossiter headed to the rear of the line.

Jason had just finished making his sandwich when he heard Winona gasp.

"Naomi!"

―――

WINONA RAN to where Naomi lay in the dirt. "Are you okay?"

Naomi pressed her fingers to her temples. "I feel … funny."

Then Chaska was there, kneeling beside his wife. "What happened?"

"She just sank to the ground."

"I've had a headache, and then I got so dizzy."

That's when Winona noticed the swelling in Naomi's ankles.

Oh, God.

She met Chaska's gaze, tried to show him she was serious without upsetting Naomi. "She needs to go to the ER *now*."

Naomi shook her head. "We've got all of these volunteers here. I don't have much time before the baby comes. Someone needs to start making the stew for—"

"These guys can order pizza if they have to." Chaska fished out his keys, handed them to Winona, and scooped Naomi into his arms. "We're taking you to the hospital. Nothing is more important than you and our baby."

Kat ran down the steps of the mess hall toward them. "Is she in labor?"

Winona shook her head. "She got dizzy and sank to the ground. We're taking her to the ER. Can you watch over everything until I get back?"

"Of course." Kat waved her away. "Go."

Winona hurried to the SUV, unlocked the doors, and stood back while Chaska lifted Naomi into the front passenger seat. "Do you want me to drive?"

"I'm fine." He helped Naomi buckle her seatbelt.

Winona found the button that reclined Naomi's seatback. "I think you should lie back and rest, okay?"

Naomi nodded, clearly anxious. "Thanks, Win."

Winona smiled, doing her best not to let her fear show. "What are sisters for?"

She got into the back seat and saw Grandpa hurrying toward them. "Hang on, Chaska. Grandpa's coming, too."

Grandpa climbed into the back seat. "*Hoka hey*! Let's roll."

They kept the conversation light on the drive down to Scarlet, talking about the morning's progress and how kind and helpful the volunteers had been. But Winona couldn't shake her fears.

Naomi had been under so much stress since the fire. First, she'd believed for a few hellish hours that her husband, her grandfather, and people who had depended on her had burned to death. Then she'd had to face rebuilding the camp. That much stress would be hard for anyone, but for a woman in her third trimester…

Winona wasn't an obstetrician, but she *was* medically trained and had cared for lots of pregnant animals. Stress put both mother and baby at risk, no matter the species.

"That Jason Chiago—he knows how to use a hammer," Grandpa said. "He worked construction in college."

Chaska met Grandpa's gaze in his rearview mirror. "You did some construction work back in the day, didn't you, Old Man?"

"That was a long time ago. In those days, living was

hard. You had to build and repair your own house if you didn't want to freeze to death."

Not that life on Pine Ridge was easy now.

The charred landscape gave way to green forest as they reached the edge of town. Chaska took the shortest route to Mountain Memorial Hospital, where he parked outside the emergency entrance.

Winona opened her door, climbed out. "I'll go get a wheelchair."

Naomi shook her head. "I can walk."

"I've got you." Chaska carried Naomi inside and hurried over to the check-in desk. "My wife is three weeks from her due date and just collapsed. She said she was feeling dizzy and has a headache."

"I'll need her insurance card and a photo ID." A young man at the check-in desk held out a clipboard with several sheets of paper on it.

Winona was about to tell the guy what to do with the clipboard when Ellie Moretti, an RN and wife of Jesse Moretti, a friend and Team member, walked out. "Bring her back. We'll deal with the paperwork later."

Thank God.

Chaska carried Naomi into an exam bay and set her gently down on the gurney. Winona stood off to the side so as not to get in the way.

Grandpa motioned toward the waiting area. "I'm gonna sit out here and pray."

Naomi and Chaska explained what had happened and answered Ellie's questions, while Ellie took Naomi's temperature, checked the baby's heartbeat with a fetal doppler, and hooked her up to an automatic blood pressure monitor.

"The baby's heartbeat is strong, so that's good news."

Ellie gave them all a reassuring smile. "Do you know if it's a boy or a girl?"

Naomi shook her head. "We wanted to wait."

But when the blood pressure monitor had to try a second time to get Naomi's reading, Ellie's demeanor grew more serious. "You're at thirty-seven weeks, right?"

"Yes."

"You said you've had a headache?"

"I've had it off and on for the past few days."

When the monitor finally gave its result, it put a knot in Winona's chest.

Much too high.

Ellie gave them the news. "Your blood pressure is dangerously high. I'm going to start an IV and page the on-duty OB. We're also going to need to draw some labs. In the meantime, try to rest. We'll take good care of you and your baby, Naomi."

Naomi's eyes filled with tears, her fingers twining with Chaska's. "Thank you."

Chaska kissed Naomi's cheek, smiled, his voice projecting calm strength. "It will be okay, Tanagila. They're not going to let anything happen to you or the baby."

Tanagila was their Lakota nickname for Naomi. It meant *hummingbird*.

Ellie returned quickly and set up the IV, stepping back for the lab tech, who drew four vials of blood. "We're checking your kidney and liver function and several other things, too. We should have the results soon."

A few minutes later, a woman in a white lab coat stepped in. "I'm Dr. Peterson, the OB-GYN. You must be Naomi. And you're the baby's father?"

"Yes. Chaska Belcourt." Chaska shook the doctor's hand.

"I'm Winona Belcourt, Chaska's sister."

"Nice to meet you all." Dr. Peterson glanced at the blood pressure monitor. "It looks like you've developed severe preeclampsia, Naomi. While we wait for the results of your blood tests, we're going to give you IV medication to bring down your blood pressure and prevent seizures. Then it will be time to have this baby."

Chapter 3

JASON HAD no idea what had just happened, but it was clear that people needed to step up to keep things moving. He helped McBride and Rossiter clear what was left of lunch off the picnic table and carry it into the Mess Hall.

They found Kat talking on the landline. "Tell Naomi not to worry about anything, Win. We can manage. Let us know how things go. If *you* need anything… Okay. Thanks for keeping me in the loop. Bye."

She hung up, a worried expression on her face.

Rossiter set an armful of condiments on the counter. "What's going on?"

"Naomi has preeclampsia. Her blood pressure is so high that it's life-threatening to both her and the baby. The doctor wanted to induce labor, but her blood tests showed her condition was more serious. They're doing an emergency C-section."

"Ah, hell." Rossiter shook his head. "Is there anything we can do?"

"Pray."

Jason nodded. "I'll gather everyone into a circle."

Most of the volunteers were already back at work, their mood somber.

Jason raised his voice, shouting to be heard. "Listen up! Gather around!"

When everyone had formed a circle, Kat shared the news and then led the prayer, holding her husband's hand. "Creator, we thank you for the gift of life and ask for strength for our sister Naomi as she gives birth to her child. Keep her and her baby safe. We also pray for our brother Chaska, her husband, that he might be strong for her. May they walk in beauty always."

There was a moment of silence afterward.

Then Jason led the volunteers in a quick strategy session. Rossiter offered to help Kat in the kitchen. Chaska's team needed someone with construction experience to take his place. The three teams that were shorthanded would do their best. Any team that finished quickly would divide up to help the others.

He did his best to encourage them. "I know most of us don't know Naomi and Chaska well, but we came to help anyway because of what this camp represents. They can't be here, so let's put our hearts into this for their sake and get it done."

"*Aho!*"

"Yeah!"

"Let's do this!"

They went back to work with a new sense of urgency, Adam joining Jason and McBride, apparently feeling better now.

Jason pointed to the rolls of insulation with his hammer. "Let's insulate the corners before we put on the sheathing."

Roof rafters would come next and then the front wall, which was already framed.

They were halfway through getting the sheathing onto the cabin when Kat and Rossiter walked out of the Mess Hall, both smiling.

They came to stand in the center of the cabins. "We've got news from Winona. It's a boy!"

A cheer went up.

"The baby weighed seven pounds three ounces and is healthy and doing well. Naomi isn't out of danger yet, but she…" Kat's words trailed off as three vehicles drove up the dirt road and parked, a small army piling out. "Oh!"

"Nice of you all to show up," Rossiter called out to them.

"Who are they?" Adam asked.

McBride grinned. "They're friends. Remember the Rocky Mountain Search and Rescue Team I mentioned, Chiago? Chaska and Winona are both Team members. It looks like some of them have come to help. In Scarlet, folks take care of their own."

Jason watched as they put on hard hats.

"What?" McBride shot him a look. "You seem surprised."

"I guess I didn't expect this kind of community off the reservation." Jason had never gotten to know his neighbors in Phoenix.

Then again, maybe he hadn't tried.

McBride seemed to study him, as if trying to understand this. "There are only about fifteen hundred people in Scarlet, so everyone knows everyone."

Jason followed McBride down to meet the new arrivals, the volunteers stopping work to listen. Kat, Rossiter, and McBride hugged the newcomers or shook their hands, Kat sharing the news about the new baby.

Then an older woman turned toward the volunteers. "I'm Megs Hill, director of the Rocky Mountain Search and Rescue Team. We heard about Naomi and the baby and came to help. This is Mitch Ahearn, my quieter half. This is part of our motley crew. Sasha Dillon. Creed Herrera. Bahir Acharya. Conrad and Kenzie Harrison. Someone give us hard hats and hammers and show us what to hit."

As it turned out, Creed and Conrad had both worked in construction. They focused on making roof rafters for the cabins, while the others were divided up and kept busy helping in the kitchen, carrying plywood sheathing, hauling lumber, fetching nails or house wrap, or doing whatever else needed to be done.

When it came time to put sheathing on the roof rafters, these Team members seemed to have an advantage, especially Sasha, the young blond woman, and Megs.

Jason took a water break, watching as the two walked like cats along the edges of the wall frames, helping settle the roof sheathing into place. "They're all like Rossiter, aren't they?"

McBride nodded. "Yep."

"They're not afraid of heights at all."

"Nope." McBride chuckled. "Sasha is a five-time world champion sports climber. Megs Hill is a climbing legend, one of the first women to make it in rock climbing. Mitch, her partner, was a big name in climbing in the Seventies. Conrad Harrison has climbed Mount Everest more than once and had his face all over magazines."

Jason crossed his arms over his chest, watched Sasha jump, catch the top of a wall frame, and pull herself up with seemingly little effort. "The only climbers I've met are the ones who trespass on our land and want to climb at sacred O'odham sites. They don't care about our customs or beliefs. They think they should be able to climb anywhere."

"That's not who these people are. Megs would kick their butts if they climbed on sacred land. Team members are dedicated, man. They save lives all the time—and they don't charge a dime."

"Really?" Jason was impressed, but there was work to be done. "Let's get this cabin wrapped."

———

"ISN'T HE ADORABLE?" Winona turned off the highway onto the dirt road that led up the canyon to the camp, her heart full, her emotions caught somewhere between elation about the baby and worry for Naomi.

Grandpa hadn't stopped smiling. "He looks just like his father."

Winona had gotten to hold the baby for a few precious moments, Chaska carefully placing the tiny bundle in her arms. "We named him Shota. It was Shota who saved Naomi's life, after all. He brought us together."

Winona's eyes had blurred with tears. "That's … *perfect*."

Little Shota Belcourt had felt so tiny in her arms. She hadn't known she'd fall instantly in love with the little guy or that the intensity of that feeling would turn her world upside down. The best part had been watching Chaska, tears in his eyes, place his newborn son in Grandpa's arms.

Grandpa's expression had been one of wonder. "My great-grandson."

If only Naomi's blood pressure would go down…

Winona had already called Naomi's father, Doug Otter Tail, and his wife, Star Tall Grass. They were driving down from Pine Ridge today to help with Shota. Winona had gotten to see Naomi for a few minutes. She'd been resting, the baby in her arms, contentment on her face, IVs carrying life-saving medications into her veins.

The doctor had warned that delivery wouldn't make her preeclampsia go away but was hopeful that her condition would quickly improve.

All they could do now was pray.

Grandpa's stomach growled. "I didn't get to eat my sandwich."

Winona hadn't had lunch either. "Hopefully, there will be plenty of stew left for us. If not, I'll take you to Knockers."

She needed to get Grandpa home and check on the animals again, but first, she wanted to see if there was anything the volunteers needed. They had been short-handed today, but she hoped they'd made at least some progress.

As they drew closer, she saw vehicles she recognized. That was Megs and Ahearn's Outback. The red Forester belonged to Creed. "The Team is here."

She parked, climbed out—and stared.

The six cabins the volunteers had started on this morning all had their walls and roofs, and the volunteers had begun work rough-framing the other four.

"Look, Grandpa. Look what they've done. The Team came to help, too."

Grandpa glanced around. "They've been busy beavers."

That's when people noticed Winona. Work came to a halt, volunteers and Team members alike setting down their tools and gathering around her.

She swallowed the lump in her throat. "Thank you. Thank you all. This is more than I imagined. I'm so grateful. This will mean so much to Naomi."

"How is she?" Megs asked.

"She's doing better. They're monitoring her."

"I hope you took photos of the baby." That was Sasha.

"I did. I need to get my grandfather something to eat, and then I'll show you." She led Grandpa to a picnic table. "Sit here, Grandpa."

"I'll get him some stew. It should be ready now." Kat walked over to the cookfire, stirred the stew with a large wooden spoon, and dished some into a bowl. "Are you brave enough to be the first to eat it, Grandfather?"

Grandpa chuckled. "It smells good enough to me."

While Grandpa ate, Winona shared the photos of her nephew. "They named him Shota. Grandpa says he looks just like Chaska when he was born."

"He's precious." Smiling, Kat scrolled through the photos, then handed Winona's phone to Sasha.

"Aww!" Sasha held the phone so Megs could see over her shoulder. "Look at all that hair. He's so tiny."

"Uh-oh." Megs shook her head. "He *does* look like his daddy. He'll be breaking hearts before he's in high school."

Laughter.

Winona thanked Kat and Gabe for making the meal and helped them serve it, filling bowls and handing them to volunteers, the rich scent making her mouth water. When everyone else had been fed, Winona filled a bowl for herself and sat beside Grandpa, who was now on his second serving.

The sun had sunk behind the mountains, the camp slipping into shadows, heavy clouds threatening rain. Some of the volunteers had built a campfire in a fire pit in the middle of the ring of tents and sat around it, one of them playing a guitar. Jason, Zach, and Gabe sat together at one table, ribbing one another. Most of the Team members sat at another, laughing and talking.

Winona closed her eyes for a moment, exhaled, willing

herself to relax. She had so many reasons to be grateful today. So many people had helped her and her family— volunteers, her fellow Team members, Ellie, Dr. Peterson, the hospital staff.

She sent up a prayer of gratitude to Creator.

Pilamayaye. Thank you.

She made a spirit plate, setting aside a little bit of everything she was eating as an offering. When she'd finished her meal, she set the spirit plate on the porch of the Mess Hall, cleared the tables, and went inside to help Kenzie, who was three months pregnant, wash the heavy stew pot and other dishes.

By the time they had finished, it was dark outside. Winona thanked Kenzie, Megs, and the other Team members, who promised to be back in the morning if they weren't toned out for a rescue.

"Taylor and Hawke wanted to be here, but Taylor is on duty, and Hawke…" Megs didn't have to finish.

Austin Taylor was a park ranger and worked most weekends. Eric Hawke, the town's fire chief, had been badly burned on one leg during the fire and wasn't yet back to his regular routine.

"Thanks, Megs. This means so much to us."

Megs gave Winona a motherly pat on the arm. "I know."

Winona spotted Jason standing with Gabe and Zach on the creek bank, and she knew what they were doing. She walked over, heard Gabe recounting the day of the fire. Even two months later, the story sent chills down her spine.

"We stood on the banks of the creek, knowing we were trapped. Then I saw it."

Jason looked up, frowned. "I don't see a cave."

"That's because it's hidden behind that arete." Gabe

took a few steps to his left. "We didn't see it either, not at first. Look now."

Jason stood where Gabe was standing, then his jaw dropped. "Holy … *shit*. You climbed up there?"

"I climbed up, hammered a pulley into the rock, and pulled the others up."

Jason was still looking up at the cave. "That cave is a geological accident that's millions of years old. It's amazing to think it's been waiting there all this time just for that day."

"Yeah, we got lucky."

"That wasn't luck, man. That was a damned miracle."

Winona couldn't have agreed more.

———

FIREARM IN HAND, Jason moved as quickly as he could through the darkness, fresh blood on the spines of an ocotillo and the distance between footprints telling him the suspect was getting careless and running now. Jason knew where the bastard was heading. He thought he'd slip across the border and disappear. Jason wasn't going to let that happen. The son of a bitch belonged in a prison cell.

As the ground leveled out, Jason picked up his pace, the border less than a half-mile away. He watched for movement, listened for footfalls or heavy breathing.

There you are, cabrón.

A dark shape moved through the night, a gray-on-black shadow running toward the vehicle barrier that marked the US-Mexico border. The fucker was angling for one of the gates intended for use only by the O'odham. If Jason didn't stop him before he made it through, he would lose him.

Jason ran. "¡Alto!" Stop!

But he was too late.

The suspect slipped through the gate into Mexico and kept running.

Fuck that.

Enraged, Jason pushed his way through the gate, closing in on him.

Then the suspect turned, raised his weapon.

But it wasn't a man at all.

"Elena!"

Jason jerked awake, his pulse pounding. He found himself in his tent, the day's first light filtering through the mesh flap. He was in Colorado. Camp Mato Sapa.

Hell.

He sat up, drew in a breath, a sick feeling in the pit of his stomach. Elena had been his world. He'd believed that what they had was real, that they would get married, raise a few kids. How could he have been so wrong?

Let it go.

That was easier said than done.

These past six months, he'd been trying to figure out who he was without Elena. Now, he might have to figure out who he was without the Shadow Wolves.

He closed his eyes, focused on the world around him.

The morning's chill. A raven's throaty *caw*. The lingering scent of rain in the air. The solid earth beneath him.

There was no point in trying to go back to sleep, so he crawled out of his sleeping bag, slipped into his jeans, and put on his boots and fleece-lined denim jacket. Then he left his tent, took a leak, and washed his face and hands with water from his water bottle, the cold helping to clear his head.

McBride poked his head outside his tent, looking half asleep, stubble on his jaw. "Jesus, Chiago. It's six-thirty."

"Tell me about it."

"You okay, man?"

Jason didn't know how to answer that. "I'm going to make coffee."

He got his fire-starter kit out of his pack and walked down to the picnic area. Once he had a good fire going, he walked to the Mess Hall, where the door had been left unlocked in case anyone needed anything during the night. In the kitchen, he found both ground coffee and the big, enamel coffee pot.

He had to give the Belcourts and their friends credit. At least they made real rez coffee instead of that designer soy mocha latte shit.

Jason filled the pot with water, carried both pot and coffee out to the fire, and set the pot over glowing coals. When the water had begun to steam, he poured two cups of grounds straight into the pot then waited for it to boil.

A vehicle pulled up and parked.

Winona.

"It looks like someone already started a fire. Go sit where it's warm, Grandpa. I'll carry the food inside and then make you some coffee."

Jason stood. "The coffee is already brewing."

"Oh! Jason. Hey." She huddled against the cold in a blue puffer jacket, jeans hugging her hips. "Thanks."

"Sorry to startle you. Good morning, Grandfather."

The old man smiled. "It *is* a good morning. I have a great-grandson."

"Congratulations." The old man's pride made Jason smile. "Can I carry something?"

"Thanks. That would really help." Winona opened the liftgate. "All of this needs to get to the kitchen. Kat can't make it today. Her youngest, Noelle, has a fever."

"Sorry to hear that." Jason walked to the rear of the vehicle.

Winona stood close enough that Jason could smell the feminine scent of her shampoo. "Before the day gets busy, I wanted to thank you."

"For what?" He hadn't done more than anyone else.

She looked at him through those big, brown eyes. "Kat said you stepped up and played a leadership role yesterday after we left for the hospital. You kept everyone focused and made sure construction moved forward. That means a lot to us—to me."

"You're welcome." He lifted a stack of egg crates out of the vehicle, trying not to notice how her words warmed him. "Have you heard anything from the hospital?"

"Not this morning, but Chaska sent me a text late last night saying little Shota is fine and Naomi is doing better."

"That's good news."

Still looking sleepy, McBride walked toward them, probably searching for coffee.

Jason motioned him over with a jerk of his head. "Hey, Sleeping Beauty, help us get all of this into the kitchen."

Chapter 4

WINONA TOOK OFF HER JACKET, poured herself a cup of coffee, and sat at one of the tables in the quiet of the Mess Hall. What a relief it was to have breakfast and lunch behind her! Thank goodness for Jason, Zach, and Kenzie, who had each helped in their own way. She didn't have to worry about making dinner tonight because Caribou Joe, the owner of Knockers, had donated a coupon for a free meal for every volunteer.

She sipped the coffee, needing a jolt of caffeine. She hadn't had nightmares last night, but, even so, she hadn't gotten much sleep. She hadn't wanted Grandfather to be alone, so she'd slept on Chaska and Naomi's sofa. The sofa wasn't uncomfortable, but it wasn't her bed. With so much to do and so few hands to help, she'd gotten up extra early, getting the guest room ready for Naomi's parents, doing her rounds at the clinic, and loading up her Subaru with provisions for the day.

Everything seemed to be going well. Jason had told her the cabins would all be watertight by this evening, just as Naomi had hoped. Winona prayed he was right.

She folded her arms on the table, rested her head, and closed her eyes. That's all she needed—just a few minutes of rest before the coffee kicked in.

Just a few minutes…

"Winona?"

She gasped, springing to her feet on a burst of adrenaline and knocking over her chair with a clatter.

Jason reached across the table, caught her by the arm to steady her. "I'm sorry. I didn't mean to scare you."

Heart thrumming, she tried to get her bearings. "I … I must have fallen asleep."

He released her, concern on his face. "Are you okay?"

Way to embarrass yourself—again.

"I'm fine." She righted the chair. "Sorry."

"Don't apologize. I came to tell you that we're done. All of the rough-framing is complete, and the cabins are wrapped and dried in."

"Already?" How long had she been asleep?

"Come see."

She slipped on her jacket and followed him outdoors. Even from the Mess Hall's porch, she could see them—ten cabins with walls and roofs covered in house wrap. "You said you would finish, and you did. I'm so grateful, Jason— to all of you. Naomi is going to be so happy."

Team members and volunteers alike gathered around the cookfire, drinking coffee, warming themselves, smiles on their faces. Grandfather was with them, sitting close to the fire, talking with Megs.

Winona made her way toward them, stopping first to get the Knockers coupons out of her vehicle. She climbed on top of a picnic bench near Grandpa, the crowd of about thirty falling quiet. "You did it. *Pilamayaye.* Thank you. I can't believe how much you accomplished this weekend. I know that if Naomi were here, she would be amazed, too. We are all deeply grateful for your help. What you've done will enable us to operate next summer and make a difference in the lives of Lakota children."

She held up the Knockers coupons, explained that they were good for a free meal. Then she invited anyone who was leaving right away to make sandwiches for the road using leftovers in the fridge. Anyone who wanted to camp here for another night and drive home in the morning was welcome to do that, as well. "Thank you all again."

She snapped a photo with her cell phone to show Naomi, then hopped down to the ground. She shook each volunteer's hand, thanked them, and gave them their coupons. The out-of-town volunteers began taking down their tents and packing their gear into their vehicles, while Team members gave her hugs and headed back into town. Within an hour, everyone had gone except Zach and Jason.

Jason approached, carrying several long boards. "Where do you want the scrap lumber and the extra sheathing?"

"I think everything should go in the garage, along with all the tools and the leftover house wrap."

The oversized, steel garage at the north end of the property had been built to hold the school bus Naomi planned to buy next spring. For now, it served as a tool shed.

While Zach, Jason, and Grandpa cleaned up the area around the cabins, Winona packed up the leftover food, washed the remaining dishes, and wiped down the kitchen. By the time she had finished, Zach and Jason were packing their gear in the back of Zach's SUV.

"Are you heading home?" She fought to ignore a stab of disappointment.

It's not like you and Jason hit it off.

No, they hadn't. She'd blundered into him, and then

she'd freaked the heck out when he'd woken her. Besides, Kat had said he was taken.

Zach shook his head. "I thought Chiago should experience Knockers at least once in his lifetime. There's no place else like it."

"So, we'll see you tonight then." Her disappointment ebbed. "I'm going to drive Grandpa home so he can have a nap and then check on the animals at the sanctuary. I've got a golden eagle who's always hungry."

"Do you mind if we tag along?" Jason asked. "I'd love to see an eagle up close—that is, if you don't mind."

Winona's spirits lifted. "I don't mind at all."

━━

JASON FOLLOWED Winona's vehicle down a winding road toward Scarlet Springs, McBride in the passenger seat, watching him. "What?"

"Have you got a thing for Win?"

Jason kept his expression impassive. "I'm not looking for a relationship."

"That *wasn't* a denial. So, you and Elena are truly done."

"Yeah."

"I'm sorry, man."

"Don't be." Jason hoped McBride would let it go.

"Chaska is a pretty good tracker, by the way. He helped the Marshal Service with a couple of cases in the past."

Jason couldn't resist. "You couldn't handle it yourself after spending a whole week learning to cut sign with the Wolves?"

McBride snorted. "All I learned in that week is that you guys are *really* good, and I have no fucking clue what I'm doing."

The drive to Scarlet took less than a half-hour. Winona pulled into the driveway of a large Victorian house, climbed out of her car, and walked to Jason's window. "I need to carry the food inside and get Grandpa settled."

"You take care of your grandfather. Let us handle the food." Jason parked, and he and McBride carried the boxes of leftovers inside, setting them on the kitchen counter. Winona disappeared upstairs with her grandfather, the soft sound of her voice drifting down to him.

Jason glanced around. "Nice house."

It was bigger than any home in Sells.

"This is Chaska and Naomi's place," McBride told him. "He works for an aerospace engineering company building rocket parts or some shit. She's an artist—jewelry mostly."

Engineering and jewelry-making—two skills that could surely be put to better use on the reservation.

Winona came downstairs. "Grandpa thinks I fuss over him, but he's ninety-three."

McBride leaned back against the counter. "I bet he loves the attention."

"Let me put all of this away." She stuck the leftovers into the fridge, then walked to the back door. "We can get to the clinic faster through the back gate."

As it turned out, the rear entrance to the clinic was only a short distance from Chaska and Naomi's backyard.

Winona opened the door with a key card, reached inside, and flipped on a light. "This was a hectic summer because of the fire, but things have slowed down now."

She gave them a tour, showing them the treatment rooms, the two operating rooms, and the indoor rooms lined with cages for smaller animals.

Jason was impressed. "You run this by yourself?"

"No." Winona laughed. "I have an army of volunteers

who clean cages and handle a lot of the feedings. I also get several interns from the university each summer. That's my busiest time."

She opened a door and turned on the lights. "We've got a raccoon and a beaver back here. The raccoon was hit by a mountain biker and has a broken leg. The beaver got tangled in barbed wire, and the lacerations on her little webbed feet were infected."

Jason stayed back so as not to scare the animals. Winona checked them, speaking to them in what he assumed was Lakota, her voice sweet, her devotion to the animals shining on her face—and stirring something inside him.

McBride bent down to get a better look at the beaver, which sat, tail between its legs, chattering to itself. "Hey, buddy. What's the biggest animal you've ever treated?"

She closed the raccoon's cage. "That would have to be a bull moose last fall. He had a volleyball net tangled in his antlers and was dragging it everywhere, along with every branch and twig it caught. Eventually, he couldn't move at all. A game warden freed him, but he was hungry and badly dehydrated. I had to tranq him to get close enough to treat him."

Jason had to ask. "Who pays for the animals' care—the state? It's not like wild animals have owners."

She led them from the room. "The sanctuary runs on donations. I get some grants from the federal and state governments, but most of it comes from ordinary people who want to help injured wildlife. Let's go outside."

They stopped at a snug enclosure that held a red fox.

"You can smell why I don't keep this guy inside. Red foxes have a musk gland that would make the entire building stink."

Jason had wondered what the odor was. "I believe that."

McBride wrinkled his nose. "Good decision."

"The aviary is over here." Winona led them to a tall enclosure with thick, wooden perches—and an enormous golden eagle.

Jason stared. "It's … *huge*."

McBride was also impressed. "I've never seen one up close like this."

"I measured its wingspan at just under seven feet. When the warden first brought it in, I wasn't sure I'd be able to save it. Broken wings are tricky. We'll be releasing it into the wild in the next few weeks."

McBride rested a hand on her shoulder. "Well done, Win."

The eagle eyed them from its perch, sharp talons gripping wood. Then it flew from one side of the aviary to the other.

"Isn't it beautiful?" Winona gazed up at the raptor.

"Beautiful." But Jason wasn't looking at the eagle.

———

JASON FOLLOWED Winona through the parking lot toward the entrance of Knockers, already able to hear the band. Given the pub's name, he'd thought it must be one of those places where women wore short shorts and skimpy belly shirts. He was glad to be wrong.

"The name honors the Tommyknockers, little gnome creatures that supposedly inhabit the mines here," Winona had told him on the way here. "My friend Lexi believes one saved her life."

Jason knew better than to disrespect another culture's

beliefs and legends. There was more to this world than could be understood or explained.

McBride held the door open for both of them. "The food here is good, and the brews are fantastic. But the atmosphere is what makes it."

It was like stepping into happy chaos. The place was packed, a band on stage, the dance floor crowded, people milling about near the front door waiting for tables to open.

Winona had to shout for him to hear her. "This is the heart of Scarlet Springs."

She didn't wait for the hostess, but grabbed a couple of menus and led them toward the rear of the restaurant. "Joe always sets aside a table for the Team. It's his way of thanking us for saving lives."

As soon as they reached the table, Jason understood why the Team sat here and not toward the front. Not far from the table was a climbing wall with brightly colored handholds that went up to the ceiling.

A climbing wall in a pub?

You're in Colorado, man.

Right.

Jason recognized some of the faces—Megs and Ahearn, Sasha, Creed Herrera, Bahir Acharya, and Conrad and Kenzie. There were new faces, too.

When the Team spotted Winona, heads turned.

A woman with red hair called out and waved. "Win!"

"Everybody, scoot closer. Move!" Megs stood, moved her chair. "Pretend we like each other or something."

Winona introduced Jason to the people he hadn't yet met. "This is Lexi, my friend. She's the Team's accountant and volunteers at the clinic. This is Austin Taylor, her husband. This is their little girl, Emily, in case you couldn't tell by the red hair. This is Eric Hawke, our fire chief, and his son, Caden. Eric's wife, Vicki, runs Knockers' deep dish pizza business and is expecting their second."

Jason shook their hands in turn. "Good to meet you all."

"Any news about Naomi and the baby?" Lexi asked.

"I heard from Chaska just before we came here. The baby is fine. Naomi is pretty uncomfortable from the surgery, but her blood pressure is better. Her dad and stepmother just got into town from Pine Ridge and are at the hospital now."

"Do you have photos? Have they named him?"

Winona's smile was tinged with sadness. "They named him Shota."

Lexi's eyes went wide. "Oh, Win! That's perfect!"

"Isn't it?" Winona passed her phone to Lexi so she could see the photos. "Isn't he adorable? I got to hold him for a few minutes."

As if the word *baby* were magic, several women who worked at Knockers hurried over to their table to see the photos, passing Winona's phone around.

Grandpa beamed, his gaze meeting Jason's. "I can remember people makin' a fuss like this when Chaska and Winona were born. They grew up there—on the rez. The years pass so fast—like wind over the grass."

A pretty woman with tattoos of skulls and roses on her arms rested her hand on Grandpa Belcourt's shoulder. "Congratulations, Grandfather. You must be so happy."

Grandpa Belcourt chuckled. "I've been waitin' for my grandchildren to settle down for a long time."

The woman turned to Jason. "I'm Rain Moffat, co-owner and general manager. If there's anything you need, let me know."

"Jason Chiago. I'm here with McBride."

"We came to cash in our coupons for free meals." McBride waved his around, a grin on his face.

"Right on. Do you know what you'd like to order?" Rain took their drink and dinner orders, and, finally, there was a moment of relative quiet.

Winona leaned across the table. "The first time Chaska brought me here, I was completely overwhelmed. I didn't know anyone. I'd never seen a climbing wall. Everything was so new."

Jason could understand that. "Why did you leave Pine Ridge?"

"Chaska left to study engineering at CU and fell in love with climbing. I missed him—we'd never been apart before—and I wanted to study to become a vet. CSU in Fort Collins has a great veterinary medicine program, so I followed him here."

"Don't you miss being home with other Lakota?" Jason had seen how respectful she was toward her grandfather and other living creatures. It made no sense that she could turn her back on the reservation.

"Sure, but Scarlet Springs is home, too. We visit Pine Ridge when we can, and Grandpa spends part of the year here with us."

"My place doesn't have the air conditioning," Grandpa explained. "I like the air conditioning."

Jason understood that.

A shadow fell across the table.

McBride got to his feet. "Hey, Jack, good to see you, man."

"How have you been? It's been a while." A tall man with gray hair and sun-browned skin shook McBride's hand.

"Is the rest of the family here?"

"It's just me and Janet tonight. My wife had a craving

for Vicki's pizza." The man—Jack—turned to Winona. "I'm happy to run into you, Winona. Can I have a moment of your time?"

Winona looked surprised. "Of course."

She stood and followed Jack.

"What does Jack West want with Winona?" Megs asked.

McBride leaned closer, filled in the blanks for Jason. "Jack West is one of the wealthiest men in the state. He's also about as honorable and generous a person as you could hope to meet—and a good friend. He and his family have been running cattle and breeding quarter horses for generations. He hosts the best barbeques."

Then Winona was back. "Jason, can you come with me? We need your help."

Chapter 5

WINONA LISTENED while Jack explained the situation to Jason, the three of them standing outside Knockers, the cold wind making her wish she'd worn her jacket.

"My son and I run black Angus on our ranch north of town. I've lost a few prime steers, and it looks like wolves could be to blame. The strange part is that we haven't had wolves in Colorado for about eighty years."

Winona couldn't deny that the idea of wild wolves in the state excited her. "There have been confirmed sightings of lone wolves who've wandered down from Wyoming, but they never stayed. If wolves have settled in the mountains north of Scarlet, that's going to be big news."

Jason raised an eyebrow. "You want me to confirm that it's wolves?"

Jack shook his head. "Based on the size of the tracks, I'm pretty sure it's wolves. I want to know whether we're talking about a pack or a lone wolf passing through. I was hoping Chaska could help me, but he's doing more important things right now. Winona tells me you're one of the best trackers in the country."

Jason crossed his arms over his chest. "What do you plan to do if we find wolves on your land? Are you going to eradicate them?"

"God, no!" Jack looked appalled at the thought. "You've got my word on that. If it's wolves, I need to change how we're managing the herd—put a couple of ostriches in the pasture or something."

"*Ostriches?*"

The look on Jason's face almost made Winona laugh.

Jack grinned. "Ostriches make effective guard animals —llamas, too."

"I've told Jack that I'm happy to help." Winona owed Jack a favor, but she would have helped no matter what. "I'll ask Dr. Keene to cover for me at the clinic. I can examine whatever remains are left and see if the scene looks like the site of a wolf kill, but I can't track."

Jason considered it for a moment. "I'm in. I need to get McBride home. He and I drove here together in my truck. I'll spend the night at his place and pick Winona up from her house early tomorrow morning."

"I'll meet you at the gate to the ranch at ten. Is that too early?" Jack asked.

Winona met Jason's gaze. "Does that work for you?"

"Yeah. No problem."

"I'm much obliged to both of you. Lunch will be on us." Jack's brow furrowed. "We don't want this reaching the media, so it's best to keep it quiet. That's why I dragged you out here in the cold. Word travels fast in Scarlet."

Winona knew he was right. Wolves had been eradicated in Colorado in the 1940s, and people had strong feelings about their return to the state. Many supported it for environmental reasons, while others were vehemently opposed and believed they should all be hunted.

If the media got wind of a pack of wolves north of Scarlet…

"We'll keep it to ourselves."

"I'd best get back to my family, and you need to get inside before you freeze." Jack opened the door, held it for them. "See you tomorrow morning."

Winona walked back to the Team table, one thought chasing another through her mind. If wolves truly were returning to Colorado on their own, there would be no need to fight legal battles to reintroduce them. It would improve the health of the entire mountain ecosystem. Ranchers wouldn't be happy, but the state would reimburse them for lost livestock like it already did.

Jason walked beside her. "You're excited. I can see it on your face."

She *was* excited. "I love wolves."

"We get Mexican gray wolves moving through TO land once in a while."

"Have you ever seen one?"

"Only from a distance. Sadly, my job doesn't involve tracking four-legged creatures, just the two-legged, criminal kind."

They ended the conversation before reaching the table.

"You going to tell us what that was about?" Megs asked.

"I'll tell you when I'm sure what's happening." Winona took her seat, tapped out a text message to Dr. Keene, the local vet.

Megs' eyes narrowed. "My imagination will run wild."

Their drinks were waiting for them—Winona's Blackberry Izze, Grandpa's root beer float, Jason's brew.

"What'd you get?" Zach asked him.

"Smoke and Fire IPA." Jason took a sip. His eyebrows shot up. "Damn."

Zach raised his glass. "Told you."

Their food came a few minutes later, the conversation at the table ranging from the new gear the Team hoped to buy to predictions for the first snowfall to Sasha's upcoming photoshoot for *Rock & Ice* Magazine.

Then Sasha, who'd clearly had one too many margaritas, turned her attention to Jason. "What do you track as a Shadow Wolf?"

Jason seemed amused. "Bad guys."

"What kind of bad guys?"

"The kind that wouldn't hesitate to kill every single one of us just to make a buck—drug smugglers and human traffickers, mostly."

That seemed to sober Sasha up. "Oh. Wow."

Zach tossed back the last of his beer. "I met Chiago when I was still working the line. Our paths didn't cross often, but when they did, I knew he had my back."

"Back at you, man."

Winona found it hard to keep her gaze off Jason. He was everything she'd been raised to admire in a man—courageous, respectful of his elders, willing to take responsibility. He was what Grandpa would call a true warrior. Even when he was relaxed, there was an air of danger about him. If that wasn't enough, he was so good-looking that she found herself wondering about things she shouldn't.

Things like how it would feel to kiss him. And what he'd look like without that T-shirt. And what it would be like to have sex with him.

Stop torturing yourself! He's taken, remember?

Yes, she remembered.

And tomorrow, she was spending all day with him.

WINONA WAS JUST DRYING off after her shower when Jason knocked at her front door. *Damn.* "Coming!"

She slipped into her bathrobe and hurried on bare feet to answer, her hair hanging uncombed and wet. "Sorry. I forgot to set my alarm. I'll get dressed."

"No worries. I'm early. We've got plenty of time." He stepped into her living room, faded jeans riding low on his hips, a fleece-lined denim jacket covering a gray T-shirt, black boots on his feet. His gaze slid over her.

Great.

He probably thought she looked like a half-drowned cat.

"Make yourself comfortable. There's coffee in the kitchen if you'd like some."

"Thanks."

Winona hurried into her bedroom, dressed in layers—jeans, a warm silk jersey camisole, her purple long-sleeved T-shirt with the yellow feather on the front, and warm socks. Then she combed the tangles out of her wet hair, squeezed the moisture out of it with a towel, and left it loose to air dry.

She found Jason sitting on her sofa with a cup of coffee in his hands. "Have you had breakfast?"

"Yeah, thanks. I'm good." Jason wasn't much taller than Chaska, but he dominated the space, the coffee mug seeming small in his hands.

She stuffed things she might need into her backpack—a water bottle, gloves, a hat, a notepad, and pen—and laced into her hiking boots. "The local vet is covering the clinic later today, but I need to do morning rounds."

She let Jason feed the eagle, his fascination making her smile.

He sucked in a breath when the big bird flew down, talons out, to dig into its meal. "Look at that."

The morning was cold and crisp as they walked to Jason's truck, the air fresh with the scent of pine and golden aspens.

Winona had to hurry to keep up with his long stride. "I texted Jack for directions to the Cimarron last night."

Jason touched a button on his keychain fob, starting the truck's engine. "It's already programmed into my GPS. McBride gave me the address. He has nothing but praise for Jack West and his family."

Neither did Winona. "When the fire hit, most people were at work and couldn't make it home to evacuate their livestock. Jack and Nate showed up with trailers and rescued other people's horses. No one asked them to do it. No one paid them. They just showed up. They helped me evacuate the clinic, too."

"They sound like good people." Jason opened her door, then walked around to the driver's side and climbed in.

They headed toward the Peak to Peak Highway.

Winona stowed her backpack by her feet. "Naomi was so happy to see the photos of the cabins. Thanks again for all you did to see that through."

"I was glad to help." Jason turned up the heater.

"I got to hold little Shota again." Winona had kissed his toes and held his tiny fingers. "I had no idea how much I would adore him."

Jason smiled. "What does his name mean?"

"It's the Lakota word for 'smoke.' It's an old-fashioned boy's name. But, really, they named him after my wolf."

Jason stared at her as if he hadn't heard her correctly. "Your … *wolf?*"

She laughed. "Yeah. What? Doesn't everyone have a wolf?"

He chuckled, the sound warm. "I don't even have a

dog—well, unless you count that stray that comes around sometimes."

She told Jason how Shota and his two littermates had been rescued from a smuggler by a game warden and how she'd managed to save only Shota. "I got a special permit and built an enclosure for him. We became a pack—me, Shota, and Chaska. We brought him inside, played with him, took him for long hikes."

"You went hiking with a wolf?" The disbelief on his face made her laugh.

"That's how Chaska met Naomi." Winona told him how Naomi had been taken captive by a couple of fugitives while camping in the mountains west of Scarlet. "She escaped, but they shot her in the arm. She fell into a ravine trying to hide from them and broke her tibia. She lay there all night alone in the rain. Shota found her the next morning and saved her life. That's how she and Chaska met. He helped Zach track them."

"Did they catch the bastards?"

"One died in a shootout. They caught the other one a short time later."

"Good." He glanced over at her. "I understand your nephew's name now. That's a good name. But where's Shota, the wolf?"

Winona had known he would ask. "During the fire, I had to evacuate him to the Forest County Fairgrounds. I sedated him, but it just wasn't safe for him there—so many people, so many other animals. I found a wolf sanctuary that would take him for as long as he needed a safe home. I dropped him off there."

Her throat went tight, tears blurring her vision, an ache in the part of her heart that belonged only to Shota. "When I went to get him, I saw that he had bonded with a female—a beautiful white wolf named Aput. He had a much larger enclosure and a new pack. I couldn't take that from him, so I … I left him there. I let him go."

She blinked her tears away, hoping Jason hadn't noticed.

He took her hand, squeezed, his fingers warm. "That must have been hard."

"It was best for him, but I miss him." She willed herself to smile. "I visit when I can. He's always excited to see me."

"I bet he is. You saved his life and raised him. You're his mother. Now I know why you love wolves."

Winona was touched that Jason seemed to understand.

For a time, they drove in silence.

Jason glanced down at the GPS screen. "McBride tells me that if Jack offers us his chili or a steak, we can't say no. He says the Cimarron is like nothing I've ever seen."

Winona couldn't deny that she was curious. "I've never been there, but from the stories I've heard, Zach is right."

———

JASON FOUGHT to keep his eyes on the road. "McBride wasn't kidding."

"Holy smokes!"

The Cimarron sat in an open valley surrounded by white-capped peaks, the mountainsides gold with aspen. Nestled in the middle of the valley was perhaps the largest family home Jason had ever seen. Constructed of stone and logs, it had a steep, multi-gabled roof, high cathedral windows, and a portico driveway accented by a colonnade of polished logs.

"It looks like a Swiss chalet that grew up, married rich, and became a mansion." There was a note of awe in Winona's voice.

Jason laughed. "Good description."

"Can you imagine living here?"

"Hell, no. For most of my childhood, our house didn't have plumbing or electricity."

Off to one side stood several large outbuildings, including horse barns, a bunkhouse, an enormous riding hall, and several corrals.

Jason followed Jack's pickup around to the back and parked. "Check that out—a five-car garage."

Jason climbed out and met Winona at the back of his truck.

Jack walked up to them, hand out. "Welcome to the Cimarron. I'm grateful to both of you for coming up today. What do you say we head inside so you can refresh yourselves after the drive? Then we can talk."

Jason and Winona followed Jack through a heated garage into a mudroom and then down a hallway into a spacious, modern kitchen, the mingled scents of coffee, cinnamon, and something tangy and savory making Jason's mouth water.

"Make yourselves comfortable. We've got coffee and fresh-baked cinnamon rolls if that tempts you." He pointed to a large pot. "I've got my world-famous chili heating up for lunch."

Winona glanced over at Jason. "We've heard about your chili."

Jack grinned. "It wouldn't be world-famous if you hadn't, now would it?"

Winona sat at the table. "I'd love some coffee and a cinnamon roll. Thank you."

"Milk or sugar?" Jack asked.

"Milk, please."

Jason took the seat across from her. "Just coffee for me, thanks—black."

From upstairs, came the happy sound of children's laughter.

"Where's Emily?" Winona filled Jason in. "She's Jack's oldest grandchild."

"She's at school—second grade now." Jack handed Winona her coffee first, then poured Jason's. "My wife, Janet, would love to meet you both, but at the moment, she has her hands full with our grandson and daughter, both in their terrific twos. My daughter-in-law Megan is in court this morning with a client. I'll tell you what—I never thought I'd welcome a child and a grandchild three weeks apart."

While they drank their coffee and Winona savored her cinnamon roll, Jack gave them the whole story. "Six weeks ago, we lost a steer. Nate found only its skull, the bones picked almost clean. Other than blood in the grass and a few wolf tracks, there was nothing else—no bones, no hide. Nada."

"Would a wolf take down something as large as a steer?" Jason had no idea.

Winona dabbed her lips with a napkin. "Yes, but wolves typically stick with wild game and only go for livestock if other prey isn't around."

"A month ago, it happened again. No remains apart from the head. There were lots of canine tracks in the area, including a couple of prints the size of my hand." He held up a callused hand, fingers splayed. "It sure looked like a wolf to me."

"Have you ruled out disease?" Winona asked. "Lots of prey animals will take advantage of carrion, including wolves."

Jack nodded. "Our vet checked the herd and found nothing but healthy animals. In all my years running cattle, we've lost livestock to cougars, black bears, coyotes, even a bobcat or two. But I've never seen a cow's carcass *disappear*. Even if the animals got at it, we'd find something."

Winona picked up her coffee, clearly thinking this through. "Wolves are messy eaters. A pack of wolves will typically tear a kill apart, each wolf dragging its share to a different spot to feed, but they wouldn't carry the entire animal away. You typically find bits of bone and other parts of the carcass around."

Jason had never raised cattle, but he'd seen his share of dead animals in the desert. "I've seen cougar kills in the wild. There's not much left, but there's always something—antlers, hide, bone, viscera."

"We found another steer killed yesterday morning. It rained the night before, so there are lots of tracks. I had Nate cordon off the area and cover it with a tarp to protect whatever sign is there. We bagged the head and set it aside. I thought maybe there'd be a way to determine what killed the animal."

"Smart." Jason drained his coffee mug. "When do we get started?"

Winona glared at him. "When I finish my cinnamon roll."

Chapter 6

THE PASTURE where the latest steer had been killed was a forty-minute drive on dirt roads through tall glades of aspen and stretches of towering pines. It was some of the most beautiful scenery Winona had seen in Colorado.

"This herd is headed for market in the spring." Jack parked his truck near a gate. "I expect losses—every rancher does—but I can't let predators pick off my profits one steer at a time."

Winona climbed out of the truck. The sun was high in the sky now, but the wind was cold, the air carrying the unmistakable scent of autumn. In the distance, black cattle grazed on the last of the sun-dried summer grass. "It's beautiful up here."

The sound of an engine announced Nate's arrival. He stepped out of his truck looking like the quintessential cowboy, brown hat on his head, denim and plaid on his body, cowboy boots on his feet.

He introduced himself to Jason and then shook Winona's hand, a grin on his scarred face. "Good to see you again, Winona. I hear you're an aunt now. Congratulations."

"Thanks."

"Son, why don't you show Chiago where you found the kill? I'll stay here with Winona while she checks out the remains."

"Sure thing." Nate walked to a nearby gate, opened it. "This way."

"I've got the head on ice in a cooler back here." Jack opened the tailgate and reached for a plastic cooler. "There's a box of nitrile gloves in the back seat."

"I already grabbed a pair." Winona slipped the gloves over her hands. "Just to be clear, I'm not a forensic specialist or an expert in bite marks."

"No, but you know a hell of a lot about wolves." Jack drew a plastic garbage bag out of the cooler. "This won't be the prettiest sight you've seen—and it doesn't smell good, either."

Winona laughed, her gaze on Jason as he walked away with Nate. What was it about him that drew her like a magnet? "I take care of wild animals. Have you ever smelled skunk poo?"

"No, and I don't think I want to." Jack pulled the head out of the cooler, spread a plastic bag on the tailgate, and set the head on top of it. "All right, boy, let's see what Winona has to say about you."

There wasn't as much flesh left on it as Winona had imagined, the skull intact, the bones unbroken but exposed, a few vertebrae still attached. She worked as methodically as she could, examining every surface.

She canted the head so Jack could see the left jawbone. "These are tooth pits where the animal bit down. These grooves are called scores."

Jack pointed. "What about those deeper grooves?"

"Those were probably made by rodents."

"Rodents?"

"They eat bones and antlers for calcium, and they've got those big front teeth. See how those marks are deeper at the bottom than the top?" She pointed with a gloved pinky finger. "I sometimes give bones to rodents at the clinic. Their bite marks look just like this. I bet these came from a squirrel."

Jack leaned closer. "I had no idea."

Winona went on with her examination. "I wish I'd taken more time to study the bones from the roadkill I fed Shota. Most of the time, he got frozen blocks of meat to gnaw on. There was nothing left by the time he'd finished."

Still, the bite marks looked like they *could* be from a wolf, but she couldn't be certain. For all she knew, they might just as easily come from a mountain lion or black bear. "It's possible that these marks weren't left by the predator that killed the steer. Kleptoparasitism is very common. A mountain lion kills an elk, feeds, and caches the rest. A black bear finds the cache, drags the kill away, and feeds on it for several days. While the bear isn't looking, foxes or coyotes take their share."

Nature wasted nothing.

She turned the skull to see what she could of the vertebrae. "A mountain lion typically attacks the neck and crushes the vertebrae and part of the skull. That didn't happen here, but…"

She ran a gloved finger over a mark on the bottom of the lowest vertebra. It was too narrow to be scoring from a tooth. It was almost razor-thin, like a...

"I think this was made by a knife." She held it out so Jack could see.

"A knife?" He leaned in, brow furrowed. "Well, I'll be damned."

"It looks like a cut mark to me, but I don't know enough about forensic science to be certain. I could be making this up."

"I appreciate that disclaimer, Winona, but that doesn't mean you're wrong."

She set the remains down on the plastic. "I'd probably be more helpful to you if I took a careful look around the pasture. That's where the story is."

Jack bagged the remains and set the bag inside the cooler. "Let's head out there and see what Chiago has for us."

———

WHILE NATE HUNG back so as not to tread on sign, Jason walked around the site of the kill, studying it, and snapping photos with his phone.

A large depression in the grass where the steer had fallen. Lots of dried blood and small bits of tissue drawing flies. Scattered sign—overlapping tracks from squirrels, coyotes, humans, and possibly a wolf.

Click. Click. Click.

Jason knelt beside a single clear print of a front paw that was as wide as his palm. It certainly looked like a wolf, but he needed to see a complete set of tracks to be certain.

Click.

He tried backtracking, following bent and broken grasses and the occasional partial print in a straight line back toward the fence. He hadn't gone far when he found what he'd been searching for—tracks from both the front and hind paws—and beyond that, gray fur snagged on barbed wire.

This was where the animal crossed into the pasture.

But where had it gone afterward?

Click. Click.

He walked back to the site of the kill, looking for drag marks or places where the grass had been flattened. There were none, except…

He backtracked the way he and Nate had come, heading toward the gate. He'd assumed that Jack and Nate had trampled the grass when Nate had entered the pasture to examine the site and cover it. But maybe Jason was wrong about that. He stepped carefully, his gaze moving over a two-foot-wide path.

Boot tracks. A front and hind paw print. And there— dried blood on the grass.

Click. Click. Click.

He saw that Winona and Jack had joined Nate and made his way carefully over to them. "I'm pretty certain I know what happened here."

He walked them through it, starting at the site of the kill and moving toward the barbed wire with the bit of fur, which he plucked off and handed to Winona. "This is where the wolf entered the pasture. It can be hard to tell a wolf track from that of a large dog, but there are differences."

He pointed to the toes. "See how the claw marks are visible for each of the toes and how they point forward? We often don't see all of the claws on dog tracks, and the outer toes tend to be splayed outward. But the biggest difference is the way they walk."

"The way they walk?" Nate asked.

"Wolves walk in a straight line. Dogs don't. See where the rear paw track is right in front of the larger front track? You wouldn't see that with dogs."

The three bent to examine the track.

"So, we've got ourselves a wolf." Jack lifted his gaze

from the track to Jason. "Can you tell how many wolves were here? Is it a pack?"

"So far, what I've seen looks like a lone wolf."

"It wasn't a pack." Winona glanced around the pasture, the wind catching strands of her dark hair. "If a pack had attacked that steer, there'd be several drag trails and depressions in the grass where pack members sat down to feed. They would have left some of the larger bones, maybe hide. There would be something here."

Jason motioned to them to follow him. "There's more."

He led them back to the kill site, knelt, and pointed. "There are lots of boot tracks around the place where the steer fell. At first, I figured they belonged to you, but you're both wearing cowboy boots. Some of these tracks have deep tread with a circle in the center of the heel. What kind of boots were you wearing when you covered the site?"

Nate lifted a foot, showed Jason the tread. "These same cowboy boots."

Jack scowled. "I don't like where this is going."

Jason stood, led them back toward the gate. "There are drops of dried blood on the grass. I also found tracks with that same deep tread, as well as a few wolf tracks. The wolf left the pasture the same way you entered it—through that gate."

Winona met his gaze, understanding in her eyes. "The wolf didn't kill the steer."

Jason looked from Nate to Jack. "Your predator walks on two legs."

"Son of a bitch." Jack removed his cowboy hat, ran a hand through his gray hair.

Nate swore under his breath. "A poacher."

"That fits with what Winona found on the remains of the head." Jack left it to Winona to explain.

"There are tooth pits and scoring on the bones, which could be from a wolf. I think coyotes and a squirrel got at it, too. But on the last vertebra, there's a striation that must have come from a knife."

Jason put the pieces together. "Someone killed the steer, probably with a firearm. Then he dressed it, cut it into manageable pieces, bagged it, and carried it away. The wolf probably fed on the viscera and the head."

Nate glanced back down at the wolf track. "The wolf must have been drawn by the scent of carrion."

Jason wasn't sure about that. "Winona's the wolf expert."

"A wolf would definitely be drawn by the smell of the kill. Wolves aren't obligate carnivores, so, unlike mountain lions, they do eat the digestive organs of ungulates, including the rumen. It could have followed the scent trail left by the blood droplets over to the gate. An adult wolf would have no trouble jumping over the fence. But there's another possibility."

"What's that?" Jack asked.

Winona seemed to hesitate. "It's just a hunch."

"Let's hear it."

"It's strange that you found wolf tracks at all of the kills. I would expect a lone wolf to range over a territory of hundreds of square miles. There's a chance that the wolf might belong to the poacher."

———

WINONA HELPED Jason cover the spot where the steer was killed to protect the evidence. She was conscious of his every movement, every breath, every glance, her senses heightened, some kind of awareness stretching between them.

He's taken. Don't forget that.

"Hold the tarp down so I can hammer in these stakes."

She dropped to her knees and held down one edge of the tarp, fighting to keep the wind from taking it.

Jason glanced up, his gaze catching Winona's. "Are you disappointed that it's not a wolf pack?"

"A little." Winona couldn't deny it. "I would love to see wild wolves back in Colorado. I'm also relieved. At least now, I don't have to worry that ranchers are going to start killing them out of fear for their livestock."

"You can't shoot what isn't there."

"I'm impressed with how quickly you put it together." She'd only watched him work for a few minutes, but she'd found it mesmerizing—the way he moved, the concentration on his handsome face, his ability to read the land at a glance. "Who taught you to cut sign?"

"My grandfather. He and my grandmother took me in after my parents were murdered. They taught me about the Tohono O'odham *himdag*, our way of life. They made sure I learned the traditional skills so I could pass them down one day."

Winona stared at him. "Your parents were ... *murdered?*"

The word cut through her like cold barbed wire, sent chills down her spine. Some part of her wanted to tell Jason that she'd almost been murdered, too. But she wouldn't open that door. She couldn't. Besides, this wasn't about her.

"The police said it was drug traffickers." Jason hammered in another stake, his face downturned so she couldn't see his expression. "They were shot execution-style while coming back one night from my grandparents' home on the Mexican side, their bodies left in the desert."

"I'm so sorry. How old were you?"

"Twelve."

"So young." She'd been only ten when her mother had died. "I guess that's why you became a federal agent."

He hammered in another stake. "Yeah."

"I'm glad your grandparents were there for you. You grew up on the Mexican side? You must speak Spanish."

"*Sí, por supuesto.*" He grinned. "All O'odham speak English and Spanish, as well as our own language. We all have dual citizenship, too—US and Mexican."

"Our grandparents taught Chaska and me Lakota. There aren't that many Lakota people who still speak the language, especially young people."

"Have you thought about going back to Pine Ridge to teach Lakota classes? It sounds like they need you."

She shook her head. "I'm not sure I'd be a good teacher. I wouldn't want to leave the clinic or move far away from Chaska."

Jason reached for another stake. "You two are close."

"When I was little, our mother had too much to drink one night and got lost in a snowstorm. Chaska and I found her the next morning, frozen to death, just ten feet from our front door."

Jason's head came up, sympathy in his dark eyes. "I'm sorry to hear that."

"Our dad had a girlfriend and wasn't around much, so Chaska took care of me. For a time, all we had was each other. He kept me safe, got me to school, and made sure I had something to eat every day until our grandparents came for us."

"He sounds like a good big brother."

"The best."

"Where's your father now? Or maybe I shouldn't ask."

"I've had a hard time forgiving him for being unfaithful to our mother and abandoning us. He and Chaska were on speaking terms for a while after Chaska completed his fourth Sun Dance. But then Chaska caught him taking money from non-Native tourists for bogus ceremonies—vision quests, naming ceremonies, and the like. That was the last straw for both of us."

Jason frowned. "That's not okay. I'm sorry."

With the tarp in place, they made their way back to the truck.

"I called the sheriff's department," Jack told them. "They're sending a deputy this afternoon. I was wondering if we could head over to the other pasture to look at the other two sites before lunch."

Winona had taken off the entire day. "I've got time."

"Fine by me." Jason turned and walked toward the trees. "Before we go, I want to check the edge of the forest, see if I can find anything else. The poacher left the pasture heading this way."

Winona walked beside him, amazed at how quickly he moved. She'd have been on her hands and knees, crawling along with a magnifying glass if she'd been looking for sign, but he walked at a normal pace. Did he have laser eyes?

He stopped, knelt. "Do you have any more of those nitrile gloves?"

There, lying in the duff, was a brass shell casing.

"I'll get some." She ran back to the truck where Jack and Nate stood talking, grabbed a pair of gloves, and hurried back to Jason.

He slipped a glove onto one hand, picked up the shell casing, and examined it. "Thirty-ought-six. Absolutely big enough to put down a steer."

He dropped the brass inside the other nitrile glove, tucked it into his pocket, and got to his feet.

Winona turned, glanced back to where the steer had

died. "The shooter would've had a clear line of sight from here. What distance is this—fifty yards?"

"I'd say that's about right. An easy shot." Jason turned, walked twenty or so paces into the forest. "He passed through here."

Jack and Nate joined them.

"Did he find something?" Jack asked.

"So far, a thirty-ought-six shell casing and some tracks."

Jason walked back to them, handed Jack the nitrile glove with the shell casing. "It looks like he shot the steer from the edge of the forest here. Then he loaded the bagged meat onto some kind of four-wheeler and headed deeper into the mountains."

"Into the mountains?" Jack's expression went dark. "That's our land."

"Is there a highway or road he could have used for his exfil?"

"There are a couple of old mining roads, but it's mostly untouched wilderness."

Nate met his father's gaze. "We need to find this son of a bitch."

Chapter 7

JASON WALKED through the pasture where the other two steers had been killed but found little. Whatever sign there'd been had washed away in the rain or been trampled by grazing cattle. But based on what he'd learned about wolf behavior from Winona, what they *didn't* find was revealing.

No bone fragments. No drag marks. No depressions in the grass where a wolf might have sat down to feed.

A quick walk along the edge of the forest had yielded three more .30-06 shell casings. He'd be willing to bet that ballistics tests would reveal they'd been fired from the same firearm as the first.

Before they made it back to the house for lunch, the sheriff arrived.

"I appreciate you coming out here yourself, Sheriff Pella." Jack shook his hand. "This is Jason Chiago. He's an ICE agent with the Shadow Wolves. He's been helping us piece together what's happening here."

Pella, an older man with salt-and-pepper hair, shook

Jason's hand. "That's an impressive resume. Let's see what you've got."

They drove back to the other pasture where the evidence was preserved, and Jason walked Sheriff Pella through the scene, ending with the tread marks from the four-wheeler. Winona answered Pella's questions about wolves and what they ought to expect at the site of a wolf kill.

Sheriff Pella looked up from his notepad. "It sure looks to me like you've got a human problem, Jack. Those can be the toughest to resolve."

"Don't I know it." Jack looked up at the mountainside behind them. "We've had poachers on our land before—hunters who camp illegally and take deer, elk, and moose. But we've never had a poacher go for our beef herd. We're organizing the men, putting armed riders in the pastures this afternoon. Nate also plans to take some of the men and ride patrols in this area to make our presence felt."

"That all sounds good. I can increase patrols on the highway near the ranch." When this failed to impress Jack, Pella went on. "My two best deputies are in Denver giving depositions, but I could send one of them out here tomorrow morning and try to pick up that trail left by the four-wheeler—if Agent Chiago has the time."

"I'll do it—provided Winona comes along. There's only one of us here who knows how to handle a wolf."

You just want to spend time with her.

He brushed that thought away.

Winona looked up at him through those big, brown eyes. "If I can get coverage for the clinic again, I'm happy to help."

They worked through the details with Sheriff Pella. They would meet the deputy at the ranch house tomorrow at nine and see where the trail led. If Jason and Winona wanted to carry a firearm, they were welcome to do so.

"I don't think there's much chance of finding this bastard, but it might help to figure out where he's getting onto your land." Sheriff Pella held his hand out to Jason. "Agent Chiago, I'm impressed. I've never seen a Shadow Wolf in action. If you ever get sick of working for the feds, you've got a spot on my team."

Jason didn't tell the sheriff that it would be a cold day in hell before he left Sells. "Thank you, sir."

As the sheriff drove away, Jason, Winona, and Jack piled back into Jack's truck and started the drive back to the ranch house.

"I'm grateful to both of you for your help today. Tomorrow is bound to take most of the day. My family and I would love to have you both as guests of the ranch. We can grill some steaks, put you up in our cabin, where you can soak in our hot tub. I'll make you a good breakfast the next morning, and then we can saddle up some horses and go riding. I make wicked buttermilk pancakes."

Jason was about to turn Jack down, but Winona's face lit up like it was Christmas.

"I would love that. Thank you, Jack. I've heard about your barbeques."

"Well, of course, you have." Jack chuckled.

It was on the tip of Jason's tongue to decline. The Wests were good people, but they were strangers. Jason could drive up separately, let Winona come in her vehicle, and then leave at the end of the day.

But he'd be damned if the Cimarron wasn't one of the most beautiful places he'd ever seen. And it had been ages since he'd sat in a saddle.

Against his better judgment, Jason accepted. "McBride

told me not to turn down one of your grilled steaks if you offered, so I won't."

"Well, then, it's settled." Jack grinned. "We'll get the cabin ready."

Almost immediately, Jason regretted his decision.

You're not here for horseback riding or scenery. You're here for Winona.

Something about her tugged at him, made him want to be near her. Yes, she was attractive, but it was more than that. There was something about her—her way with animals, her unguarded smile, her sincerity, her openness, her willingness to help others. She was everything Elena was not.

You don't really know her.

No, he didn't. He'd been with Elena for four years. He'd thought he knew everything about her, but he'd been wrong.

He was probably wrong about Winona, too.

———

BACK AT THE HOUSE, Jack thanked them and handed Winona a paper bag with a large container of leftover chili and cornbread wrapped in aluminum foil.

"Thanks for your help today," Jack said. "We look forward to treating you to some Cimarron hospitality tomorrow."

Winona waited until they were back in Jason's truck and on the highway to say it. "I told you the Wests were good people."

"Jack certainly makes a mean chili." Jason glanced over at her, his eyes hidden behind sunglasses. "Can I ask what happened to Nate?"

"He was burned in an IED explosion while serving

with the Marines in Afghanistan. No one expected him to survive." That's all Winona knew. She hadn't lived here then. "I can't imagine how painful that must have been."

Jason winced. "He must be one tough guy."

Winona's mind went to Eric Hawke and what he'd endured since being burned in the fire just two months ago. "Scarlet Springs has more than its share of heroes."

They drove for a time in silence, Winona mulling over their day, her head filling with questions. She spoke aloud without realizing it. "How much does a steer weigh—a thousand pounds?"

"Something like that."

She did some quick math. "Three steers in six weeks with maybe five hundred pounds of edible meat per animal would be fifteen hundred pounds of beef. That's a *lot* of burgers."

"Maybe this guy is filling up a freezer or selling it on the side."

She supposed that made sense. "Why poach steers? Why not go after wild game?"

"I can think of a couple of reasons. Wild game is unreliable. You can hunt all day and go home with nothing."

She could understand that. "The steers are captive, fenced in."

Jason nodded. "Not only that, but they don't run. They're domesticated. Shooting a steer in a pasture takes no skill at all. It would be easier than shooting a sitting duck."

"Do you hunt?"

"My grandfather used to take me hunting for feral hogs and javelinas. That's how I learned to shoot."

"And track."

He nodded. "If you want a successful hunt, you have to know what the animal wants, where it's going, what it needs. You have to anticipate its movements, know the landscape, and learn to be patient. That's as true for people as it is javelinas."

It struck Winona that Jason had probably spent most of his life on the hunt. "I'm sure people are the more dangerous prey."

"For sure." He shrugged his right shoulder. "I caught a round in the shoulder a couple of summers ago. I have friends, fellow Wolves, who've been shot—and killed."

"I'm sorry." Winona hurt for him.

"It goes with the job—but thanks."

"I can't imagine doing what you do and dealing with that kind of danger every day. A criminal held me at gunpoint once, and I still haven't gotten over it."

John Charles Ready had done more than that. No, he hadn't raped her, but he'd talked about it, saying filthy, racist things to her. Then he'd tried to kill her. If not for Lexi, he would have succeeded.

Jason reached over, took her hand, his touch comforting. "I'm sorry, Win. I hope they caught him."

"He's dead." She shivered. "That's when we met Zach. Chaska helped track him. I'm not sure why I told you that. I don't usually talk about it."

"We were talking about bad guys doing bad things." He released her hand. "I can see why it came up."

She tried to let it go, to shift the conversation back to safer paths.

"We'll need to leave an hour earlier tomorrow. You can stay at my place if you want." The moment her words were out, she worried he might get the wrong impression. "I've got a spare room. You can get an extra hour of sleep. But if you think that would make your fiancée uncomfortable, I understand."

"My fiancée?" A dark eyebrow arched. "Who told you

I had a fiancée—or is that your way of asking whether I'm attached?"

Heat rushed to Winona's face. "Kat said you're engaged. I—"

"Oh. Kat doesn't know. That relationship ended a while back."

This revelation took a moment to sink in.

He's single.

Her cheeks burned hotter. "I'm sorry. I didn't mean to—"

"Don't apologize." He seemed to find her blunder amusing, the hint of a smile on his lips. "You could only believe what Kat told you."

There was a moment of awkward silence—or at least it felt awkward to Winona. It had been one thing to feel attracted to him when she'd believed he was already in a relationship. It was something altogether different to know that he was available.

Just because he's available doesn't mean he's available to you.

"Thanks for the invitation, but don't you want to hang with your family?"

"I'll probably visit Naomi and the baby, say hello to her parents, check on Grandpa, and then reheat Jack's chili. You can come with me or just hang out at my place and watch TV. I have cable."

"It's a good thing I brought my gear. I'll call McBride and let him know."

━━━

JASON FOLLOWED Winona into her house, the sweet scent of her skin teasing him, her windblown hair making his fingers itch to touch it.

Why had he done this to himself? Staying overnight

with her was putting himself in the danger zone. It had been six months since he'd been with a woman, and Winona was everything he'd love to get his hands on. She was intelligent, beautiful, compassionate—and attracted to him.

Nah, man, forget it.

He'd learned long ago that casual sex wasn't worth it. It took the edge off his sexual need, but instead of contentment afterward, there was only emptiness. Besides, there was too much of a chance of someone mistaking physical pleasure for love and getting hurt.

Winona deserved better than that. All women did.

She set her backpack down inside the door and put the chili Jack had given them in her refrigerator. "Just make yourself at home."

"Thanks."

She led him to the spare bedroom, showed him where to find towels and washcloths, then gave him a quick tour of the kitchen. "Glasses are here. The coffee is in here. There's wood outside the back door if you want to start a fire. The remote is on the coffee table, and my wireless password is taped to the fridge. I'll be gone for about an hour, maybe an hour and a half."

"Don't worry about me."

"You've got my cell number, right?"

"Yeah."

"Call if you need anything. See you in a bit." She hurried out the door, locking the deadbolt behind her.

Jason took out his laptop and caught up on his email. An update about Ren's condition. A reminder that the premium on his auto policy was coming due. And something from his supervisor—a notice of his disciplinary hearing date.

Shit.

He closed his computer, gave McBride a call, and explained the situation.

"West never asked *us* to spend the night." McBride sounded hurt.

"You jealous?"

"Hell, yes." McBride chuckled. "So, you and Winona?"

"It's not like that."

"That's what you keep saying."

"Hey, she offered me her spare room to save me time in the morning."

"Right."

Jason changed the subject. "She told me that you helped catch a guy who held a gun to her head."

"Yeah. That was five years ago, I think."

Jason didn't think it was his place to ask what had happened, but McBride shared the story anyway.

"The asshole robbed a bank and got badly burned when the dye pack in the money bag exploded. He went to her clinic and forced her to give him medical care at gunpoint, then injected her with a lethal overdose of ketamine."

"Jesus."

"From the reports I read, he got ugly with her before he injected her, made all kinds of violent sexual and racist threats. I think the worst part of it for her was knowing that the dose he was giving her would kill her. If her friend Lexi hadn't wandered in and gotten a call off to the police, Winona would have died on the clinic floor."

Good God.

Jason could only imagine how terrifying that must have been. "Tell me you're the one who killed this son of a bitch."

"Nah, man. I didn't have to. The bastard abducted Lexi and dragged her with him into an abandoned mine shaft. Chaska helped us track them. We'd just found them when the shaft collapsed. He died, but Lexi survived with the help of a tommyknocker—or so she claims. The Team got her out."

"There are some sick fuckers out there." Jason had spent his life tracking them.

"True that."

Jason finished the conversation, got to his feet, and went out back for firewood, the details McBride had shared running through this mind. It sickened him to think of some asshole taking advantage of Winona's skills and repaying her by trying to take her life. She'd drifted into unconsciousness, believing she was dying.

Fucking bastard.

Jason knew so many Native women whose lives had been destroyed by violence—child abuse, partner violence, sexual assault, murder. He'd rescued dozens of Indigenous women and children from trafficking operations. He'd witnessed their helplessness, their terror, their desperation. All he'd been able to do was bust the bad guys, one by one.

It didn't feel like enough. It was never enough.

Jason wasn't especially religious. He didn't attend Mass regularly. But he had no trouble believing that evil was real and alive in the world.

When the fire was going, he turned on the TV, but he was too restless to sit. He carried in more wood, then found a pot and set Jack's chili on the stove to reheat. While that simmered, he sorted through his gear and checked his Glock, making sure he was ready for tomorrow's hunt.

He'd just put the pistol back in its case when he heard Winona's key slip into the lock. Certain the sight of his pistol would unnerve her, he tucked it into his pack.

She stepped inside, a bright smile on her face. "Hey."

He got to his feet. "Hey."

"Oh! You started dinner."

"I can't claim any glory. I just dumped the leftover chili into a pot." Still, he liked the way her eyes lit up.

"Look what I got you." She held up a six-pack of amber bottles. "I saw that you liked the beer at Knockers, so I brought you this—Golden Aspen IPA."

"Thanks." Jason thought he just might be in love.

Chapter 8

WHILE JASON WASHED UP, Winona got dinner on the table—an easy task when it was already made. She set butter next to the warmed cornbread, got a glass out for Jason's beer, poured seltzer water over ice for herself, and set out an old plastic coffee can lid for the spirit plate.

She'd never actually had a man over for dinner—if you didn't count her brother or her grandfather. The last time she'd set two places at her table, Naomi had been out of town, and the second plate had been for Chaska. She couldn't help feeling a little nervous, especially now that she knew Jason was single.

"That smells good." Jason twisted the cap off a bottle of beer and poured it into his glass. "Want one?"

"No, thanks." Winona sat. "I don't drink."

"Got it." He took his seat across from her. "How are Naomi and little Shota?"

While they ate, Winona shared the news. Naomi's preeclampsia had improved, but she was still in pain from the C-section. Her doctor thought she'd be able to come home by the end of the week. Shota was thriving and had the nurses wrapped around his tiny pinky finger. Chaska had slept at home last night and had finally gotten a shower. Doug and Star were watching over Grandpa. Chaska had been approved for eight weeks of paternity leave.

"The last time I saw my brother so happy was on their wedding day." Winona realized Jason didn't know any of these people. "I'm boring you to death."

The warmth in his gaze made her pulse skip. "I asked, remember?"

She broke eye contact, shifted the conversation to him. "Do you have any nieces or nephews?"

"I've got three older sisters, and between them, they've got seven kids—three boys and four girls. They moved away, one by one." There was a disapproving edge to his voice. "I do my best to stay in touch. I don't want the kids to grow up not knowing what it means to be Tohono O'odham."

"Your sisters will teach them."

Jason didn't look sure of that. "They all married non-Natives. They don't speak the O'odham tongue to their kids, and they've never brought them home to Sells. How can you teach someone what it means to be O'odham—one of the Desert People—if they've never seen the desert and don't speak the language?"

Winona could see how much this bothered him. "Do you think they left because of what happened to your parents? After my mother died, I couldn't walk out the front door, not even with Chaska holding my hand. I had to go out the back way. I was so glad when our grandparents took us away from that house."

"I'm sure that was part of it. More than that, I think they just wanted easier lives." He sounded disappointed.

"Is that so wrong? After centuries of suffering and

trauma, isn't it a good thing when one of us finds happiness?"

"If everyone with a college education or special training leaves the reservations, where does that leave the Nations? How will anything get better for our people? What happens to our cultures, our languages?"

"We carry them with us." Winona tried not to take what Jason was saying personally, though she couldn't help but feel judged. "We speak for those back at home. We are the voice of our people to the outside world."

Jason didn't look convinced.

Winona didn't want to lose her temper, but she needed him to see her point of view. "Naomi has a gift shop that sells jewelry made by Native people from reservations all over the country. If not for her and her shop here in Scarlet, they wouldn't have that income. Don't forget Camp Mato Sapa. I've seen it change kids' lives."

"And Chaska? Couldn't his engineering skills be put to better use at home?"

Winona leaned back in her chair, crossed her arms over her chest, irked now. So much for her silly hopes for a romantic evening. "Sure—when the Oglala Lakota start launching rockets. And, yes, I probably could have started a wildlife sanctuary on the reservation. It would have taken years to get the funding and all the permits. But I don't want to live far from my brother. Once my grandfather makes the journey, he and Naomi will be all the close family I have."

"I get that. Family is important. But do you think little Shota will grow up to have the same sense of what it means to be Lakota that you and your brother have?"

Winona hoped so. "Chaska plans to speak only Lakota to him, and he will spend time on Pine Ridge visiting relatives, even if he doesn't grow up there."

Jason's gaze dropped to the table for a moment. "Sorry. I don't mean to question your choices."

"Yes, you do." Winona let go of her frustration. "But I understand why."

She understood something else, too. No matter how attractive or courageous Jason was, she couldn't afford to let herself develop feelings for him. He would never leave Sells, and her home was in Scarlet Springs.

———

JASON WATCHED the news while Winona packed for their stay at the ranch, brushed her teeth, and got ready for bed. He did his best to ignore the sight of her as she moved back and forth from her bedroom to the bathroom, but it wasn't easy. He wasn't sure what he found sexier—her sleeveless white sleepshirt with pink sheep on it that showed off her smooth, slender legs or the blue bathrobe she'd left open.

She'd been wearing that same bathrobe this morning, except it had been tied, and she'd been soaking wet and naked beneath it. Yes, he'd noticed. How could he not?

He dragged his gaze away from the hallway and back to the TV, where CNN had aerial footage of a fire at an apartment complex in Miami. But Jason was too restless to take in the news, their dinner conversation on loop in his head. He shouldn't have pushed Winona the way he had.

No matter how strongly he felt about the issues, he was a guest in her house. How she lived her life wasn't his business. She and her family were doing a lot of good in this world, which is why he was here in Scarlet in the first place.

Sometimes it pays to keep your mouth shut.

Yeah, well, that was a lesson he was still learning.

He turned off the TV and walked toward his room, colliding with Winona in the hallway when she stepped out of the bathroom. He caught her around the waist, her body soft against his, her hair like silk beneath his palm. "We keep bumping into each other."

She looked up at him through wide eyes, the minty scent of her toothpaste making him want to kiss her. "I … uh…"

For a moment, neither of them moved, his gaze locked with hers.

He could tell by the way her pupils dilated and her body tensed that she felt it, too, this attraction between them.

You're playing with fire.

"Do you … uh … need anything?" There was a slight quaver in her voice.

It was on the tip of his tongue to tell her that he needed her tonight, but he let her go, stepped back. "No. Thank you. I'm turning in."

"Goodnight then."

"Goodnight."

She walked to her room and closed the door behind her.

Well, he had passed that test.

Damn.

He walked to his room, grabbed his toothbrush, and went to the bathroom to brush his teeth, his gaze fixing on his reflection.

Idiot.

He could have kissed her, and she would have melted in his arms. It would have been sweet. But then morning would come, and things would be awkward between them. There was no chance that they could be together, so there was no point in crossing the line and getting physical.

Strange that he could feel so drawn to a woman who wasn't right for him.

Remember Elena?

Yeah. Maybe it wasn't strange. Maybe it was a pattern. Jason had felt drawn to Elena, and she'd turned out to be the enemy.

Moral of the story? Don't let your cock make decisions for you.

He finished brushing his teeth, walked back to his room, and stripped down to his boxers. Then he turned out the light and crawled beneath the covers.

He willed himself to relax, to let the sexual tension ebb away—or tried to, anyway. Images of the day passed through his mind. Winona, wet and naked in her bathrobe. Winona, listening as he interpreted the sign, dark hair caught in the breeze. Winona, excitement on her face when Jack invited them to stay at the ranch.

He had no idea how long he'd been sleeping when something woke him. He sat up, listened. Was Winona crying?

He got out of bed, slipped into his jeans and a T-shirt, opened his door, and stepped into the hallway.

A stifled sob.

He walked to Winona's door, knocked. "Winona, are you okay?"

"I'm fine."

Ah, hell.

He stood there for a moment, trying to decide whether to let her lie stand. "I know that's not true."

Footsteps.

The door opened.

Winona stood there in her sleepshirt with the pink sheep, her face wet with tears, misery mixed with embarrassment on her pretty face. "I woke you, didn't I?"

"That's okay. What's wrong?"

She leaned against the doorjamb, her dark hair tangled around her shoulders. "Just a bad dream. I have nightmares about it sometimes."

"About the time the bastard attacked you in your clinic?"

She nodded, sniffed. "The dreams always seem so real."

Jason understood a thing or two about that. "Why don't I make you a cup of tea or warm some milk, and we can talk?"

"I should be making *you* the tea. You're my guest."

"Hey, you told me to make myself at home, remember? Follow me to my kitchen."

———

WINONA SAT on the sofa with a fleece throw around her shoulders and a cup of chamomile tea in her hands, while Jason put wood on a fire that had burned down to glowing coals.

He closed the wood stove. "That ought to warm things up."

"Thanks." She sipped her tea. "Sorry again to wake you."

"Don't apologize." He sat down on the other end of the sofa, one long leg tucked beneath him so that he faced her. "Some nightmares are a lot worse than others."

That was the truth.

She wasn't sure where to start. "It's hard for me to talk about this."

"If it makes it any easier, Zach told me what happened."

"He did?" That was a huge relief.

"He didn't go into the finer details, but he told me

enough." Jason's brow furrowed, his gaze dropping to the sofa for a moment. "Truth is, I brought it up with him. I hope that doesn't upset you."

She shook her head. "Of course not. You two are friends. You're both federal agents, and you both know me. After what I told you today, it's understandable that you'd be curious."

"Not just curious, Winona. You and I haven't known each other for long, but I consider you a friend. I hate it when bad guys hurt good people."

She got the feeling he'd seen a lot of that—and not just with his parents. "What did Zach tell you?"

"He said some fugitive came into your clinic to get you to treat the burns he got from the dye pack on a money bag. He said the bastard forced you to help him at gunpoint, made all kinds of awful threats, and then injected you with a lethal overdose of ketamine. He said you were sure you were dead."

Winona nodded, her throat going tight. "He came through the front door. I was in the back with my friend Bear, who'd brought in an orphaned fawn. He barged in on us, gun pointed straight at us, and demanded I help him. I didn't have any choice."

"No, you really didn't."

"He had bad second-degree burns on one hand, and it had become infected. I told him he needed to be seen at a hospital by a burn specialist, but he jammed the barrel of his pistol into my temple and told me to shut up."

"What did this friend of yours, Bear, do?"

"Bear is a big guy with a big beard, but he suffered brain damage from a fever as a child. He has the mind of a little boy. He's one of the most wonderful people I know, but he couldn't do anything to help. He was terrified."

"You felt like you needed to protect him."

"Yes." Winona's stomach knotted at the memory of terror. "I put a topical anesthetic on the man's burns and cleaned them as best I could. The whole time, he was saying terrible things. 'When you're done, I'm going to make you suck my dick. I think this pistol turns you on. Maybe I'll fuck you with the barrel. Would you like that? I bet a bitch like you loves taking it up the ass. Do you fuck the animals?' Stuff like that."

"*Jesus.* I'm so sorry."

"I was so afraid." Winona didn't realize how much her hands were shaking until Jason gently took her tea mug and set it on the coffee table. "I thought maybe I could inject him with anesthetic instead of antibiotics, but he demanded to see the vial. I gave him an IM injection of amoxicillin. Then he demanded the ketamine."

"We catch people trafficking small amounts of that from time to time."

"Yes. It's an anesthetic." Winona hugged the blanket tighter around herself. "I thought he wanted to steal it. Vet clinics get burglarized all the time by people trying to steal ketamine."

"It makes sense you would think that."

"He took a syringe and the ketamine and drew a big dose—more than enough to anesthetize two or three bull moose. I asked him what he was going to do with it, and he told me that firing his pistol would attract attention. He walked over to Bear and jammed the needle into his thigh. I tried to stop him, but he was stronger than I was. He shoved me away. I fell and hit the floor hard. Then he walked over and injected me. I knew Bear and I were dead, that someone would find us there on the floor."

Winona could still feel the prick of the needle, the sting of the medication in her muscle, the racing of her own heart.

Jason moved closer, took her hand, held it, his fingers warm. "It was Lexi who found you—and just in time, from what McBride says."

Winona blinked back tears. "He abducted her and almost got her killed."

Jason leaned forward, cupped her face in his palms. "But you're a daughter of this land. The very earth that raised you saw what he'd done and decided he didn't deserve to be in this world. It crashed down on him, ending him, but sparing Lexi."

Winona had never thought of it like that before. "Yes."

"He's gone, Win. He can never hurt you or Bear or anyone else again."

"My mind knows that, but there's some part of me inside that is still terrified."

"I know." Jason drew her into his arms, held her, stroked her hair, the heat of his body chasing away the chill inside her, the strength of his embrace soothing.

Chapter 9

WHILE WINONA MADE her rounds at the clinic, Jason loaded her bag and backpack and his duffel into his truck and went to get gas at Frank's Pump 'N' Go, the only gas station in Scarlet Springs. He paid inside, tossing a pack of condoms on the counter.

What are you doing, man?

Hell, he didn't know.

He climbed into his truck and shut the door—a bit too hard.

He was out of sorts this morning, on edge. Listening to Winona talk about her ordeal had triggered something in him, a sense of protectiveness mingled with rage. He'd done his best to comfort her, but he knew nothing could take away the horror of what that bastard had done.

God, she'd felt sweet in his arms.

Holding her had done nothing to curb his growing infatuation with her. In fact, it had made things worse. He'd wanted to kiss her, but that would have made him a world-class asshole. She'd bared her soul to him. She'd been vulnerable and upset, her face wet with tears, her body shaking. The last thing she'd needed was him coming onto her.

No matter what he'd like to believe, his dick wasn't magic. It couldn't heal that kind of pain.

That's why you're going to keep your junk in your pants.

He found Winona locking up, the bright smile on her face, a strange tenderness for her blossoming in his chest. "Ready to go?"

"Let's hit the road."

Jason knew the way now and followed the signs toward the Peak to Peak Highway. "It's beautiful up here."

"I'm sure it's beautiful in the desert, too."

"It's a different kind of beauty."

"Tell me about it."

Jason searched for a way to put a lifetime of experience into words. "The colors are always changing depending on the light. In the mountains, you can see the different geological strata—dark gray, red, white, tan. In spring, the land explodes with life. Prickly pear and giant saguaro in bloom. Tadpoles in every puddle. Tiny yellow flowers on the greasewood trees. A sky that goes on forever. You can see a rainstorm coming from miles away, ghost rain falling like a gray curtain, evaporating before it hits the ground, the sky purple."

"It sounds amazing."

"Maybe you can visit and see for yourself one day."

"I'd like that. I…" She seemed to hesitate. "I wanted to thank you for your kindness last night. I feel a little ashamed that I fell apart like that."

"You shouldn't. We're friends, right?" It was too damned bad they couldn't be more than that. "What you went through would give anyone nightmares. Look at who you are and all the good you do. You should feel proud of yourself."

"Thanks."

"It's the truth. I've never been through anything like what you experienced, but I've been shot. I've witnessed a lot of violence and seen more than my share of dead and decomposing bodies. I have nightmares, too."

"You do?" She seemed genuinely surprised by this.

He couldn't help but laugh. "Hell, yeah."

"Do you ever cry all over your guests?"

"I haven't cried since the day we buried my parents."

She rested her hand against his arm. "That must have been so hard."

"Yeah." It had been hell.

They reached the Cimarron just before nine. Jack and Nate welcomed them, took their bags, and invited them in for a quick cup of coffee.

"One of the hands will take your bags to the guest cabin," Jack told them. "They'll be waiting for you when you get there."

No sooner had they finished their coffee than the sheriff's deputy arrived.

Deputy Julia Marcs introduced herself to Jason. "It's a pleasure to meet a Shadow Wolf. You sure impressed Sheriff Pella yesterday."

"I was happy to help."

While Deputy Marcs went over the day's plan of action with Jack and Nate, Jason geared up, setting out his Glock, holster, and two extra loaded magazines. As a Shadow Wolf, he carried an M4 rifle in the field, so it felt strange to be armed only with his pistol.

"You brought a gun?" Winona came up behind him.

"I usually carry concealed. Drug runners sometimes target Wolves and their families. I haven't had it on me since I arrived in Scarlet, but I always have a firearm. Does that bother you?"

"I'd rather have the gun in your hands than someone else's."

"Fair enough." He racked the slide on the pistol and holstered it.

They climbed into the cab of Jack's truck, Jason and Winona in the back, Nate riding shotgun, Jack at the wheel, and drove to the pasture where Jason had found the four-wheeler tracks, Deputy Marcs following in her sheriff's vehicle.

Jack turned the truck's radio to a weather station. "They're saying that a cold front will move down from Wyoming this evening, bringing snow to the high country. We'll need to keep our eyes on the weather. I don't want to get benighted in the middle of a winter storm."

"It's good we're doing this today then." Jason met Jack's gaze in the rearview mirror. "A snowfall could destroy the sign."

—

"I THINK you might be right, Win."

"Of course I am," Winona teased. "About what?"

"The wolf sign disappears here. My guess? The animal rode with the poacher in the four-wheeler."

Nate turned to Winona. "Could a wolf do that?"

"Shota did. I never took him four-wheeling, but he rode in my vehicle at least once a week when Chaska and I took him out for trail runs."

They set off again, Jason following the four-wheeler's tracks. While Winona could see those plainly enough— the wheels had torn through the duff to the mud beneath —she would never have noticed the minute details that were obvious to Jason. A bit of gray thread from a wool sweater caught on a pine branch. A log overturned by tires, its sun-bleached side now facing the ground. The mud pushed up onto a slab of rock by one of the vehicle's tires.

"When it's pushed up on this side of an obstacle, it means the four-wheeler was heading that way—toward the ranch. He used this route both to get on and off your property."

"Damn, you're good." Deputy Marcs was clearly impressed. "That's Newton's third law of physics right there."

Winona understood now. "Every action has an equal and opposite reaction. A vehicle heading that way would push the mud this way."

Jason grinned. "Exactly."

Oh, that smile.

She felt it from her ovaries to the tips of her toes.

She'd noticed a change in him since last night. Something about him seemed gentler. He was still every bit the intense, serious Shadow Wolf she'd met a few days ago, but his attitude toward her seemed … softer, warmer.

You're imagining things.

She hadn't imagined the way he'd made her feel last night—protected, safe, sheltered. She hadn't imagined the hard feel of his body either, or that scent that was uniquely his, a mix of musk, sage, and spice. She'd soaked it all up, and it had left her longing for more.

He stopped, knelt. "Scat."

Winona went to examine it. "Coyote. It's shiny and too small to be wolf scat."

Deputy Marcs knelt beside her. "Do they teach you how to identify animal poop in vet school?"

Winona laughed. "There weren't any courses on that

particular subject when I was in school, but when you take care of animals, you learn pretty quickly."

They moved onward, the tracks leading them steadily uphill, through a glade of willows and aspens that had been badly gnawed.

She stopped, ran her fingers over the scarred bark of a stunted aspen. "It looks like you have a lot of elk up here."

"We do." Jack drew his water bottle out of his pack, screwed off the top. "They move back and forth between our property and National Forest land. They've taken out some of our aspen stands entirely."

"When they reintroduced wolves in Yellowstone, they witnessed a trophic cascade." When this drew blank looks, she explained. "The wolves created an ecological shift. They fed on the ungulates—elk and deer—and reduced their populations. The remains left by the wolves fed other species and put nitrogen into the forest soil. The lower population of elk meant that aspen and willow glades could thrive, and that helped the beaver bounce back because they eat willows. The increased number of beaver dams helped aquatic species to thrive. The ecosystem began to heal itself."

Nate adjusted one of the straps on his backpack. "Mother Nature knows what she's doing. I would welcome wolves on our land—provided we got compensation for our livestock losses."

They stopped at noon to hydrate and eat the bagged lunches Jack had made for them—roast beef sandwiches, celery and carrot sticks, apples, and homemade brownies.

Jack drew out his sandwich. "Mountain air makes a person hungry."

While they ate, Deputy Marcs peppered Jason with questions. How old had he been when he'd first learned to cut sign? What had made him want to work with the

Shadow Wolves? Would he be willing to come back and do a training for the Forest County Sheriff's Department?

As Winona ate, she couldn't help but feel the peace that came with being in the wild. The landscape here was so vast that it seemed to swallow up everything but the present moment. Up here, there was only *now*.

She breathed it in, closed her eyes, let her senses go.

The wind in the trees. The staccato chirp of a downy woodpecker. The angry chatter of a squirrel. The scent of pines and fresh, clean air.

When she opened her eyes again, she found Jason watching her.

She met his gaze, felt a stab of longing, looked away. "It's beautiful up here."

"That's what my great-grandfather thought." Jack reached into his lunch bag and drew out his apple. "He bought this land after fighting in France in World War One. He wanted to escape the world and find some peace."

Winona unwrapped her brownie. "Did he? Find peace, I mean."

"I surely hope so."

After lunch, they moved on again, heading across the mountainside but no longer gaining elevation. The wind picked up, got colder, a bank of gray clouds moving in from the northwest.

Nate looked up. "That storm is coming."

It was around three in the afternoon when they reached the western property line of the Cimarron and found the fence down.

"This is the old mining road." Jack pointed with a gloved hand. "That's Forest Service land on the other side."

Jason held up one end of the severed wire. "Wire

cutters. This is where he's coming onto your property. You could repair the fence, put up more warning signs, let him know you're aware of him, maybe even put up some kind of surveillance camera."

Nate turned to his father. "I'll bring up some men and repair it as soon as I get a chance. He could just cut the fence again or enter somewhere else, but at least the bastard will know we're watching."

Jason knelt by the road. "The tracks lead that way, down the mountain. But there are a lot of other tracks mixed in—bike tires, other four-wheelers, horses."

Deputy Marcs knelt beside him. "It looks like this road is popular with mountain bikers, hikers, horseback riders, and all-terrain vehicles. Are you able to discern one set of tire tracks from another in all this mess?"

"Yeah. I could lose it farther on, but for now, it's pretty clear."

Winona walked over, looked down at the overlapping tracks. "How is *that* clear?"

Jason touched a finger to the track. "See the flying chevron here in the center of the tire tread? That's our guy. Let's see where this goes."

―――

JASON FOLLOWED the four-wheeler's tracks down the road, the others behind him, the wind ice-cold. They moved faster now, partly because the sign was easier to see than it had been in the forest and partly because they were heading downhill.

Jason stepped over a large pile of horse manure. "I wonder why he's getting onto your property at that location. Why drive all the way up this road? This is Cimarron land here to our left, isn't it? Why not cut the fence somewhere closer to the pasture?"

"Good question." Deputy Marcs fell in beside him, ponytail swinging. "There are miles of fence line here. He could have cut through at any point. Why spend the fuel and the time driving up here?"

"There has to be a reason the poacher chose that spot." Jason considered the possibilities. "Jack, are there any natural obstacles?"

"There's a steep ravine. He could be trying to avoid it."

"Why wouldn't he try to enter your land below the ravine?" That seemed a lot easier to Jason. "The pastures are down here, not up there."

Nate had that answer. "That would put him near the Forest Service parking area—and a lot of potential witnesses who might wonder what a guy with a rifle, a freshly bagged kill, and a wolf is doing out here."

Jason turned to Winona. "Would a wolf be a problem around people?"

"If he has a wolf, he'll do his best to avoid people and other canines. Wild wolves never become pets. Even hand-reared ones like Shota and wolfdog crossbreeds remain pretty wild. Their behavior can be unpredictable. They can be wonderful, but people have been mauled and even killed by animals they thought were tame."

Then Jason saw another breach in the fence. "Someone cut through here, too."

"Is it the same guy?" Deputy Marcs asked.

"I don't know how long ago this happened. There might not be any sign left." Jason searched the ground for wolf tracks, tire treads, boot prints, or anything else that might offer information about who had done this. "There."

Under the canopy of a tall pine was a small section of tire tread. In the center was the telltale flying chevron.

Nate knelt beside Jason. "The bastard must have tried here first and found himself cut off by the ravine. Then he did some recon and moved farther up the mountain."

"Looks like it."

They kept going down the road and soon came to a creek. About ten feet wide from bank to bank, it bisected the trail. Someone had placed a couple of boards over it to act as a bridge. The water wasn't deep, but the erosion and sand deposits on the downhill side told Jason that the creek frequently overflowed.

"This part of the road floods in the spring," Jack said.

Jason crossed the makeshift bridge—and the trail went cold. He stopped, doubled back, tried again, moving more slowly. When that yielded nothing, he walked farther down the road, hoping to pick up the trail again, but he found nothing. "The trail stops here. He might have driven up the creek bed. We can follow this onto Forest Service land and see what we find."

Deputy Marcs zipped her parka to her chin. "We get squatters on Forest Service land sometimes. I've helped rangers clear off more than a few."

Jack stopped, looked up at the sky. "I think we ought to call it a day. Those storm clouds are headed this way, and the temps are dropping fast. It will take us longer to get back up this trail than it took to get down. I'm guessing it will be a few hours before we get back to our vehicles."

They turned and hiked back up the road.

They hadn't gone far when Jason spotted a rough-looking man with a long beard, long hair, and a sidearm standing off to the side of the road, a grin on his face.

"I don't like the feel of that guy," Deputy Marcs whispered.

Neither did Jason. "He looks like one of those squatters you mentioned. No backpack. No winter coat. No vehicle or mountain bike."

Jason wasn't one to judge someone based on their appearance, but there was something about this guy. It wasn't the hair or the beard. It was that smile—and the way he was looking at them. Jason had long ago learned to trust his instincts.

He caught up with Winona. "Stay close, okay?"

She nodded.

They drew even with the man, who hadn't taken a single step.

"Well, look at that." The man chuckled. "A lady deputy."

Deputy Marcs ignored him.

"Ain't you gonna ask for my ID?"

"Not today."

"Good, because I ain't got one. I'm a freeman, not a federal citizen like the rest of you. My flesh has been freed."

"How nice for you." Deputy Marcs' voice dripped with sarcasm.

But the man went on. "The other little lady—she's that Indian gal from Scarlet, ain't she? Yeah, she is. She's that pretty little Indian gal. What's your name, sugar?"

Jason bit his tongue and took Winona's hand. He didn't like this bastard's tone or his language—or the fact that he was singling out the women.

Deputy Marcs lowered her voice. "He must be one of those crazy sovereign citizens—anti-government types who live out of vehicles and tents. We get a fair number of them around here. Most of the time, they just want to be left alone."

Jason was familiar with them. "Once in a while, we

find one living in the desert on our land and escort them to our borders."

He glanced back to make sure the guy wasn't following them and saw that he was watching them, that idiot grin still on his face.

Chapter 10

BY THE TIME they reached their vehicles, the first snowflakes were beginning to fall. While Jack and Nate spoke with Deputy Marcs, Winona and Jason waited in Jack's truck, out of the cold and the wind.

"I'm sorry for how that bastard spoke to you, Win." Jason took her hand. "I can tell it upset you. It pissed me off, too."

Jason was right. The bastard's words *had* upset her. They had left a weight in the pit of her stomach, a sense of dread. "It's not your fault."

Jack and Nate had also apologized, though they weren't to blame, either.

Jason's jaw clenched. "I wanted to shut his mouth for him."

Winona squeezed his fingers. "I'm glad you didn't, given that Deputy Marcs was standing right there."

"It might have been worth it."

"You know what bothers me most?" After last night, Winona felt safe telling him this. "He knows where I live. He must have seen me somewhere in Scarlet. What if he comes to town? What if he comes to the clinic? He scares me."

"Maybe it's time to boost security there, install flood-lights and cams and put a system on the front door that requires someone to buzz people in."

"Buzz people in? In Scarlet?"

"If the people of this little town are as warm-hearted as you say they are, they'll want you to feel safe at work."

She supposed he was right. "I put a bell on the door after the attack so I would know when someone enters the clinic. Every time it rings, I tense."

"We can look into your options when we get back to Scarlet."

It touched her to think he cared. "Thanks."

Jack and Nate climbed into the truck, prompting Winona to release Jason's hand. They started the drive back to the house.

Nate glanced back at them over his shoulder. "We're mighty grateful to the two of you for your help today. We know a lot more today than yesterday, and I learned a few things about cutting sign."

Jason answered Nate with a nod. "You're welcome."

Winona couldn't take any credit. "Jason did all the work. I identified animal poo and talked about ecosystems."

But Nate wouldn't accept that. "Hey, we learned from you, too, Winona."

"I wish I'd gotten a look at the tread on that guy's boots," Jason said.

"I talked with Deputy Marcs about him." Nate faced forward, took off his gloves. "She doesn't think it's him. He had no four-wheeler, no rifle, no wolf that we could see. Plus, he doesn't look like he has money. To get a four-wheeler of that size up here, he'd need a trailer and a truck to hitch it to."

"We're looking for someone with a bit of disposable income, not some idiot who thinks he's Daniel Boone." Jack turned on the truck's windshield wipers, the snow falling harder now. "I'm going to run it all by Janet tonight."

Nate grinned. "My father's wife used to work for the FBI. When they first met, he threw her off the property."

"Which neither of you will ever let me forget."

"Is that true?" Winona had a hard time imagining someone as kind as Jack throwing anyone off his land.

"It wasn't my finest moment."

Janet West was much younger than her husband—probably in her mid-forties. She met them outside the garage, her daughter on her hip, her dark hair pulled back in a ponytail. "How did it go?"

"Hey, Lily-bean." Jack scooped the toddler into his arms, quickly brought his wife up to date, then introduced Janet to Winona and Jason. "We're hungry, woman. What's cookin'?"

Janet kissed his cheek, a teasing smile on her face. "Whatever you make, of course. The salad is done, and the baked potatoes are in the oven."

While Jack and Nate fired up a big gas grill and handled the steaks, Janet gave them a tour of the house—they hadn't had time for one this morning—and then invited Winona and Jason to kick back in front of the fireplace in the living room. She walked with a noticeable limp, and Winona seemed to remember something about her having been shot in the line of duty.

"Can I bring either of you something to drink—beer, wine, whisky?"

Jason sank onto a long leather sofa. "Whisky. Thanks."

Winona sat beside him. "Do you have any flavored seltzer water?"

"We sure do—raspberry, I think."

"Perfect."

Janet disappeared, returning quickly with their drinks.

"Thank you." Winona glanced around, feeling strangely safe and at home here, the stress of their encounter with the creepy guy melting away.

Or maybe she was just stunned by their surroundings. She'd never seen a house like this before. She'd never known that anyone lived like this. Not only did they have a gym and a sauna, but they also had a two-story library with a fireplace. More than once, she and Jason had exchanged looks, both of them astounded.

"They call this a *house*?" Jason had whispered.

Jason took his whisky from Janet. "Thanks. I'm looking forward to one of these steaks. McBride swears they're the best."

Janet nodded like she'd heard that before, her lips curving in a smile. "I would have to agree with him."

Then Emily came bounding down the stairs in jeans and a pink, sparkly sweater, a pair of fuzzy bunny ears on her blond head, Megan, Nate's wife, back from Denver and following her daughter with little Jackson in her arms.

Emily's face lit up. "Winona!"

Winona was surprised the child remembered her. "Hey, Emily. How was school?"

"It was okay. I like my teacher, but Ms. Walker made us do odd and even numbers again, and that's boring. How is Shota?"

"I went to visit him a few weeks ago, and he was doing very well. I have a newborn nephew named Shota now."

Emily's nose wrinkled in confusion. "You named a baby after a wolf?"

Winona couldn't help but laugh and saw that Jason was smiling, too. "Shota is a boy's name in my language."

The little girl's eyes widened with understanding. "Oh."

Megan introduced herself to Jason. "I'm Megan, Nate's wife. This is Emily, our daughter. She's eight."

Emily grew indignant. "I'm eight and a *half*."

Winona thought she was adorable. "That half is important, isn't it, Emily?"

"This is Jackson." Megan lowered the toddler to the floor. "He's two and a *half* and into everything."

Then Jack and Nate stepped through the sliding glass door.

Jack glanced around, as if confused. "Who are all you people?"

Emily hopped over to him. "Silly Grandpa Jack! We're your family."

Jack waggled the girl's bunny ears. "My family?"

Nate shook his head, a grin on his face. "Don't let my old man fool you. He loves a full house. Get your jackets on and join us on the patio. Dinner's ready."

———

"OKAY, Chiago. Let's hear it. What's your verdict?"

Jason looked from Nate to Jack. "That was the best steak I've had—and the best chocolate cake, too."

Winona dabbed her lips with a napkin. "It was all so good."

The two men clinked their beer bottles, broad grins on their faces.

Jack took a drink. "Glad you enjoyed it."

Jason had never eaten outside during a snowstorm. He had expected it to be a cold and awkward experience, but the West family had the art of the winter barbeque down. With big propane heaters placed around the patio, a fire pit, and a canvas shade overhead to keep in the heat and protect them from snow, he'd been toasty warm. There was something about the combination of fresh air and flame-grilled food that provoked and satisfied hunger like nothing else.

"Okay, Emily." Megan got to her feet, Jackson in her arms, his chubby hands and little face covered with chocolate frosting. "It's time to wash up and get ready for bed."

Emily glared at her mother, clearly not happy about this. "Damn it!"

"Miss Emily!" Jack pinned his granddaughter with his gaze. "What have I told you about using those words?"

Emily rolled her eyes. "Don't cuss in front of Mama or our guests."

"That's right—and you'd best listen."

Jason had to fight not to smile and saw Winona was doing the same.

"Come now, Emily." Megan opened the rear sliding glass door.

Emily got to her feet. "Can Winona read me a bedtime story?"

Winona picked up her dishes and stood. "How about I tell you a story instead? I know lots of stories that aren't in books."

The little girl's face lit up. "You do?"

"Yes, I do."

The two disappeared inside with Megan.

Janet handed Lily to Jack and carefully got up from the bench, one hand on Jack's shoulder to steady herself. She winced as if lifting her leg over the bench were painful.

"You get inside. I'll bring Lily-bean." Jack noticed

Jason watching. "My wife took a high-caliber round to the hip a few years back while on a protection detail."

"I'm sorry to hear that." Jason was surprised she could walk at all.

"It's a lot better. I used to walk with a cane."

Jack kissed his little girl, got to his feet, and followed Janet indoors, his daughter giggling in his arms. "It's time for you to have a bath, chocolate monster."

And then it was just Nate and Jason.

"How is Win doing?"

Jason knew why Nate was asking. "That bastard shook her up."

"I thought so. I don't know her well, but we all read what happened to her and Lexi in the newspaper."

"I'm going to help her upgrade her security. She's afraid that guy knows where she is or will try to find her. He sure seemed to have an unhealthy interest in her. Besides, there are drugs in her clinic that have real street value—anesthetics, narcotics, sedatives. They could attract bad elements."

"I've got a contact in Denver who handles security systems. I'll give you his card when we get back inside. I'd like to help pay for it if she'll let me. This happened while she was up here at our request. I need to make this right for her."

"That's a kind offer. The clinic is completely dependent on donations, so I doubt she has much of a budget."

Jason helped Nate clear the remaining dishes off the table, the two talking about horses and ranch operations while Nate loaded the dishwasher.

Then Megan walked into the kitchen, a smile on her face. "Come. You should hear this. Winona has Emily completely mesmerized."

The three of them walked upstairs and down the hallway, stopping outside what must have been Emily's bedroom to listen.

"Iktomi saw what Porcupine had done with that hawthorn branch and how the thorns had pricked Bear when Bear had tried to gobble up Porcupine. It gave Iktomi a crazy idea."

The sweet sound of Winona's voice put a hitch in Jason's chest.

"Iktomi took many hawthorn branches and peeled off the bark. Then he put a thick layer of good, sticky clay all over Porcupine's back and stuck the thorny branches to the clay, making them a part of Porcupine's skin. What do you think happened when Wolf came that night to eat Porcupine?"

"The thorns poked it, and it ran away crying, 'Ow! Ow! Ow!'"

"That's right. What happened when Bear came back?"

"He saw all of those thorns and said, 'I'm sure as hell not touching you again, you thorny son of a gun.'"

Winona sounded like she was choking back laughter. "Yes! Bear ran away, too. And that's why all Porcupines have quills now."

"Tell me another story, please, Winona?" Emily pleaded.

"I need to rescue her." Megan walked into Emily's bedroom. "Can you thank Winona for the stories? Winona and Jason are going up to the cabin, and you need to sleep. It's a school night."

"Thank you, Winona."

It was the saddest *thank you* Jason had ever heard.

"You're welcome, Emily. Sweet dreams." Winona stepped out of the room, the same light on her face Jason had seen when she'd been caring for the animals at her clinic. "That was good practice for being an auntie."

"Shota is a lucky little boy."

As they walked downstairs together, Jason wondered what kind of perverse bend in the road had brought him to a woman as wonderful and beautiful as Winona when she couldn't be a permanent part of his life.

———

WINONA SAT in the back seat in the cab of Nate's truck as he drove her and Jason to the ranch's guest cabin, snow falling heavily now.

"We built the cabin some years back. We invite friends to stay up here and rent it to hunters. I've stayed here with Megan when we needed some peace and quiet. We expanded the deck this summer and added an outdoor hot tub. There's food in the fridge, as well as beer and wine. I hope you'll enjoy yourselves and unwind."

Winona was looking forward to the hot tub after hiking in the cold. "Thanks, Nate. I'm sure we will. It's very generous of you to have us."

"It's our pleasure." Nate told them how lonely Jack had been after his first wife, Nate's mother, had died suddenly of an aneurysm. "He lived in that big house and had no one to share it with. I was deployed, serving with a Marine Special Operations Team. When I was nearly killed, it hit him hard, but I think it gave him a new sense of purpose. Then Megan came along and, after that, Janet. He loves having a full house with lots of kids and noise. The more, the merrier."

"I'm so glad you're okay now and that he's no longer alone."

"Thanks, Win." Nate glanced back at her. "Do you know why he cooks so well?"

Winona had no idea. "Because he likes to eat?"

"That's part of it." Nate chuckled. "Learning to cook with my mother's old recipes made him feel that she was still with us."

"Oh." That put a lump in Winona's throat.

"I can understand that." Jason's voice held a hint of sadness. "There are things my mother made, like her mole poblano, that were special. No one made mole sauce the way she did. I think she sweetened it with *sitol*—saguaro syrup."

"If you've got the recipe or can get a hold of it, you should give it a shot—or let my old man try to make it. He'd love the challenge, I'm sure."

"I just might do that."

Nate drove the truck around a bend in the road. "There it is."

The cabin wasn't the small, rustic cabin Winona expected, but a log home, its porch light on to welcome them.

"This is beautiful." The place was bigger than Winona's house.

Nate parked near the front stairs, handed Jason the keys. "They brought your bags here earlier. I think one of the men got a fire going in the wood stove, so it should be nice and warm. I'll pick you up tomorrow at nine for breakfast, and then we can see the horses and do some riding if you like."

Winona and Jason thanked Nate and climbed out, Winona waving as Nate backed up and drove away. They walked up the stairs through about three inches of accumulation, Winona inhaling the scents of snow and wood smoke, coyotes yapping and howling in the distance.

"It's so peaceful up here."

"They call this a cabin?" Chuckling, Jason pushed

open the door and stepped back so that Winona could enter.

She flicked on the lights and found their bags sitting in a short hallway just inside the door. "This is nice."

They gave themselves a quick tour. A leather sofa sat across from a flat-screen TV, a wood stove in one corner, a fire roaring inside. The blinds were drawn back so that she could see the sliding glass door and the hot tub that glowed blue on the deck beyond, steam rising off the water.

There were two bedrooms. One was off the living room and had a queen-sized bed and an en suite bathroom with a large tub. The other was off the kitchen and had a bunk bed and a leather recliner. There was a second smaller bathroom near the back door.

"These Wests don't do anything halfway, do they?" Jason picked up his duffel. "You can have the big bedroom. I'll take the bunk."

Before they could debate the issue, he disappeared into the back.

Winona carried her bags to her room. "I don't know about you, but I'm heading straight for that hot tub."

She set her bags down on the bed, closed the bedroom door, and changed into her bikini. She'd forgotten to bring a towel, but there were plenty of those in the bathroom. She tucked one under her arm and stepped out of the bedroom.

She stopped mid-stride and stared.

Jason stood there in a pair of black swim trunks, a towel in hand, his torso beautifully bare from his muscular shoulders to the rounded slabs of his pecks and his well-defined abs and obliques. The man was a walking anatomy lesson. Could he possibly be any sexier?

His gaze slid over her, pausing on her breasts and belly, sending a trill of excitement through her. It had been such a long time since she'd been with a man, so long since a man had made her feel desired or even desirable.

You'll be sorry if you sleep with him.

Yes, she probably would. But she might regret it even more if she didn't.

"You ready?"

Yes. Yes, she was.

Chapter 11

JASON HAD ONLY himself to blame.

He could have turned down the Wests' offer of a night at the ranch and gone back to McBride's. He'd be shooting the shit with Zach over a couple of beers now instead of wondering how he was going to keep his hands off Winona.

God, she was perfect. Everything about her made him want her—the gentle curves of her breasts, the flare of her hips, her slender legs, the way her gaze moved over him. But he'd been down this road before, and it led nowhere.

None of those women were Winona.

They sure as hell weren't.

Winona started toward the door. "This water is going to feel *so* good after hiking in the cold wind."

"Yeah," he managed to say, following her, his eyes drawn to the irresistibly sweet mounds of her ass, which shifted enticingly as she walked.

She opened the sliding glass door and stepped outside into the snow without the slightest hesitation.

Jason had never walked barefoot in snow before. "That's cold."

"Don't tell me a little snow is too much for a Desert Person," she teased. "In the winter when we do the *inipi*—our name for the sweat lodge ceremony—we often have to walk barefoot through snow. When I walk from the lodge to the women's tipi to change afterward, my hair and clothes freeze almost instantly."

He couldn't imagine that. "Don't you worry about hypothermia?"

"We're so warm from the lodge that the cold feels good." She held the handrail and stepped down into the hot water, her sigh of pleasure as she sank up to her chin sending a rush of blood to Jason's groin. "Oh, this is wonderful."

Jason did his best to hide his growing erection as he made his way down into the water, the heat sending tingles of pleasure up his spine. "Is now the time to tell you I've never been in a hot tub before?"

She gaped at him. "Never?"

"Never."

Snow fell steadily from the sky, melting on the surface of the water and landing in their hair and on his bare shoulders, the forest around them silent. Even the coyotes were quiet now. Overhead, storm clouds hid the stars. It felt magical.

Or maybe that was Winona.

She moved toward him through the water and ran a finger over the scar on his shoulder, concern on her pretty face. "Is this where you were shot?"

His pulse tripped.

He looked down at the line of heat her fingertips traced over his skin. "Yeah. A trafficker took a shot at me from behind some rocks. It wasn't bad—just a deep graze."

"I bet it was painful."

"At the time, I was just pissed."

"Did he get away?"

Jason shook his head. "The Wolf pack surrounded him and brought him in."

She ran her fingertips over his tattoo. "Does this mean something?"

He watched her as her fingers explored the maze, his blood hotter than the water now. "It's the Man in the Maze. The little guy here is I'itoi, who helped Creator make our people. He's a bit of a trouble-maker. We call him Elder Brother. The maze represents the journey of life and death—the choices we face, the unexpected turns, the dead ends. The center represents your dream, the purpose of your life, the end of your journey."

Lips he wanted to kiss curved in a smile. "I like that."

Then she touched the scar above his left nipple. "Were you shot here, too?"

Jason sucked in a breath, his control dangerously close to shattering. Was she doing this on purpose? If she was, it was working.

"That was a knife." Jason fought to remember what had happened, his thoughts scattered, his senses and his mind focused entirely on her. "I was cuffing a guy. He went for my throat. We fought. His blade got beneath my body armor."

"God, Jason." Her fingers caressed the ridge of puckered flesh, her body mere inches from his now. "I'm so sorry."

Jason knew he shouldn't do this for both their sakes. He'd be leading them both down a path that went nowhere. He couldn't abandon his people to be with her. She would never leave Chaska and her family. If they turned this corner, they would both pay for it later. But, God, he wanted her.

He cupped her face between his palms, touched his forehead to hers. "I want you, Win. I want to kiss you. I want to go back inside, strip off that bikini, and do all manner of things. But there's no way we can be together, and I don't want to hurt you. Tell me to keep my hands to myself, and I'll back off."

She moved closer, ran her palms over his chest, and looked straight into his eyes. "Kiss me."

WINONA FELT Jason's heartbeat quicken beneath her palm, saw the heat in his eyes, sensed the battle inside him. Her heart was beating fast, too, her body shaking.

His gaze searched hers, a big hand coming to rest on her hip, then sliding slowly up her back, the heat of his touch making her gasp.

"*Jason.*"

He brushed his lips over hers, again and again, burning little hints of kisses, the contact sending shivers up her spine, making her lips tingle.

He drew back and exhaled, a slow, shuddering breath. "Tell me to stop, Win."

"I don't want you to stop. Can't we have tonight?"

He moaned and drew her hard against him, strong arms enfolding her, his lips at last claiming hers.

God, yes.

He didn't rush her, but took his sweet time, exploring her, tasting her tongue, nipping her lips with the sharp edges of his teeth. She gave herself over to his kisses, sliding her hands up his chest and over his shoulders, arching against him, reveling in the hard feel of his body against hers. Her pulse thrummed in her ears, her heart racing.

Oh, he was *so good* at this.

She'd never been so turned on by a kiss, heat pooling in her belly, her body already aching for more. She shifted to straddle his thighs—and took control.

His eyes flew open as she ran her tongue over his upper lip, nipped his lower lip, and then claimed his mouth with hers. But it wasn't enough.

Hungry for him, she pressed kisses to the side of his throat, tasting him, teasing him, the scent of his skin filling her head, his pulse pounding against her lips.

In a heartbeat, he turned the tables, sliding his fingers into her wet hair, turning her head to reclaim her mouth with his.

Oh, it felt good to surrender.

He tilted her head to the side, his lips leaving her mouth to trace a path along her throat just as she'd done to him, kissing, licking, nipping, the sharp edges of his teeth raising goosebumps on sensitive skin. Then one hand moved to the ties of her bikini top, and with two quick tugs, her breasts were bare.

Anticipation made her belly clench.

He gazed down at her breasts, his brow furrowed. "*Winona.*"

He cupped one breast with his hand, rubbed its puckered nipple with his thumb, tremors of pleasure shivering through her.

Winona couldn't help but moan.

He nuzzled her throat. "You like that."

"*Yes.*"

Owooooo!

Winona froze, chills skittering down her spine. "The wolf. It's *here*! *He* must be here, too—the poacher."

The two of them were exposed and vulnerable. If the poacher *was* here....

Jason drew her closer, his gaze moving over the forest on the other side of the deck railing before meeting hers. "On the count of three, I'm going to get out of the water. You climb out after me and head straight inside. I'll be right behind you."

She grabbed her bikini top out of the water, held it against her breasts, her heart pounding. "Okay."

Owooooo!

It was closer now, probably standing just outside the circle of light shining from the cabin's windows and porch lights.

"One... two... three."

Winona rose out of the water, followed Jason up the stairs, hurrying toward the door, Jason right behind her, shielding her body with his, one strong arm around her waist. She pushed open the door, stepped inside.

"Get dressed." Jason shut and locked the door and drew the blinds. "Stay away from the windows."

Owooooo!

She ran into her room, grabbed her bag, and hurried into the bathroom, where she stripped off her wet bikini, dried off, and dressed, questions chasing one after another through her mind. What was the wolf doing here? Why would the poacher come to the cabin? Was he just out trolling for beef?

When she walked to the doorway of her room, she found Jason standing in the kitchen, wearing jeans and a T-shirt, pistol in its holster, phone in hand.

"It sounded like it was twenty or thirty feet away at most. If your poacher is traveling with the wolf, then he's likely here, too, and he's almost certainly armed. Thanks. We'll see you shortly." He ended the call. "Nate will be here in about thirty minutes. He's bringing a group of men to get us. He'll take us back to the main house for the night. You'll be safe there."

But Winona wasn't sure she'd feel safe anywhere tonight. "Do you think the poacher followed us?"

Jason considered that. "I don't know. Maybe seeing the armed riders in the other pastures drove him this way in search of steers. Or maybe the wolf is out for a run. I won't know until I can get a look at the tracks."

She nodded, crossed her arms over her chest, and sat, her back to the wall outside her bedroom door where she wasn't in line with any windows.

Jason crossed the room, knelt before her. "I'm sorry, Winona. I know this is scary, but I'm not going to let anything happen to you."

⸺

JASON WANTED to kick his own ass. He'd gotten so caught up in his need for Winona that he'd let his guard down. He'd let his dick do the thinking—and it could have gotten both of them killed. If the poacher *was* here, he could have opened up on them with that rifle and killed them both.

Owooooo!

"It's farther away now. They're leaving."

Jason blamed himself for the fear on Winona's face. "Why don't you come sit at the table in the kitchen? It's a lot more comfortable than the floor."

He took her hand, helped her up, and walked with her to the kitchen. "Would someone just let their wolf run free?"

"I let Shota run off-leash on Forest Service land, but I never just turned him out to roam by himself. I was too afraid something would happen if…" Her words trailed off, a look of comprehension on her face. "The poacher *has* to be here. Either that, or he lives nearby. I don't know how the wolf could get here otherwise."

"Why do you say that?"

"Wild wolves lope along at no more than five or six miles an hour, and they don't travel more than thirty miles in a day. Either the poacher brought the wolf with him like he did when he killed the steers—or he lives a lot closer than you all think."

Jason thought through what Winona had said, images from the day moving through his mind. The two cut sections of fence line. The four-wheeler tracks disappearing at the creek. The creek flowing onto Forest Service land.

Jack had turned back at that point, so Jason hadn't gotten a look at the creek or its banks. It was entirely possible that the poacher had turned off the road at that point and driven up the creek.

We get squatters on Forest Service land sometimes. I've helped rangers clear off more than a few.

Jason needed to get back up there while there was still snow on the ground.

Winona sat at the table. "Sorry to act like such a chicken."

He sat across from her. "Hey, don't apologize. It was a scary situation. I think most people would be a little freaked out to discover that a criminal with a wolf had crept up on them, and most people don't have your history."

She didn't look convinced.

Jason tried to shift the conversation. "What was it like raising a wolf pup?"

"I had to be available around the clock. I lost a lot of

sleep, but he was so adorable that I didn't mind." She pulled out her phone. "I have photos and video."

"Show me."

She handed the phone to him. "Just scroll."

Winona feeding a tiny gray fluffball from a small bottle. A short video of the tiny gray fluffball, eyes now open, doing its best to howl like one of the big boys. The pup now several months old and asleep on Winona's lap. Winona outdoors with her arm around an enormous, fully grown wolf's neck, its yellow eyes looking into the camera.

"Whoa. He grew up to be huge." Jason could see how much she loved the animal in every image. "You had shorter hair then."

She ran her fingers through her long, damp strands. "I cut it after my grandmother made the journey. It's one of the ways we mourn."

"Right." He handed the phone back, heard the sound of approaching truck engines. "I think they're here."

They grabbed their bags and were at the door when Jack and Nate knocked.

Jack wasn't happy. "I'm awfully sorry about this. We'll get you back to the house so you can enjoy the rest of the evening. I've asked my men to stay close to the truck, so they don't step on sign."

Jason was glad to hear it. "Thanks. Got a flashlight?"

"In the glove box of my truck."

Jason got Winona safely into the cab of Jack's truck, but he didn't climb in after her. He grabbed the flashlight. "I'm going to have a quick look around."

Nate climbed out of his truck, rifle in hand. "I'm coming with you. Someone has to watch your six."

Shining the flashlight onto the snow, Jason walked to the rear of the cabin and then toward the line of the forest in the direction of the wolf's howls. He hadn't taken more than a few steps into the trees when he found the tracks—those of a wolf and a man's boots, size ten or eleven, with deep tread that had a circle in the heel.

Jason swore under his breath. "The bastard was here—tonight. It scared the hell out of Winona."

"I bet it did."

Jason turned, looked back toward the deck. Whoever this asshole was, he'd had a clear view of the hot tub and anyone in it. He'd probably watched them kissing. Worse, he'd also had a clear shot. "We need to get up to the old road tomorrow while the snow is fresh. I want to see what we find if we follow that creek."

Chapter 12

FIGHTING A SENSE OF DREAD, Winona sat in front of the fire with Megan, the two of them sipping hot chocolate and talking about what had happened. Winona left out the intimate parts, of course. The house was quiet, the children asleep, the men and Janet talking in Jack's office. "Then came this howl. The wolf couldn't have been more than twenty or thirty feet away from us."

Megan shivered. "That sends chills down my spine. I would have jumped out of my skin."

"It's not the wolf that scares me."

Megan laughed at that. "You're braver than I am."

Winona wanted to cry. "I'm not brave at all. I'm overreacting."

She was safe now. What was wrong with her that she still felt afraid?

"No, you're not overreacting at all. That guy doesn't care that he's breaking the law. He's a poacher, an armed trespasser, and he's got a big wolf with him. That's pretty disturbing."

Winona had to smile. "When you put it that way…"

Megan's eyes were warm with understanding. "This isn't the first time you've felt threatened. Experiences like that—they're cumulative."

"You're right. Thanks." Winona felt the truth of Megan's words down to her DNA, as images from today dredged up memories of what that bastard John Charles Ready had done to her.

Megan gave her a rueful smile. "I've got experience, unfortunately."

Winona didn't know Megan well, but she'd heard that Megan had suffered from heroin addiction and had served time in prison. There were even rumors that she'd killed a man. Whatever her past, she had overcome it and made a good life for herself. She was a mother, a wife, and an attorney.

"How do you get past it?"

"I suppose it's different for everyone. I had to get help. It took lots of counseling and medication. Nate's love made the biggest difference. He accepted me as I was, and that gave me room to heal."

Is that what Winona needed to do—ask for help?

Megan changed the subject. "Nate tells me that you're a climber and part of the Rocky Mountain Search and Rescue Team."

"My brother, Chaska, is the climber. I'm not nearly as good as he and the others are. Mostly, I help with rescues that involve animals."

"You rescue animals?"

She shared rescue stories with Megan until her hot chocolate was gone and Janet and the men reappeared. She could tell from the resolve on Jason's face that they'd decided on a course of action.

"Morning comes early," Jack said. "Time to put these

old bones to bed. Have the two of you been shown your rooms?"

Winona got to her feet, empty mug in hand. "Yes. They're beautiful. Thank you."

"I'm awful sorry about what happened tonight, Winona, but you're safe under our roof." Jack's eyes held no reproach, only concern. "I hope you rest easy tonight."

"Thank you, Jack."

Nate helped Megan to her feet. "We've got a state-of-the-art security system, not to mention two ex-military men and a federal agent here. And that bunkhouse we passed? It's full of men, a few of them ex-military, who know how to deal with trouble."

Winona willed herself to smile. "I'll remember not to cause any trouble then."

"I hope you'll sleep well." Janet slipped an arm around her husband's waist. "We're just down the hall from you if you need anything. Goodnight!"

"Goodnight."

Megan took Winona's empty mug. "I'm glad we got a chance to talk, Winona. I'll see you in the morning."

"Thanks, Megan."

"Of course."

Winona walked with Jason upstairs and down the hallway to their adjoining rooms. She stopped outside her door. She didn't want to be alone, and there was so much to say to him. *Be brave.* "Goodnight."

"Hey." He caught her hand, looked into her eyes. "Are you okay?"

She nodded, lied. "I'm fine."

"Nate and I will be heading out early tomorrow with some of their men to cut sign and see if we can't find this bastard."

He didn't ask her to join them this time.

He probably thinks you're not up for it.

Maybe she wasn't. "Please be careful."

"We will. Thanks. Goodnight, Win." He bent down and pressed a kiss to her cheek. "Our rooms have adjoining doors. Just knock if you need me."

"Thanks." Winona walked into her room, closed the door behind her.

Her room *was* beautiful, with a queen-sized poster bed, a fireplace, a velvet chaise, and a huge flat-screen TV on one wall. Best of all, the bathroom floor was heated, something she'd never experienced before.

Relax and go to bed. Nothing bad happened. You'll be fine in the morning.

She took a quick shower to wash away the chlorine from the hot tub. Then she dried her hair with a towel and brushed her teeth. She pulled down the duvet on the queen-sized poster bed, then crawled beneath the covers and turned out the light. She closed her eyes, drew deep breaths, willed herself to relax.

But she couldn't sleep.

Her mind jumped from one thing to another, a jumble of images and emotions. Jason cutting sign in the forest. The howl of the wolf. Jack and Nate arriving at the cabin, armed. The jerk near the road who'd called her "pretty little Indian gal."

If you so much as make a peep, I'll put an extra hole in your pretty little head.

She sat up, John Charles Ready's voice echoing in her mind. Then she noticed light coming from beneath the door that separated her room from Jason's. He was still awake. She hopped out of bed, turned on her bedside lamp, and walked to the door, hesitating for a moment. Was she truly so desperate?

Ask for help.

She knocked—and immediately felt stupid.

He opened the door wearing only a towel, his hair damp. "Hey."

"I-I can't sleep."

———

JASON COULD TELL that Winona was on the edge. Fear was written in every feature of her pretty face, her arms wrapped protectively around her, her breathing a little too rapid. "Let me get dressed, and we'll talk. I'll leave the door open."

"Okay."

"What happened tonight was pretty scary." Doing his best to keep her talking, he walked over to his bed, dropped the towel, and grabbed his flannel pajama bottoms.

"It all runs together—tonight, that guy today, what happened at my clinic."

"That makes sense to me." He stepped into his pajamas, grabbed a condom, and slipped it into his pocket.

What the hell are you doing? She doesn't need your dick.

He took it out and then put it back—just in case.

"But nothing really happened today." She sounded angry at herself, ashamed.

"That's not true, Winona." He walked to the doorway, found her sitting on her bed, arms still hugged around her middle. "Some asshole singled you out and said he recognized you. Then this armed trespasser showed up with a wolf. I can see how what happened today would awaken memories from five years ago."

"You can?"

"Yes."

Then it hit him.

Winona was trapped in a trauma loop. Nothing was real for her now except the fear churning inside her.

Jason didn't have a lot of experience with post-traumatic stress, but he had buddies who did, Wolves who'd suffered in the line of duty or who'd served in the military. Too bad he hadn't learned anything that could help Winona now. Should he try to distract her, urge her to talk about it, tell her she was safe until she actually felt safe? Hell, he didn't know.

He wasn't used to feeling helpless.

He took a throw off the chaise, wrapped it around her shoulders, and sat close beside her. "I know you're scared, Win, and I understand why. I'm listening if you want to talk about it. If not, then we'll just get through tonight, one moment at a time."

"Thanks." She looked up at him, a wobbly smile on her face and tears in her eyes. "Tell me about your home."

So, he told her about life in the desert. Harvesting saguaro fruit and cooking them down to syrup. Going on Salt Pilgrimage with other young O'odham men. Playing basketball with boys from the local youth club every Friday night. Growing tepary beans and corn with his grandfather. Watching his grandmother weave baskets. Learning the hard way not to get stuck by the spines of a cholla cactus.

"Those are painful—let me tell you. They'll make you bleed."

"Ouch." Winona scooted back until she was sitting with her back against the headboard. She seemed more relaxed and less afraid now. "I bet that's a mistake you don't make twice."

"Truth." He sat beside her. "The fruit is tasty, but you have to get the spines off first. My grandmother made it look easy, but it isn't."

"Why did it end—your relationship with your fiancée?"

The question took Jason by surprise. So, too, did the realization that he didn't mind talking about it with Winona.

She mistook his silence for something else. "I'm sorry. I shouldn't have—"

"No, it's okay. I was just surprised." Jason took a breath, wondering where to start. "Elena is O'odham, too. We met in high school."

Jason told her how he'd lost track of Elena while he was away at college and then the training academy and how they'd gotten reacquainted one night at a party that his friends had hosted to welcome him back to Sells.

"We started dating. She had a hair salon and wanted to make life better for our people—or so I thought." Jason saw it all differently now—her love of nice things, her constant talk about money, her focus on appearances. She'd only wanted to make life better for herself. "Every weekend when I was working, she went to visit her auntie in Tucson, taking her food, picking up her medicine for her, doing her hair and nails."

"That was kind of her."

Jason had to laugh. "That's what I thought."

"I don't understand."

"A little more than six months ago, I was working, cutting sign along the border. I got a text from my boss to come to his office. A DEA officer was waiting for me there. He told me that they had just arrested Elena for trafficking cocaine—part of a long investigation. They recorded her bragging about how she was engaged to a Shadow Wolf and how she'd learned by listening to him how to avoid feds."

It had felt like a physical blow—a bullet through his chest.

"Oh, Jason!"

"When prosecutors questioned her, she told them how drug runners dropped off cocaine at her salon in shampoo boxes and how she transported it to a house in Tucson for five grand per trip every time she visited her auntie. She'd gotten away with it for years, right under my nose. She just didn't want to live on my salary."

Winona shifted so that she faced him. "I'm so sorry. That must have hurt. You trusted her. You *loved* her."

"I'm grateful I found out when I did and not a few months later when we would have been married." He'd have had a divorce to contend with then. "But, yes, it hurt."

"You broke up with her?"

"The same day." Elena's tear-stained face flashed through Jason's mind. "I went to the jail. I needed to hear from her why she'd done it. She expected me to bail her out and help her pay for an attorney. Instead, I ended things. She knew drug runners had *murdered* my parents. She knew I'd spent my entire adult life busting people who did what she'd done, that I'd lost fellow Wolves, that I'd been shot. Still, she'd gone to work for the enemy. That's what hurt the most. It felt like a betrayal of everything I am."

Winona laced her fingers through his. "It *was* a betrayal."

Jason looked into Winona's guileless eyes, saw nothing there but compassion. He tried to hold back, but he couldn't. He leaned forward—and kissed her.

━━━

THE SWEET SHOCK of Jason's lips against hers made Winona's breath catch. Heart skipping, she leaned into the kiss, resting her palms against his bare chest. All else faded from her mind, the world around her melting away until there was nothing left but the two of them.

The searing press of his lips. The silken caress of his tongue. The spicy scent of his skin. The rapid beating of his heart beneath her palms. The hard feel of his body.

Oh, yes.

He sat fully upright, slid one big hand into her hair, and turned the two of them, bearing her back onto the mattress, his lips never leaving hers.

Anticipation shivered through her, just the weight of him arousing. It had been so long since she'd been with a man. But Jason wasn't just any man. He kissed her like he meant it, paying attention to the tiniest details—the dip at the center of her upper lip, the outline of her lower lip, the corners of her mouth.

At last, he broke the kiss, the intensity of his gaze making her pulse skip. "Are you sure you want this?"

She caught his face between her palms, looked into his eyes. "Yes."

He groaned and claimed her mouth once again with a blistering kiss that was as fierce and raw as it was perfect. She matched him stroke for stroke, tongues teasing, tasting, twining, her need every bit as desperate as his.

But he was ruthless, relentless.

She surrendered, lost in the rush of being overwhelmed by him. Needing more, she slid her palms up his chest and over his shoulders, savoring the satin texture of his skin, caressing the shifting muscles of his back.

God, even touching him turned her on.

He dragged his lips from hers and straddled her hips—and pulled her sleepshirt over her head, tossing it aside, leaving her completely naked.

His gaze dropped to her breasts then moved down her

body, breath leaving his lungs in a rush when he saw she wasn't wearing panties. He whispered words in his own language, then spoke in English. "You're so damned beautiful."

She shivered, her nipples drawing tight—and he hadn't yet touched her.

Then a big hand closed over each breast, and she arched into him, her eyes drifting shut as he toyed with her nipples, palming her, circling her areolas with his thumbs, grazing the sensitive tips, his touch sending darts of arousal to her belly.

Oh, she wanted him, heat building between her thighs.

"*Jason.*" She moaned his name, opened her eyes just a sliver, and found him watching her, his pupils dilated, a smile on his lips.

She sucked in a breath, watching him as he watched the effect he had on her, the heat between her thighs now incandescent. "You're tormenting me."

He chuckled, gave her breasts a gentle squeeze. "I hate to tell you, but it's going to get worse before it gets better."

Then he stretched out beside her, lowered his head, and sucked an aching nipple into the heat of his mouth.

"*Oh, God.*" She moaned, her eyes closing again, her fingers sliding into his short hair. It felt *so* good as he feasted on one nipple and then the other, his lips tugging on her, the sharp edges of his teeth teasing her, his tongue flicking her. The heat inside her became a backdraft, her body twisting beneath him, her hips rocking upward, her body instinctively seeking release.

Without realizing it, she crossed her thighs and squeezed.

He slid a hand down her belly, nudged her thighs apart, and cupped her. "You've got to let me in."

"*Yes!*" That's what she wanted—him inside her.

She bent her knees, let her thighs fall open for him.

"That's better." He went to work on her, fingers parting her, exploring her, finding ... *just the right spot.* "Like that?"

"*Mmm, yes.*"

Then his mouth closed over her nipple once more.

The combined sensations rocked Winona, sexual need like a fever now, his clever fingers driving her to the brink. She heard herself babble a mixture of Lakota and English, words mingling with moans. "*Wasté kstó...* aah ... so good ... *aké* ... more ... *oh, Jason.*"

Then he slid a finger inside her, stroking her inside and out.

She moaned his name, each deep thrust carrying her higher until she was hanging on the shimmering edge of an orgasm. And then she was soaring, the bliss of climax rushing through her, lifting her up, giving her body wings, then leaving her to float slowly back to earth.

When she opened her eyes, she found him still watching her, his eyes dark, the hint of a smile on his face. "Welcome back, beautiful."

Chapter 13

JASON WAS AN IDIOT. He'd led the two of them around this corner. Yes, Winona had come willingly, but he had started it.

Even so, he couldn't bring himself to regret it. Watching her open up for him, seeing the bliss on her sweet face when she'd come—it had left him feeling more alive than he'd felt in months, not to mention horny as hell.

Maybe you should stop here. This doesn't have to go any further.

Yeah, right.

She smiled up at him, a sensual, sexy smile, then pushed him onto his back, straddling him, her beautiful breasts swaying as she settled herself, dark nipples peeking out from between tangled strands of black hair. She ran her hands over him, explored his pecs, his shoulders, his biceps, taking her time and clearly liking what she saw, her touch making his skin burn.

"This is my favorite muscle." Her fingertips grazed his obliques, making his abs tense. "I wish we had a condom. I'm not on the pill or—"

"One of these?" Jason pulled the condom out of his pocket and held it up.

Her face lit up, her lips curving in a sensual smile. "Oh, thank God."

He lifted his ass off the bed so she could yank down his pajama bottoms and was about to open the condom when she stopped him.

"Wait! I haven't gotten to see you or touch you."

He couldn't help but laugh. "I'm all yours."

Her gaze shifted to his cock, her quick inhale telling him she found the sight of him arousing. Then she took his cock in hand, moving slowly from tip to base and back. "Show me what you like. I want to please you."

I want to please you.

Her words were like a dart straight to his heart. Had Elena ever said anything like that? He didn't think so.

He reached down, took hold of Winona's hand, increased the pressure, sucking in a breath when she got it right. "Yeah. Like that."

He held himself still, letting her set the pace, watching as she got used to the feel of him, the sight of her hand on his cock almost as arousing as her touch. Stroke upon stroke, she built the rhythm until he couldn't help but thrust into her fist.

He caught her hand. "Stop."

He didn't want to embarrass himself by coming up short when she needed him.

He tore open the condom with his teeth, rolled it over his erection, then grasped Winona's hips. "Come here."

She moved up his body until she was positioned just above his cock, her palms on his chest for balance. He held himself in place for her, watching as she took him inside her, inch by inch, the two of them moaning in unison.

Sweet Jesus.

She felt so good, her body clenching around him, hot and slippery and tight. He willed himself to relax, let the tension in his muscles go. He wanted this to be good for her, too, and that meant he needed to last.

He held his hips still, giving her time to adjust to him being inside her, focusing instead on those beautiful breasts, the weight of them, the lush feel of them, the pebbled velvet of her dark nipples.

Then she began to move, rocking her hips slowly, grinding herself against him, her eyes drifting shut, her lips parting on a soft moan.

Hell, yeah.

What she was doing would keep him hard, but it wouldn't make him come. That was a *good* thing as far as he was concerned. Besides, it turned him on to see her so turned on, to watch her using his body for her pleasure, to see delight on her face again. She was so responsive, his every touch drawing a reaction, her nipples drawing tighter, goosebumps rising on her skin, sweet little sighs and moans.

Yeah, he could do this all night.

She was breathing faster now, her lips parted, her brow furrowed.

He slid his hands down her body, savoring the feel of her—her ribcage, her narrow waist, the soft curve of her hips. Then he pressed against her dark curls with both thumbs, applying pressure just above her clit.

Her eyes flew open. "Oh … *yes.*"

Her head fell back on a moan, silken strands tickling his thighs, her hips moving faster, his cock buried deep inside her. She was getting close now, every muscle in her body tense, her nails biting into his chest, every exhale ending with a moan.

He was so turned on that his hips instinctively bucked,

and she moaned. He thrust upward again and was rewarded with another throaty moan. He thrust again—and she shattered, coming with a cry, ecstasy shining on her face.

Jason stayed with her until her climax passed. She sank against him, her cheek on his chest, her body languid, her hair spilling over them both. He gave her a moment, ran his fingers along her spine, kissed her hair, the feel of her precious in his arms.

She raised her head, smiled, kissed him.

In a single move, Jason rolled her onto her back, his cock still inside her.

She gave a little gasp of surprise, her hands coming to rest on his shoulders. "Is the Shadow Wolf going alpha on me now?"

He could tell from the way her pupils dilated that she liked that idea.

He ducked down, gently bit one nipple. "Oh, angel, I'm always the alpha."

He flexed his hips, thrust into her, going slowly at first, then building an easy rhythm, wanting to savor this. Oh, but she felt so good, so fucking good, her body gripping him like a fist, the first hint of orgasm uncoiling inside him.

Winona met him thrust for thrust, her moans urging him on, one of her hands clenched in the sheets, the other gripping his shoulder. He willed himself to relax, to focus on her, grazing her clit with his cock, grinding himself against her—anything to slow him down and give her what she needed.

Oh, Winona…

God, she was too much. Soft curves … musk… tight heat.

Lust for her thrummed in his chest, his control unraveling thread by thread, his body trapped on that razor's edge, caught somewhere between pleasure and pain.

She cried out his name, arching off the bed as she came, her muscles clenching around him. And the last thread of Jason's control snapped.

With a groan, he drove into her again and again, his mind blank, instinct taking over. In the next heartbeat, it hit him, climax burning through him, molten and radiant, the bliss of it consuming him, leaving him to lie spent, his head against her breast.

———

WINONA LAY in Jason's arms, deliciously drowsy, her leg tucked between his, her head on his chest, her body replete. She traced a finger along the furrow that bisected his abdomen, his heart beating slow and steady beneath her cheek, his fingers lazily stroking the length of her spine.

When had a man left her feeling so satiated, so safe?

Never. That's when.

The first time she'd had sex, she'd been sixteen. Nathan had been a sweet boy, but sex had hurt and had made her bleed. Then Chaska, who'd been home from college, heard Nathan bragging to friends about taking her virginity and had threatened to kill him. Chaska had also driven her to a clinic to get the morning-after pill—and had made her swear never to have unprotected sex again until she found her half-side.

She'd been more cautious in college. During her sophomore year, she'd met a boy named Mitch, who was also a biology major. She'd ended their relationship when he'd yelled at her for confronting his roommate, who'd kept calling her Pocahontas.

She'd met Kyle in vet school. They spent a year together, Winona helping him with bio-chem until he dropped out of the program and transferred to an art school in another state. Two months later, he'd called to tell her he'd met someone new. She'd been surprised to realize she felt not heartbreak, but only relief.

She'd thought sex with Mitch and Kyle had been good —until tonight. Now she realized she'd had no idea what good sex truly was.

Jason had given her more than he'd taken. He'd put her pleasure first. He'd protected her by using a condom without being asked.

"Thank you, Jason." She didn't realize she'd spoken aloud until she heard herself.

He kissed her hair. "For what?"

"I've never come three times before."

He raised his head, looked down at her. "You're kidding me."

"No." She'd never been given enough time. But that's not what truly mattered tonight. "Thanks for making me feel safe."

He rolled onto his side, cupped her cheek with one big hand. "I'm not going to let anyone hurt you again. We'll take care of this. We'll catch this bastard, and Nate and I will set you up with a good security system. I don't want you to be afraid anymore."

She had to ask. "Why? Why are you doing all of this for me?"

"I've met too many Native women who've been hurt in this world. I can't know what you've been through and not want to help."

His answer disappointed her.

"So, this is just political—help your Native sister with

her security issues and ply her with fantastic sex to take her mind off the bad guys?"

He grinned. "Fantastic sex, huh?"

But she was serious. "Why?"

For a moment, he was quiet, a thoughtful frown on his face. "I can't stay here in Scarlet Springs, Win. You know that. But I do care about you. We have a connection. I know you've felt it, too. We might not be able to do anything with it, but it's there. I can't see what you're going through without wanting to make it better. Is that what you wanted to hear?"

"Yes." Winona didn't think she'd ever gotten this kind of honesty from a man—other than Chaska and her grandfather, of course.

No wonder she felt safe with Jason.

He deserved the same honesty from her.

She kissed a flat, brown nipple. "I care about you, too. No matter what happens, I'm going to remember tonight."

"So will I." He wrapped his arms around her, held her close, pressed a kiss against her forehead. "Sleep, angel."

Winona closed her eyes and drifted into a deep, dreamless sleep.

⸺

JASON WOKE at his phone's first beep, reached for the damned thing, and shut off the alarm. He didn't want to wake Winona.

She was sound asleep in his arms, curled up against his chest, peace on her face, the sight of her putting an ache in his chest.

He'd meant it when he'd said he cared about her. He'd only known her for a few days, but it seemed much longer. He was going to miss her when he returned to Sells.

You have only yourself to blame for that.

Fantastic sex, she'd said. It had been incredible for him, too. It was the first time in almost five years that he'd had sex with a woman other than Elena, and it had shown him what he'd been missing.

I want to please you.

Winona had such a generosity of spirit. Everything she did came from her heart. She was straightforward, genuine, honest.

Elena only cared about herself. She'd treated sex like a reward for good behavior, making Jason wait, using his attraction to her to get what she wanted. He'd been so blinded by lust that he'd seen only the package—the pretty face, the curvy body, the vivacious personality. He'd over-looked the excessive makeup, the fake nails, the obsession over new clothes and shoes, the selfishness, the manipulation.

The DEA did you a favor.

That was the truth.

Doing his best not to wake Winona, Jason got out of bed, grabbed his pajama bottoms off the floor, and tiptoed to his room, shutting the door behind him. He took a leak, washed up, and dressed in his warmest clothes, then grabbed his gear and headed downstairs to the kitchen.

Nate and Jack were already there, coffee ready, scrambled eggs, bacon, and hash browns on the stove. While they ate, Nate went over the plan.

"Dad will stay here with the women and kids. You and I will take one of our UTVs in a horse trailer to the Forest Service parking area. A sheriff's deputy is meeting us there. Then we'll head up and see if you can pick up a trail from last night's tracks."

"That only works if this guy got onto the property the same way he did before."

Jack poured himself another cup of coffee. "Our riders in the south pasture heard the four-wheeler last night. They formed a reception committee, but the poacher never showed himself. They figure he saw them and moved on."

Jason found that interesting. "In that case, he probably did come in the same way. That indicates to me that he's operating from a fixed position."

Nate and Jack seemed to consider this.

Jack grinned. "I can't tell you how grateful we are for your help."

Jason drained his coffee. "From what I hear, you Wests are always there for the people of Scarlet Springs. I'm happy to help."

They finished breakfast and were about to head out when Nate looked Jason over. "You're going to need warmer gear."

Five minutes later, Jason was wearing a spare pair of Nate's long underwear, as well as a winter parka, a woolen hat, and warm gloves.

Nate nodded. "That's better."

Outside, the air was fresh and cold, the scent of snow mingling with pine, the first light of dawn spilling into the valley from the east. The ranch hands had already attached an extra-long horse trailer to Nate's pickup. Nate opened the rear doors to show Jason the UTV strapped inside. Big enough to carry four people, it could definitely handle three adults plus gear.

Then he opened a side door that was closer to the front. "If we get cold and need to retreat to warm up, we can shelter in here."

Inside, it was like a small camper, complete with a stove, a bathroom, and sleeping space. Best of all, it was heated.

Jason wouldn't even ask how much that had cost.

They met Deputy Marcs at the parking lot. This time, she had a rifle, in addition to her sidearm. "I heard about what happened last night. Let's catch this bastard."

Nate backed the UTV out of the trailer, locked it up, and they piled on.

It was a bumpy half-hour ride to the creek.

Jason climbed out of the UTV and immediately saw what they were looking for—four-wheeler tracks with the flying chevron in the center. "He exited the road via the creek, heading straight up the creek bed. He's on Forest Service land."

They waited a few minutes while Deputy Marcs called this information into the Forest Service to let them know what was happening, then left the UTV and hiked into the snowy forest. The tracks were obvious and easy to follow, the snow a perfect canvas.

Jason stepped over the snow-covered trunk of a fallen pine, wind blowing snow from the branches high above them, cold flakes hitting his face. From somewhere overhead came the cry of a raven, the air fresh and crisp. "Look."

Just ahead, the tracks left the creek bed and headed up the mountainside.

Instinctively, Jason stopped, looked uphill, trying to see through the trees. "I don't like having the low ground."

Nate walked up beside him, rifle in hand, very much still the Marine. "I don't like it either. Keep your heads on a swivel, folks. Situational awareness."

Then in the distance, Jason heard it—a low growl that turned into a howl.

It could only be a wolf.

Chapter 14

WINONA WOKE with a smile on her face and stretched. She couldn't remember the last time she felt this relaxed or contented, her body languid, her mind empty. She rolled onto her side, hugged Jason's pillow, and inhaled his scent, memories from the night running through her mind—the heat in Jason's touch, the erotic sound of his moans, the sensation of him moving inside her.

Last night had been the best sex of her life.

There hadn't been any of the awkwardness she associated with the first time with a new partner—the uncertainty, the clumsiness, the nervousness. Something about Jason had put her at ease. Maybe it was his confidence. Or perhaps he was just so damned good in bed that she hadn't had time to be nervous.

She glanced at the clock on the nightstand, saw that it was already half past eight. She got up, took a quick shower, made the bed, and dressed. Then she opened her blinds and found herself staring at a landscape covered in white.

It was breathtaking—high peaks glittering white, pines and firs with snow on their branches, a bright blue sky.

Downstairs, she found Jack, Janet, Megan, and the children in the kitchen, the mingled scents of coffee, bacon, and buttermilk pancakes making her mouth water.

Emily saw her first, her little face lighting up. "Winona! Guess what? I have a snow day."

Megan was trying to get a squirming Jackson into a high chair. "Good morning. I hope you slept well."

Heat rushed into Winona's face. "Yes. Thank you."

"Come have a seat." Janet cut up a pancake and gave her daughter a little fork—which went straight onto the floor. "Lily."

Jack poured Winona a cup of coffee. "We've got eggs, hash browns, bacon, and my homemade pancakes."

Winona sat. "That sounds delicious."

It *was* delicious, especially the pancakes. "If I stay here much longer, I'll have to buy new jeans."

Jack chuckled. "I'll take that as a compliment."

After breakfast, Winona followed Jack out to the barns, Emily skipping along beside her. "Have you heard anything from Nate?"

Jack nodded. "They picked up the trail and followed it onto Forest Service land. That was about an hour ago."

An hour ago.

They'll be fine. They know what they're doing.

Jack opened the barn door. "Emily, why don't you give Winona the grand tour?"

Emily led Winona inside, the mingled scents of fresh hay, leather, and horse manure in the air.

"Buckwheat is my horsy. Grandpa Jack and Daddy gave him to me, but you can ride him if you like."

"That's very kind of you, Emily. Thank you."

Then Winona saw them—twelve beautiful palomino

mares, their coats ranging from darker chocolate tones to golden to misty silver. "Oh, Jack, they're beautiful."

She had always loved horses.

Emily led Winona to the first stall. "These are our mares. Most of them are in foal. This is Baby Doe."

"Hello, Baby Doe." She petted the horse's muzzle. "Aren't you sweet?"

The mare whickered, nudged at Winona's hand.

"Sorry, I don't have any—"

Jack handed her a carrot.

"Thanks." Winona held out her hand with the carrot resting on her palm.

Baby Doe picked it up with her lips and crunched contentedly, Winona's gaze moving over her with a professional eye.

"She's healthy. Nice straight legs. She's got flawless conformation and balance."

"You know horses."

Winona patted Baby Doe's neck. "I know a little. I considered specializing in equine medicine but decided to focus on wildlife instead. What got you into breeding quarter horses?"

"That was my father's decision. My grandfather had put real effort into breeding his mares. They're important to cattle ranchers. He sold some of the foals and made a name for himself. My father just took that a step further and invested in a few prize colts. I learned what I know from him."

Emily tugged on Winona's coat sleeve. "Come meet Clara Brown."

Winona recognized some of the names as honoring important women in Colorado history. In addition to Baby Doe and Clara Brown, there were, among others, Molly Brown, Chipeta, and Isabella Bird. Winona gave each of them a carrot and then followed Emily to another part of the barn to meet Buckwheat and a few other geldings.

Buckwheat was big for a quarter horse and very calm and gentle.

Jack lifted the saddle onto Buckwheat's back. "We use him for equine therapy. He's a big, old softie, aren't you, boy?"

Winona walked with Emily as she led Buckwheat into an enormous riding barn and over to a mounting block. "He trusts you. I can see that."

"I love Buckwheat."

"I can see that, too." Winona was eager to ride, but she could see how much Emily wanted to be in that saddle. "Can you show me how to ride?"

"Sure!" Emily climbed into the saddle.

Winona couldn't help but smile at the child's joy as she rode around the riding barn, the horse's hooves churning up sand. "She rides well."

"Of course, she does." Jack chuckled.

A buzzing sound.

He drew his smartphone out of his pocket, scrolled through a message. "It looks like Deputy Marcs, Nate, and Jason are closing in."

JASON STOPPED AT DEPUTY MARCS' signal, weapon in hand. The ground had leveled out, and there were clear signs that their poacher was living nearby—multiple four-wheeler tracks crisscrossing, trees marked with yellow tape, boot tracks with telltale circles in the center of the heel, trash, stumps of trees that had been cut down.

Marcs spoke quietly. "I can see a large tent up ahead,

and there's the four-wheeler. We'll hold here for now. I'm requesting backup."

She made the call, then turned to Jason and Nate. "Remember that the two of you are here in an advisory capacity. This is public land. Those firearms you're carrying are for personal protection, not to go vigilante."

"Copy that." The last thing Jason needed before his disciplinary hearing was some kind of firearms charge in Colorado.

Nate nodded. "I hear you Lima Charlie."

BAM!

Bark sprayed like shrapnel from the pine next to Jason's head, hitting his face.

Shit.

He dropped to the ground, crawled backward, taking shelter behind a boulder, Nate and Deputy Marcs doing the same.

BAM!

Deputy Marcs grabbed her handset, called it in. "Eight sixty-five, shots fired. I say again, shots fired."

She quickly gave dispatch the details.

Jason was used to having a radio, so it was strange to be privy to only one side of the conversation.

"They're sending in everyone they've got, locking down all roads in this area, and updating the Forest Service guys, but it will take them at least an hour to reach us. We've been ordered to back off."

"*Fuck.*" Nate wasn't happy. "We could fall back to the creek, take up defensive positions, and wait there."

That made sense to Jason. "If that's how he's getting in and out of his little camp, that might hold him in until backup arrives."

The decision ultimately rested with Deputy Marcs. "Let's do it. Stay low."

An engine revved to life.

"Shit." Deputy Marcs looked carefully around the boulder. "He's rabbiting, heading north on the four-wheeler. There's a freaking wolf with him."

She called that in as well.

Jason took the chance, broke cover, saw just the back of the four-wheeler and the wolf as the vehicle disappeared into the forest. "He's going to be easy to track."

"Where does he think he's going?" Nate looked perplexed. "There are only crags and cliffs in that direction."

Jason tried to put himself in the poacher's shoes. "Maybe he's hoping to outflank us or come up on us from behind. Or maybe he thinks he can find a way out."

"I've been ordered not to pursue, but no one said we couldn't move into his camp." Rifle raised, Deputy Marcs slowly got to her feet. "Chiago, have you seen any evidence that there's more than this one bastard?"

"No. Nothing." He stood.

Deputy Marcs looked at his face. "You're bleeding."

Jason held a hand to his cheek, found deep scratches on his cheek and forehead. "It's nothing—just some flying bits of tree bark."

He and Nate followed Deputy Marcs into the camp, the sound of the four-wheeler's engine fading in the distance. But as they grew closer, they heard something else. Yapping. Whining. Whimpers.

Deputy Marcs stopped. "Jesus fried chicken! I think I know why this son of a bitch was poaching beef."

There, locked in a large, covered dog kennel, was another wolf, but this one was a female. Close beside her were four good-sized pups.

The mother growled and bared her teeth at them, her tail up, her pups alert and clearly unsure what to make of the intruders. There, in one corner, was a size-able bone.

Nate swore under his breath. "That's a cow femur for sure."

Deputy Marcs called in to dispatch to let them know they would need a team of wildlife specialists. "Yes, I said 'wolf.' Five, actually—a mother and four pups."

Jason turned to Nate. "I'm going to look around."

Jason snapped a photo of the animals with his smart-phone, thinking he'd show it to Winona when they got back to the ranch. Then he and Nate moved through the camp.

Nate nudged open the large canvas tent with the barrel of his rifle. "He's been here a while. He's been cutting trees for firewood. He even built himself a floor out of split logs. Isn't that cozy?"

There was also a makeshift wood stove made from an old steel barrel, wood piled high beside it. The man's sleeping bag was raised off the floor by a frame of rough-hewn timber. Beneath the bedframe were tools and cans of .30-06 ammo.

Nate pointed at the ammo with his rifle. "There's evidence."

On the bed was a stack of porn mags, one of them open.

"Looks like we interrupted something." Jason saw trap sets piled in the back and what looked like a bobcat fur stretched on a frame. "He's been trapping, too."

"We'd better warn people. He might still have traplines out there." Nate shared this information with Deputy Marcs, who relayed a warning to others via radio.

Next to the tent was a large doghouse and, beside it, a heavy steel stake that had been driven deep into the ground. A thick steel chain was attached to the stake, the forest floor beneath it reduced to mud and covered with wolf tracks.

"I bet this is where he kept the other wolf."

"I think you're right." Jason moved toward another structure and realized at a glance what this must be. "He's been smoking your beef."

The suspect had built himself a small smokehouse using rough-cut lumber, river stones, and clay. There was no fire burning at the moment, but hanging inside were strips of smoked beef, ribs, and a couple of briskets.

Nate took a strip of beef, sniffed it. "He's resourceful. I'll give him that."

Deputy Marcs trudged over to them, an exasperated look on her face. "Wildlife says they can't get anyone up here today. Sheriff Pella is putting in a call to your father, Nate. He's requesting Winona's help."

Jason shook his head. "I don't want her up here. We don't know for certain that this son of a bitch won't circle back or return with friends."

"I'm just telling you what Pella said."

"Damn it." In the end, of course, it wasn't Jason's decision to make.

It was up to Winona.

And Jason *knew* what she would say.

⊏⊐

"YES!" Winona dismounted and scratched Buckwheat's withers. "Yes, I'll help. I need to get to my clinic. I'll need to tranq the mother, and I'll have to get Shota's kennel out of my garage and onto a truck. Tell them not to go near the female. A mama wolf with pups will be very protective."

Jack conveyed that information to Sheriff Pella, who

would relay it via radio to Deputy Marcs. He ended the call. "Let's get Buckwheat back in his stall, and I'll drive you to Scarlet. The poacher took off on his four-wheeler and is now in the wind. Deputy Marcs was ordered not to pursue until backup arrived. Every on-duty law officer in the county is en route."

The poacher took off. He's in the wind.

Winona pushed aside her fear. The Wests and Sheriff Pella needed her help. That wolf mama and her pups needed her help. Besides, Jack would be with her. "I'm ready whenever you are."

While Jack made arrangements for some of his men to keep a close watch on the house, Winona changed into warmer clothes and put on her hiking boots, a million thoughts running through her head at once.

Where had this poacher acquired two wolves? Had he been poaching steers to feed them? Were they healthy? Was the female wild, or had he hand-reared her as he'd obviously done with the male? How big were the pups?

Not sure whether it would be convenient for them to return to the ranch, she packed her bags and Jason's, loaded them into Jack's truck, and sent him a text message to let him know she had his stuff. Then she made a quick call to Wind River Wolf Sanctuary. Heather, the woman who ran the shelter, had taken Shota. Maybe she could take these wolves as well. "Hey, Heather, it's Winona Belcourt."

Winona explained the situation, including the fact that these wolves had been in the possession of a criminal. "I don't know what kind of shape they're in. If they need care, I can treat them at the clinic, but I can't keep six wolves."

"Of course, I'll take them. I'll get a pen ready for

mama and babies. If they find the male, I'll put him next door."

Winona shared the news with Jack. "This is the same sanctuary that took Shota. Once we have them, they'll send a truck."

"They sound like good people."

It took the better part of an hour to reach Scarlet. Winona entered the clinic through the back, leaving her bag and Jason's duffel in the hallway. She enlisted Jack's help gathering everything she'd need—protective gloves; drugs; her tranquilizer gun and darts; bolt cutters in case the kennel was locked; and several hoods and pairs of restraints. Then she went to her garage to get Shota's old crate, the sight of it bittersweet.

Jack helped her lift the large steel crate into the back of his pickup. "You travel light. How the hell are we going to get this up to the camp?"

That was a good question. That old mining road was steep and snowy.

"We can't. We need the Team." She called dispatch, explained the situation, and asked them to tone out Megs and the crew.

Jack glanced over at her, gave her an approving nod. "Good idea."

Then they were back on the highway.

By the time they reached the parking area, Winona had it all figured out in her mind, and Nate and Jason were waiting for them with Jack's UTV, several sheriff's and Forest Service ranger vehicles parked nearby.

Winona couldn't help the way her pulse skipped when she saw Jason walking toward them. Last night, he'd been naked in her arms.

She opened her door, hopped out. "Hey."

Then she saw the blood and lacerations on his cheek and forehead.

"What happened?"

He touched his fingertips to one of the lacerations. "Tree bark."

She moved his hand away. "Those are deep. I should treat them."

"Don't worry about it."

"I'm the doctor here. I'll worry if I want to." She grabbed her medical kit from the back of Jack's cab, then walked to the rear of the pickup and lowered the tailgate. "Sit."

Jack chuckled. "It sounds like you've been given an order, son."

"Right." Jason sat.

While she tended Jason's wounds, cleaning away the blood and disinfecting them, she went over her plan. "We leave the crate here and head up with my gear and the tranq gun. I tranq the mama wolf and put her in restraints. Then we get her onto a gurney, and the Team trails her out to this parking lot. We load her and the pups and drive them to my clinic. I can do a health assessment on them, and Heather from the wolf sanctuary can pick them up there."

"What about the pups?" Nate asked. "I'd say they're about thirty pounds each."

"I'll have to see how feral they are." By the time she finished with Jason, the Team was arriving, Megs and Ahearn first in Rescue One.

Megs' boots hit the snow. "Hey, Jack, Win, Jason. I should've known I'd find the three of you here. Now, will someone tell me what the hell's going on?"

Chapter 15

JASON CLIMBED onto Jack's UTV, sitting next to Winona, her gear strapped onto the back with bungee cords together with some of the Team's rescue gear.

Megs hurried over, handed something to Winona. "Take this."

A radio.

"Thanks." Winona clipped the handset to the collar of her parka, slipped the radio into her pocket, and tucked the earpiece in place. "I won't tranquilize her until you're there. I don't want to risk having to drug her twice."

"Got it." Megs turned to the Team members. "On the double, people."

Some wore skis, while others had snowshoes on their feet. Everyone carried heavy backpacks. They all set out up the snowy road.

"Win is riding, but we have to walk?" The exaggerated whiny tone of Herrera's voice let Jason know that he was joking.

The ride up to the camp seemed to take longer than it had this morning, Jason's gaze on the forest. Until the bastard who'd shot at them was caught, he wouldn't let his guard down.

Nate dropped them off at the creek and turned back. "I'll start bringing up Team members and see if we can't speed things up."

Up at the camp, they found Deputy Marcs and a ranger photographing, bagging, and tagging evidence—the porn mags, ammo cans, traps, weapons, tools.

"Look what we found." Deputy Marcs held out a small plastic bag. "He left us this lovely fake ID. Meet Thomas Jefferson. Does he look familiar to you guys?"

Nate took the evidence, glanced at the photo, then handed it to Jason. "If it isn't our sovereign citizen. Thomas Jefferson?"

Jason handed it to Jack. "I got a bad vibe off that guy."

"Always listen to your gut." Deputy Marcs took the evidence when Jack was done looking at it. "We ran the name on the ID. The name is bogus, too, of course, but we got a ping off the image from the fugitive database. His real name is Thomas Paul Graham. He's done hard time. It would be easier for me to list the crimes he *hasn't* committed than the ones he has."

Winona didn't want to see the ID. "What's he doing up here?"

"He walked off a prison work detail in Alabama more than three years ago. Don't worry, Win. We'll catch him. He's a fugitive, so the Marshal Service is involved now." Then Deputy Marcs led Winona toward the kennel. "Come see our furry friends."

Winona grabbed her gear and followed Deputy Marcs, a shocked look coming over her face when she saw the wolves. "He's kept them locked up in this tiny kennel?"

"He chained the other one up here." Deputy Marcs

rested her hand on top of the large doghouse. "I'm sure the wolf loved that."

While everyone else stayed back, Winona knelt beside the kennel, speaking Lakota in soothing tones. Jason didn't understand a word, but he recognized the care in her voice.

"She's not a wolf," Winona said after a moment. "She's a wolfdog crossbreed. You can tell by her eyes and how far apart they're set. That doesn't change our plans in any way. Her pups are about sixteen weeks old, and they're all wearing collars. You don't want us near them, do you, Mama? I understand."

Winona sat back on her heels in the snow and got her gear ready, preparing the darts, setting out the restraints. Jason could only respect her skill.

"Are those critter handcuffs?" Deputy Marcs leaned closer, trying to get a look. "Aren't they cute?"

"They'll ensure that she can't hurt herself or anyone else if she starts to come out of it early, but I'm usually pretty good at gauging how much to give. The mask is to muzzle her and protect her eyes from drying out."

"Right."

While they waited for the Team to arrive, Jason led Jack over to the smokehouse and opened the door. "He's been smoking your beef and feeding it to his animals."

Jack glanced inside. "That son of a bitch."

By the time Team members began to trickle into the camp, Winona was ready. She explained to Jason what the Team members were doing.

"Jesse Moretti is setting up the anchor. That's usually Chaska's job."

"The anchor?"

"They can't wheel the gurney on this steep, uneven ground, so they have to carry it. We don't want Team members tripping or falling and dropping the gurney, so we set up an anchor by tying the ropes to trees. It has to support the weight of the rescuers, as well as the gear, the gurney, and the person—or animal—on the gurney."

"That makes sense." Jason found it fascinating—the speed with which they worked, the way everyone seemed to know his or her job, their camaraderie.

"Anchor ready," Moretti called out.

Winona knelt next to the kennel again, the wolfdog baring her teeth, growling. "I'm sorry, sweet girl, but I need to stick you."

Winona fired two darts, one after the other, hitting the animal in its hindquarters. The wolfdog yelped—and slowly sank to the snow, darts in its hip. After a moment, she lay on her side and began to twitch.

"Is she okay?" Sasha asked.

"That's completely normal." Win motioned to the padlock on the kennel. "Can someone please grab my bolt cutters and cut that lock?"

She hadn't wanted it cut before the wolf was sedated just in case the door accidentally came open.

"On it." Ahearn walked over to the kennel, bolt cutters in hand. "Done."

Winona didn't open the door immediately. She spoke to the pups in Lakota, held gloved fingers through the holes in the fence, testing their response. They whined, wagged their tails, licked her gloved fingers, putting a smile on her face. "I think we're good. They've got collars, so he must have tried to socialize them. Let's use leashes."

One at a time, she leashed the pups, handing them off to Team members. "We've got three males and one female."

"These are *big* puppies." Taylor scratched his pup

behind the ears. "Our adult black lab isn't much bigger than this."

Winona leashed the last pup and led it out of the kennel. It hopped up on her, yipped. She patted its head. "You think they're big? Wait till you see their daddy."

Jason glanced around, still keeping an eye out for trouble. They needed to catch this Graham bastard. But what would they do about the wolf when they found him?

———

WITH THE PUPS out of the kennel, Winona worked quickly, buckling the mother wolfdog's front paws and then its rear paws together. With that done, she slipped a mask over its eyes and then checked its pulse.

"Okay, let's get her onto the gurney. Watch where you step."

With five animals in a small space, piles of poop were everywhere.

Jesse and Creed maneuvered their way inside, Winona supporting the wolfdog's head as they lifted her onto the gurney. Then she took one of the handles, Jason, Sasha, and Megs taking the other three to lift the gurney and carry it out of the kennel.

Megs took charge from there, sorting out who would be on belay, who would carry the gurney, and who would wrangle puppies. In just a few minutes, the belay crew was ready, the gurney crew was in harnesses and roped in, and the puppy wranglers, as Megs called them, were set.

Winona took Austin's pup so he could help carry the gurney. "The pups will probably want to stay close to their mama. This experience is new to them."

Down the hill they went, the crew with the gurney moving slowly over steep, slippery ground made more treacherous because the snow hid the trunks of fallen trees and rocks. When they reached the creek, they removed the ropes and carried the gurney out to the road, where Austin crawled beneath it and clipped on the large ATV tire that enabled them to roll the gurney the rest of the way.

"That's clever." Jason bent down, gave his pup's ears a scratch.

"That's Chaska's invention."

The pups trotted along behind the gurney, occasionally whimpering for their mother, their ears straight up and forward, tails wagging.

Sasha was clearly having a great time. "They're so cute!"

"This is why I love the Team—no two days are alike," Jesse said. "One day, it's a drunk kid in a Batman suit stuck on a crag, and the next, it's a wolfdog and puppies."

After that, the conversation drifted to the upcoming ski season and off-width climbing gear—mega-cams, tube chocks, gloves.

Jason leaned closer, spoke for Winona's ears alone. "Can we still be friends if I say I have no clue what they're talking about?"

Winona laughed. "Sure. Thanks, by the way. You helped find these poor creatures. Now we can put them in a good home where they can run free."

"Just doing my part." His lips curved in a smile that stole Winona's breath.

They reached the parking lot, where Jack and Nate were loading the UTV into their trailer. Under Winona's direction, Team members lifted the wolfdog, settled her inside Shota's old crate, and placed the pups beside her.

"Thanks for your help, everyone." Winona locked the crate, eager to get the mother back to the clinic as soon as possible so she wouldn't have to sedate her again. She handed her radio to Megs. "Everyone did a great job."

"You're the wolf whisperer. We just do what we're told." Megs and the others began packing away their gear. "We'll do a quick debriefing at The Cave in an hour and then hit the pub."

"I'm heading back to the ranch." Nate shook Jason's hand and hugged Winona. "I hope to see both of you at the Cimarron again soon. My old man and I couldn't have done this without you."

"I'm obliged to both of you." Jack closed the tailgate, checked it, ensuring that the crate and its precious cargo was safe. "Let's hit the road."

Winona was just climbing into the cab of Jack's truck when a US Marshal Service vehicle entered the parking lot. Several marshals got out, including Zach, who was wearing body armor and carrying a rifle.

He spotted them and walked over, a big grin on his face. "Jack, Nate, good to see you two. Looks like you've got your hands full, Winona. Hey, Chiago. I heard that bastard fired off a few shots. I'm glad you still have your head. Are those nicks from bullet fragments?"

Jason shot Zach a look. "Tree bark. The round hit a tree, and the bark splintered."

Winona gaped at him. "He almost *shot* you?"

Jack crossed his arms over his chest. "I hadn't heard this either. Anyone care to elaborate?"

Jason filled them in. "He fired off a few rounds to hold us off so he could get away. We took cover, and he hopped on that four-wheeler. No big deal."

"No big deal?" It seemed like a big deal to Winona, but then she wasn't in law enforcement. "You let me think you'd had a run-in with a tree trunk."

"I didn't want to worry you."

Zach frowned, held a finger to his earpiece, and turned away, listening. Then he spoke into his hand mic. "Copy that. We're on our way up."

Just then, a dozen pagers went off, including Winona's. She drew it out of her pocket, read through the message. "They found him. The four-wheeler flipped, and he's pinned beneath it and injured."

"Listen up! Grab your gear. We're heading back up the mountain." Megs walked over to Zach. "McBride, are my people in danger? What about the other wolf?"

Zach zipped his parka, adjusted his hand mic. "I just heard from Incident Command. The wolf ran off, and the fugitive has been disarmed. I'll be right beside you."

"That's good enough for me." Megs set off. "Let's move, people! And remember to watch for traps!"

Zach turned to Jason. "You coming, Chiago?"

"I'm sticking with Winona."

Zach's eyebrows rose. "Got it. See you later."

As Winona and Jason got into Jack's truck for the drive to Scarlet Springs, the Team headed back up the mountain, Zach and his men beside them.

———

JASON, Jack, and a group of volunteers helped unload the crate from the back of Jack's pickup and carry the sedated wolf inside, her pups scampering along behind them.

"I'm heading back up to the ranch." Jack shook first Winona's hand and then Jason's. "Thanks for solving this mystery. You are welcome under our roof anytime."

"Thanks for the hospitality." Jason had never imagined he'd enjoy hanging with a family of white millionaires. The West family and their ranch were far beyond anything in his experience. "The Cimarron is a special place."

"Then I'll see you again. Take care." With that, Jack left the clinic.

Jason watched as Winona worked, impressed with her confidence around animals that would scare most people.

She examined the mother, drew blood samples, and gave the animals rabies vaccines. "You guys didn't see that."

Her volunteers laughed, understanding a joke that sailed over Jason's head.

Winona explained. "Rabies vaccines aren't approved for wolfdog mixes, but I give them anyway. I do what's best for the animal."

She gave the wolfdog a drug to revive her, then left her and her pups in the crate with fresh water to rest. "Thanks, everyone, for your help. Heather should be here any minute. I'm going to fill out the paperwork."

While Winona filled out vaccine certificates, Jason cased out the clinic, looking at its security from a law enforcement perspective, taking photos with his phone. A criminal would have no trouble gaining entrance. Only the back entrance was truly secure. The front door was mostly glass, making it an easy point of ingress, and he had no difficulty forcing the windows open from the outside.

He carried their bags next door to her house and scoped it out, too, finding much the same thing—doors and windows that were easy to force or break, as well as a deck railing that would make it easy for someone to climb into her bedroom.

He couldn't leave it like this, but none of this was his decision to make. He'd talk to Winona tonight, give her the business card of Nate's friend in Denver.

As he walked back to the clinic, the truck from the wolf rescue pulled up. He watched as Winona, the volunteers, and the woman from the rescue transferred the still-groggy mother and her pups to a new crate.

Winona handed the woman all of her paperwork. "Thanks, Heather."

"Any word on the male wolf?"

Winona shook her head. "He ran off when the rangers and sheriff's deputies approached. I'm worried about him. He might not know how to hunt or fend for himself up there. I'm going to contact wildlife officials and ask what they plan to do."

"If they catch him, we'll take him in." Heather gave Winona a hug. "I need to get Mama and pups settled before dark. See you soon."

Winona watched them drive away, then let out a relieved breath. "I'm hungry. How about you? Want to head to Knockers?"

He was hungry—for food and something more. "How about we grab something quick and stay at your place?"

"Do you like tacos?"

"Do I like tacos?" Jason stared at her. "I'm O'odham and a Mexican citizen."

They climbed into Winona's Outback and drove to a taco truck that was doing a brisk trade, the words *Tacos Sabrosos* painted on its side—*Tasty Tacos*.

Winona ordered three tacos with shredded chicken and queso. "No jalapeños. *Gracias, Juana.*"

"No jalapeños?" Jason had to tease her just a little. "Are they too hot for you?"

Winona lowered her voice to a whisper. "I'll explain in a minute."

Jason ordered a smothered burrito with the jalapeños, the two of them standing beneath a heat lamp while they waited for their order. "Okay, let's hear it. What's the problem with jalapeños that makes you whisper in public?"

Winona leaned closer. "Chaska and Naomi got some food from Juana's one day, and they were ... intimate afterward. Naomi had eaten jalapeños, and the oils from the pepper burned Chaska on his... She says he had to spend an hour with his manly bits in a bowl of milk—which, by the way, is *not* an image I needed in my mind."

"Ouch." Jason winced at the thought of dick-burn and picked the jalapeños off his burrito, leaving them uneaten. "Okay. Agreed. No jalapeños."

He thought about it for a moment. "Wait. Does this mean you've got something specific in mind for later, angel?"

He certainly did.

Chapter 16

WINONA AND JASON ate their supper at Winona's kitchen table, talking about everything and nothing. Their shared experience at the Cimarron. How Winona and Chaska had learned to ski. Jason's first memory of snow.

"I must have been four." There was a hint of sadness in his smile as he spoke, his hand taking hers. "My mother woke me up early and told me there was snow outside. I had no idea what she meant. I remember her putting a little snowball in my hand. I dropped it because it was so cold. That made her laugh. Then, I discovered that my shoes made prints in this cold, white stuff, so I stomped all over the place."

Winona smiled, imagining Jason as a tiny child. "You were learning to track already. I bet you were adorable."

He slipped a hand into his rear jeans pocket, pulled out a leather billfold, and took out a small photo. "This is the only photo I have of my entire family."

Winona took the photo from him. Three generations stood together beneath some kind of awning made of branches, smiles on their faces, giant saguaros in the background. Jason, the youngest, stood in front of his mother, a bright smile on his face, his mother's hands resting on his shoulders. "How old are you here?"

"Six or seven."

"You *are* adorable." Winona's heart broke for that little boy, knowing what lay ahead. "Your mother was beautiful. You have her eyes."

"That's what everyone tells me." He took the photo when she finished with it and tucked it back into his wallet. "I've tried seeing her when I look in the mirror, but it doesn't work."

Winona stood, held out her hand for him. "Come."

He took her hand, stood. "Where are we going?"

She led him into the bathroom. "I smell like a wet, dirty wolfdog. I need a shower. I thought maybe you could help me out with that."

He caught her, drew her against him, nuzzled her neck. "You smell like woman to me, but the idea of getting your body wet and soapy suits me just fine."

They stripped each other naked and got the water going, Winona making sure it was nice and hot. Then they stepped under the spray together.

Winona wet her hair and reached for the shampoo, but Jason beat her to it.

"Turn around."

She did as he asked, sighing with pleasure as his fingers massaged her scalp and caressed her nape, sending tingles down her spine. While she rinsed, he washed his hair. Then she reached for the soap.

They lathered each other, hands gliding over soap-slick skin, each seeking ways to please the other. He cupped her breasts, teased her nipples, caressed her bare buttocks, making her blood hot. She explored the planes and ridges of his muscles, took the weight of his testicles in her hand, stroked his erection, her need for him building.

Hot water rinsed soap away, the air thick with steam and sexual need, her skin tingling. Then she traded places with him, looked him in the eyes, and dropped to her knees before him.

His breath hissed from between clenched teeth when she took him into her mouth, his fingers sliding into the tangled, wet strands of her hair. "*Win.*"

She'd learned a bit about him, and she put it to good use, moving her mouth and hand together along his length, teasing the head of his cock with her tongue, her free hand cupping his balls.

"*Jesus,* Win." His fingers fisted in her hair, his hips thrusting, urging her on.

In tune with his response, she picked up the pace, savoring the hard feel of him, remembering how good his cock had felt inside her. His balls drew tight, a sign that he was close to the edge now.

"Stop, angel." He shut off the water, drew Winona to her feet. "My turn."

Anticipation shivered through her as she wondered what came next.

He stepped out of the tub and scooped her into his arms, making her shriek with surprise. He chuckled. "I've got you."

He carried her, wet and naked, across the hall to his room, where he dropped her onto his bed. Before she could catch her breath, he grasped her ankles, dragged her butt to the edge, pushed her knees apart. "I want to taste you."

Winona started to tell him that this had never done anything for her when his mouth closed over her. "Oh!"

This was … different. This wasn't like anything a man had done to her before, and it felt so… incredibly … *good*.

He suckled her clit just like he'd suckled her nipples, tugging on her with his lips, drawing her into the heat of his mouth, stroking her with his tongue.

She slid her fingers into his hair, drew her knees back, surrendering herself wholly, barely aware of the moans coming from her throat. "*Jaaaa-son.*"

Then he slid fingers inside her, stroking that deep ache, pleasure twisting in her belly, coiling itself tighter and tighter. But still, he didn't stop, his mouth and fingers merciless. He gave her no quarter, no chance to breathe, her body buffeted by sensations almost too good to bear.

And then she shattered, climax washing through her, engulfing her in bliss.

He kept it up until her orgasm had passed. Then he grabbed a condom, rolled it over his erection, and buried himself inside her with a deep, slow thrust, his mouth claiming hers, his tongue carrying her musky taste into her mouth.

He took his time, slowly building up the rhythm, giving her a chance to grow aroused again, his mouth on her nipples, his deep thrusts bringing her to the edge once more. But this time when she came, he climaxed with her, the two of them falling together into paradise.

IN A POST-ORGASMIC DAZE, Jason held Winona, her head resting on his chest, her hair spilling around them, her taste still on his tongue.

Leaving her won't be easy.

It was true. He knew it. But damned if he could regret

a moment he'd spent with her, least of all having sex with her.

Winona Belcourt blew his mind. Something about her was so down-to-earth, so very … *real*.

She raised her head, kissed one of his nipples, smiled at him. "Will you believe me if I say I've never enjoyed receiving oral sex?"

He stared at her, sure she must be joking. "You're serious."

She nodded. "Until tonight, I wondered what the big deal was. Now I know."

Jason couldn't keep the stupid grin off his face. "It's all in the lips."

Don't let it go to your head, cabrón. *After this week, it will be other men giving her that pleasure.*

Maybe he could stay a little longer. He didn't have to be back in Sells until his hearing.

Do you hear yourself, man?

Lima Charlie—loud and clear.

He forced that train of thought from his mind. "What else haven't you enjoyed—in bed, I mean."

She considered his question. "Sex from behind. I don't get anything from it. I need to watch TV or read a book so I don't get bored."

That made him laugh. "That bad? Challenge accepted. Anything else?"

"I guess that's it—but there are a lot of things I haven't tried. Most of them I don't *want* to try."

This was intriguing.

"What haven't you done that you *want* to do?"

Her eyes went wide for a moment. "Well, I…"

He kissed the tip of her nose. "Hey, don't be embarrassed."

Still, she hesitated. "I … I like it when you get a little rough."

He'd noticed that. "I'll keep that in mind."

Because he couldn't yet get it up again, he changed the subject. "I cased out your house and the clinic this afternoon while you were working, and there's a lot you could do to improve security. Nate gave me a card of a company he recommends. If it's okay with you, I can give them a call tomorrow."

Her smile faded. "I'm not sure I can afford it."

He chuckled. "Jack and Nate can. They want to help. I'm sure they'd be willing to cover the entire cost."

"That doesn't seem right. It's not their problem."

"Why not? Their steers weren't your problem. They've got the money, and you helped them."

She brushed that off. "The bad guy is in the hospital. He'll be going back to prison. He's not a danger to me now."

Jason tucked a strand of hair behind her ear. "I know it scares you to be there, especially when you're alone. I know you have nightmares. It's okay to want to feel safe, and it's okay to let people help you."

"You probably think I'm a wimp."

The anguish in her eyes cut him. "No, I don't. You don't have to be brave all the time, Win. You don't have to carry the weight of this. Chaska, your grandfather, Jack, Nate, me—we want to help you. Let us. I'll stay to make sure the work gets done and gets done right."

"Wasn't the plan for you to spend time with Zach and then to go see the sights and camp? Helping to put in my security system can't be what you hoped for when you set off on this vacation."

"You want to get rid of me?" It was a joke.

She didn't take it that way. "No! No, hardly that. I just

don't want you using your hard-earned time off dealing with my stupid problems."

"Hey, now. Your problems aren't stupid." *Tell her.* "This isn't a vacation. I'm on unpaid administrative leave."

"You're … what?"

He sat up, moved to the edge of the bed, rubbed his face with his hands. "I've got a disciplinary hearing when I get back."

She sat up behind him, her hand sliding up his back. "What happened?"

He told her about Ren and the ambush and how he'd chased that son of a bitch across the border. "He turned, raised his weapon, and I fired. The next thing I knew, there were a dozen Mexican agents. They frisked me at gunpoint, cuffed me, took my weapons, badge, and ID."

"How scary."

"The rest of the Wolves showed up, and eventually, they released me. But they filed a complaint."

"I don't understand. You're O'odham and a dual citizen. That's your people's land. You have a right to be there."

"Not as a member of a Border Patrol unit."

She rested her cheek on his shoulder, one lush breast brushing his arm. "What do you think will happen?"

"I don't know." Jason had done a little digging, and there'd never been a case like his. "I might lose my job. I might find myself at a desk. I might get a slap on the wrist."

"How do you want it to end?"

No one had asked him that.

"I've spent my entire adult life working as a Shadow Wolf. I don't know who I'd be without the uniform."

She kissed his shoulder, her hand caressing his bicep. "You'll be the man you are right now—the man who helped rebuild a summer camp for kids, who helped strangers track a poacher, and who wants to help some random woman with a security system."

That last part made him smile.

He turned, caught her in his arms, and pushed her back onto the bed. "Hey, your taste is still in my mouth. There's nothing random about you."

Then he kissed her.

WINONA WOKE FIRST, the scent of Jason's skin tickling her from sleep. He lay on his back, one arm bent above his head, the other around her shoulders, her cheek against his chest. The covers had slipped down, leaving them both exposed from the waist up, his chest and belly bared to her gaze, his breathing deep and slow.

She'd met him last Saturday, and it was only Thursday —and he'd already come to mean so much to her.

He's leaving soon. You might not see him again.

The thought put an ache in her chest.

How unfair was it that life could bring Jason to her when the two of them could never be together? He had his life in Sells, and she had her clinic and her family here in Scarlet Springs.

Think of this as a gift. No regrets. No looking ahead.

The ache grew sharper.

But it was true—these days and nights with Jason *were* a gift. She shouldn't waste one moment of this time worrying about the future or weighing down the present by focusing on future sadness. They were here now, and that's what mattered.

She pushed down the covers, exposed his beautiful cock, then got onto her knees—and took him into her mouth. He'd stopped her when she'd gone down on him, thinking of her pleasure. This time, she wanted him to finish first.

She moved slowly, stroking him to fullness, his cock growing hard in her mouth.

He stirred in his sleep, his brow furrowing.

She moved faster, kept up the rhythm.

He moaned in his sleep—then jolted awake, breath leaving his lungs in a rush. "*Winona!* What…?"

She took her mouth off him, but only for a moment. "Good morning. Don't stop me this time."

He stared at her, surprise and a hint of a smile on his face. "Okay. Jesus."

Winona got back to work, putting everything she had into making it good for him, taking her cues from his responses, using her tongue, lips, and hand in tandem.

He slid his fingers into her hair, moved it aside, and watched as she devoured him, his breathing heavier. "God, you're good at this."

Winona kept at it, increasing the pressure, going faster, circling him with her tongue, focusing on the sensitive underside.

His fingers tightened until his hands were fisted in her hair, his breathing ragged, every muscle in his body tense.

She loved seeing the effect she had on him, loved seeing the erotic anguish on his face, his eyes squeezed shut now, his brow furrowed, his teeth clenched. His balls drew tight, and she knew he was on the edge.

She stopped, smiling at his frustrated groan.

"Oh, God." He thrust with his hips, seeking the release she wouldn't yet give him.

She blew cool breath across the wet head of his cock, smiled as breath hissed from between his teeth.

He slid a big hand beneath her chin, lifted her gaze to

his, the heat in his eyes sending a shiver through her. "You're cruel."

She smiled—and took him into her mouth once again.

His head fell back onto the pillow. "Oh, Win."

She brought him to the brink once more, making him wait, letting the tension build, his hips shifting against the bed, his body clearly aching for release.

He glared at her through narrowed eyes, the hint of a smile on his lips, one hand reaching to fondle her bare breast. "You're going to find yourself on your back if you're not careful."

She smiled. "Ooh, threats. I'm scared."

This time, she went all out, bringing him to the edge—and carrying him over.

He groaned, arched off the bed, drawing her head away from him as he came, his cock pulsing in her hand as she finished him, semen spurting onto his belly, her hand, her arm. With a shuddering exhale, he began to relax.

He opened his eyes, a tenderness there that made her breath catch. "You are incredible. You—"

A knock at the door. "Winona?"

"Oh, no! That's Chaska." Winona jumped out of bed, ran into her bathroom naked, and washed her hands and arm.

Another knock, more insistent this time. "Win?"

She dashed back to her room, threw on her sleepshirt, grabbed her bathrobe, and was on her way to the front door when Jason stopped her.

"You've got some of me on your cheek." Chuckling, he wiped it off with his thumb. "You're good."

"Thanks." She tied her bathrobe, hurried to the door, opened it. "*Toniktuha he?*"

How are you?

Chaska stepped inside. "Hey, what's going on? Megs

says you and Chiago spent the night at the Cimarron, that you're helping Jack and Nate with a wolf?"

"It's a long story. Coffee?" She'd just set the pot on to boil when Jason walked into the kitchen, fully dressed.

Chaska's expression went hard. "Chiago."

Jason acknowledged her brother with a nod. "Belcourt. Congratulations on the birth of your son."

"Thanks."

Winona didn't feel like she owed Chaska an explanation. She wasn't sixteen. Still, she had to say something. "Jason is staying in the guest room. Jack West asked the two of us to help him track a wolf that was killing his steers. It turns out that the wolf belonged to a poacher who was encamped illegally on Forest Service land. We found a female wolfdog and four pups at his camp, too, but the wolf got away."

That was the truth—if not the whole truth.

"What? Wait. Start over. You tracked a wolf?"

Over coffee, Winona and Jason told Chaska the story, filling in most of the blanks, leaving out only the fact that they were sleeping together.

"And this bastard is in custody?" he asked.

Jason told him what McBride had shared in a text. "He's in a Denver hospital with a broken pelvis. The four-wheeler flipped on him. But the wolf is still out there."

Winona changed the subject. "How are Naomi and Shota?"

Chaska's expression softened. "They're coming home tomorrow. Can we talk for a minute, Win?"

Here it comes.

She walked with Chaska into her backyard.

Chaska didn't mince words. "Are you sleeping with him?"

"That's between Jason and me. I'm a grown woman, Chaska."

He stopped, worry on his dear face. "I just don't want you to get hurt. What do you really know about this man?"

"I know enough."

Chaska nodded, stepped back. "You're a grown woman, and I trust you to do what's right. I just can't remember a time when you were unwilling to share your heart with me. It's not like you to shut me out, sister."

He turned and walked out through her back gate, leaving Winona to wrestle with her emotions.

Chapter 17

WHILE WINONA DID her rounds at the clinic, Jason rinsed the breakfast dishes and put them in the dishwasher, unable to get the stupid grin off his face, his mind all over her. Had he been wearing this same grin earlier when her brother had stopped by? Maybe that's why Chaska had looked like he wanted to punch Jason in the face.

Still, Jason couldn't be too hard on himself. He'd just gotten the best head of his life. He'd been surprised that he'd been able to stand upright and speak in complete sentences after Winona had finished with him.

God, she was amazing—both in bed and out.

She'd come back inside from her little chat with Chaska, worry in her eyes. Jason didn't have to ask what was wrong. Chaska didn't like the idea of Jason sleeping with his little sister. But Winona was an adult woman. She didn't need Chaska's approval to take a man to her bed.

He's not wrong to worry about her, is he, pendejo?

That thought wiped the grin off Jason's face.

Chaska wanted to see his little sister with a man who'd stick around and be a part of her life, not someone who was just passing through or using his sister to get off. He didn't want her to get hurt.

Well, Jason couldn't fault the man for that. But the last thing he wanted to do was hurt Winona. He'd been transparent with her. She knew he couldn't make a life with her here in Scarlet Springs. Their time together was a gift, and they both knew it would end.

Why did that leave him feeling desolate?

He pushed the question from his mind and spent the morning doing things around the house. He wiped down the counters and the stove, swept the floors, took out the trash and recycling, and brought in the plastic coffee can lid she'd used as a spirit plate for breakfast. Then he started a load of laundry.

Needing to stay busy, he sat down with his laptop to catch up on email. Then he brushed his teeth and took a shower. He'd just put on his jeans when Winona ran through the door, calling for him.

"Jason?"

He stepped out of the bedroom. "What is it?"

She was almost breathless with excitement, her brown eyes wide. "The Cimarron donated twenty-five *thousand* dollars to the clinic. That covers my operating expenses for the rest of the year and beyond. Can you believe that?"

Jason was impressed. "They said they'd make a donation. Those Wests never do anything half-assed."

"There's more. Someone dropped this through the front door." She held out an envelope. "It's for you from the Cimarron."

Jason read his name on the front, saw the Cimarron stamp on the back, and opened it. Then it was his turn to be surprised. "It's a check for two thousand. They didn't have to do that."

There was a letter, too, a short, handwritten message

signed by Jack, offering their thanks, praising him for his skill, and inviting him to visit the ranch anytime.

"Maybe that money will help you deal with the month of unpaid leave."

"I've got enough saved up." When he got back to Sells, he would deposit the money and donate it to Winona's clinic. "How are things with the animals?"

"The critters are doing well. My volunteers did a great job of keeping up with cleaning and feeding while I was out. I examined the beaver, raccoon, and fox, ordered some supplies, and called Dan, the game warden, to let him know we can schedule the eagle's release. He told me they've been looking for the wolf but so far haven't seen more than tracks. They're busy with that and want to wait to release the eagle until next week. Maybe you can be there."

Jason saw the hope in her eyes, a fragile hope that he would still be here in Scarlet Springs. "I would love that."

Her face lit up. "I thought we could maybe grab lunch at Knockers and then go to the climbing gym. The Team usually trains there on Thursday afternoons."

But Jason had a better idea. "How about we skip lunch, skip the climbing gym—whatever that is—and get naked. I have some things I'd like to do to that sweet body of yours if you'd let me."

Her pupils dilated, but she feigned disinterest. "Hmm. Like what?"

He grasped her waist, drew her near. "I thought I could start by stripping you naked and then kissing every inch of you."

She looked up at him through big brown eyes. "And then what?"

"I could tie you to the bed and do my best to make you scream." He ducked down and nuzzled the skin beneath her ear, inhaling her scent. "Or I could go down on you and make you wait for it like you did to me this morning. Or bend you over and fuck you from behind. I promise you won't need to read a book."

She slid her hands over his ass, her touch arousing even through denim. "Well, I do enjoy reading, but if you think you're up for all that..."

He ground his pelvis against her, let her feel his erection. "Oh, I'm *up* for it. The question is can you take it?"

"I guess there's only one way to find out."

"My thoughts exactly." He scooped her off her feet, laughing at her shriek of surprise, and carried her into her bedroom.

———

WRISTS STILL BOUND with her bandana, Winona lay face down on her bed, out of breath and spent, little tremors of pleasure washing through her as her climax slowly faded. Jason rolled onto his back beside her, and she felt him moving around—probably to get rid of the condom. Then he reached over to unbind her, warm lips pressing kisses against her shoulder.

She rolled onto her back, opened her eyes, found him smiling down at her. She tried to speak but had to swallow first, her throat dry from all the noise she'd made, all that moaning and crying out. "You are *so* good."

How could she go back to her sexless existence after this? How could she ever desire any man other than Jason?

Don't think about it.

He chuckled, kissed her forehead. "So, you didn't get bored?"

"Bored?" Then she remembered and laughed. "No."

He drew her into his arms, and for a few minutes, they

lay together in golden silence, cocooned in the afterglow of great sex, their bodies replete. His scent was all over her, and hers on him, the air heavy with salt and musk.

Then Winona's stomach growled. "I'm hungry."

He reached for his phone, glanced at the screen. "I'm not surprised. We didn't eat lunch, and it's almost five-thirty."

She stared at him. "No way! We've been at this for *five hours*? How can that be?"

They *had* done it all, all of the things he'd suggested—and more.

"There were breaks in between, and you fell asleep once, remember?"

"More like I passed out."

He grinned, his fingers caressing her spine. "It *was* sudden. One minute you were screaming, and the next you were out."

"I wasn't screaming. That's too dramatic a term for it."

He chuckled. "If you say so."

She sat up, gave herself a moment to adjust, her body like linguine. "I'm going to take a shower, and then we'll head to Knockers."

They walked the short distance to Knockers, holding hands. They ran into Bear at the roundabout. He greeted Winona with a big smile, most of which was hidden beneath his beard. "Winona Belcourt!"

"Bear, it's so good to see you. This is my good friend, Jason Chiago."

Bear looked at Jason like a shy child. "Jason Chiago. I am Winona's friend, too."

Jason squeezed Winona's hand, then released and reached for Bear's. "She told me about you. I'm so happy to meet you."

Winona's heart melted at the compassion she saw in Jason's eyes.

Bear shook Jason's hand. "She takes care of animals."

"She does—and so do you. That's what I've heard."

Bear shuffled his feet, clearly both touched and embarrassed by Jason's words. He fell back on Scripture. "Whatever you did to the least of these, you did to me."

Jason nodded. "That's right."

Winona asked the obvious question. "Have you had supper?"

Bear shook his head.

"Want to come with us to Knockers? I'll buy your favorite meal."

His face lit up.

The three of them walked the last block and a half to Knockers. It was just after six, the parking lot starting to fill, the band not yet onstage.

Rain met them at the door, her hair tied up with a red scarf, a bright smile on her face. "Hey, Bear! I've got your favorite table set aside. Come on over."

Winona grabbed a menu for Jason. "It's on me tonight, Rain. Thanks. Enjoy your supper, Bear."

Rain winked. "Thanks, Win."

A cheer came from the back corner.

"Sounds like at least some of the Team are here tonight." Winona led Jason back to the Team table, where Bahir, Megs, and Ahearn were beaming at Sasha, who was on her way down from a new route on the wall, with Nicole on belay.

Megs glanced over, saw them, and filled them in. "Hey! Have a seat. Sasha just sent a five-thirteen on the first try —nailed it."

"I'm sorry we missed it." Winona sat beside Jason,

handed him his menu. "Watching Sasha climb is watching an artist in action."

"Sounds impressive." Clearly, none of this made sense to Jason.

Megs must have realized that, too, because she started explaining the rating system and how the route-setter changed the routes on the wall regularly to keep them challenging. By the time they'd finished their meals—Jason a steak and Winona a roast chicken breast—Jason understood some of the terminology.

"Come climb with me. I'll show you how to belay." Bahir got to his feet.

But the Timberline Mudbugs had hit the stage.

"He can't be your belay slave, Bahir, because he's dancing with me—or do Desert People not know how to do the two-step?"

Jason stood, his lips slowly curving into a grin that made her belly flutter. "Oh, angel, I invented it. You come along now—and try to keep up."

They made their way to the dance floor, where Jason took the lead. She couldn't take her gaze off his face as they promenaded around the dance floor. Just like in the bedroom, he knew all the moves, and she realized at some point that people were watching. No, not people. All the *women* were watching.

Sorry, but he's mine.

That song ended, Jason and Winona applauding along with everyone else. The next song was a slow number.

Jason drew Winona close. "I think I like this better."

Buzz-buzz. Buzz-buzz.

She stopped. "My pager."

She drew it out, scrolled through the message. "I'm sorry, Jason. The Team just got toned out. I need to go. You can stay if you want. I can give you my key."

She hurried back to the table, where Megs and the others were gathering their jackets and bags.

Megs dropped a twenty on the table. "Looks like we've got someone running the Scarlet Midnight Triathlon. Let's move, people!"

Rain hurried over. She'd seen that they were leaving and understood. "Don't worry about your checks. We'll settle up next time. I've got Bear, Win. Stay safe."

"Thanks, Rain." Winona got to her feet.

Megs turned to Winona. "Chiago might be able to help us on this one. Can you track in the dark?"

Jason looked at Megs as if she were crazy. "Of course."

"Then I would be delighted to have you join us. Just do what you're told, and don't get in anyone's way."

Jason met Winona's gaze, a humorous glint in his eyes. "Yes, ma'am."

JASON SAT in the passenger seat of Winona's SUV, wearing a reflective vest over his jacket, a yellow Team T-shirt beneath. They'd left Scarlet behind and were headed downhill through a narrow canyon. He had to ask. "What exactly is the Scarlet Midnight Triathlon? Do people race at night around here?"

For some reason, Winona found this funny. "Sorry. I should have explained. The Scarlet Midnight Triathlon is Megs' term for a rescue where someone drove up the canyon drunk, went off the highway into the creek, and then ran away to avoid prosecution, leaving their vehicle in the water. Rescue humor."

Jason laughed. It wasn't funny—and yet it was. "I take it this happens a lot."

"It happens often enough to get a nickname." She

turned on the heater. "The scary thing is that we never know what we'll find. In the winter and fall, when the water is low, most people survive, though someone who is severely intoxicated could pass out and drown in six inches of water. In the spring and summer, when the water is high, it's a swift-water rescue, which is a lot more danger-ous. People have drowned in their vehicles or been swept away, even little children."

Jason caught a glimpse of the creek twenty feet below to his right. "I'm surprised they survive the crash."

"They don't always, and then we get toned out to help with body recovery."

Jason knew how hard that job was. "We just passed mile marker twenty-four."

Around the next bend, they saw flares and flashing red-and-blue lights. Just ahead, a sheriff's deputy directed traf-fic. The deputy saw Winona and waved her through. She slowed, pulled to the shoulder, and parked behind a row of vehicles, including several sheriff's vehicles, a fire truck, a rescue vehicle, and a big tow truck.

Jason instinctively assessed the situation from a law-enforcement standpoint. The dark. The narrow highway. The steep, rocky drop-off to his right. The sheer rock wall to their left. Yeah, he could see how this kind of rescue might be dangerous.

If another drunk driver came along at high speeds…

He climbed out and met Winona at her liftgate.

She pulled out her backpack and a helmet, put her radio on her belt, clipped the hand mic to her jacket, and slipped the earpiece into her ear. "Just stand off to the side until Megs calls for you."

He took her helmet, settled it onto her head, fastened the strap. "You got it."

Below them in the water was a battered, orange Ford

Pinto lying on its roof in several inches of water, both doors open. Around him, Team members worked with efficiency. Jason recognized the anchor, as they called it, its ropes leading down to the water so Team members wouldn't risk falling on the steep jumble of rocks. Uniformed officers and Team members in reflective vests moved downstream through the water, looking for any sign of the vehicle's occupant.

It was going to take them forever to find the driver that way.

Megs walked up to him. "What would you do in this situation?"

"I'd head down with a flashlight, walk along the banks in both directions on either side of the creek, expanding my search until I found sign. Then I'd follow the sign until I found the driver."

"Let's get you down there."

Five minutes later, with some expert help, he was wearing a climbing harness and a helmet and was roped in.

"I'm on belay," Sasha called to him. "Go ahead and climb down."

It struck Jason as strange that he, a guy from Sells, Arizona, was being belayed into a creek in the Colorado mountains by the world's top women's sports climber.

He reached the water safely, where Nicole freed him from the rope.

"You're set," she said. "Thanks for coming out with us tonight."

"My pleasure." He took his flashlight and got to work, Megs and the fire chief, Eric Hawke, walking along behind him. The Pinto's driver's side door faced the highway, so he started on that side.

"I appreciate your help." Hawke stepped carefully, and

Jason remembered that he'd been severely burned just a couple of months ago. "We called in the plates, so we should have the driver's name soon."

Already, the movement of law enforcement and Team members had compromised the scene. But a little further on, Jason found what he was looking for—sign. An overturned rock lay on the embankment, a thread of denim caught on a shrub beside it.

Jason plucked up the thread, held it up. "He tried to climb out here, but he was too drunk. Or maybe it was too steep."

"How the hell…?" Hawke muttered.

"I told you he was good," Megs said.

"See the stone? Someone stepped on it, turned it over. The moss is on the bottom, and the muddy side is facing up."

Hawke nodded. "It seems obvious when you put it like that."

Jason kept the grin off his face and walked a little farther upstream. "He tried again here—and threw up on the sand. Most of it washed away."

Water lapped at a small pile of vomit, peas, carrots, and mucus swirling in an eddy nearby.

Megs bent to look. "Gross."

When he found nothing more upstream, he went back to the spot where he'd found the vomit and crossed over. Almost immediately, he saw—unevenly spaced footprints rambling up the embankment, a palm print, and a slight indentation where someone had fallen onto one knee.

"Here." He climbed up, moving his flashlight back and forth.

Two eyes stared back at him from the cover of a large bush ten feet uphill.

"Hank!" Eric shook his head. "Man, I thought you

were beyond this now. You went to rehab, got clean. You've been driving to Boulder so that we won't know you're off the wagon, haven't you?"

"I'm a weak man, Hawke." Hank stood, stumbled out of his bush. He was a small, wiry man, his long, thinning hair pulled into a scraggly ponytail, a mustache on his face, his shirt stained with vomit. "I didn't think you'd find me."

"That's because you're drunk, Hank. Do you think you can run away from your vehicle without us knowing it was you? Did you forget you have license plates? You're in serious trouble now."

"Worse than when I blew up my house?"

"I think so."

"Damn, Hawke. That kind of news would drive any man to drink."

Megs called the news into dispatch, and a cheer went up around them.

Then Jason saw. "He's bleeding from his temple."

Jason climbed the embankment and helped Hank, who was unsteady on his feet, make his way down to the creek.

Hawke took hold of Hank's arm. "Come on, buddy. Let's get you checked out by medical before they take you to the pokey."

Megs turned to Jason. "What do I have to do to get you on the Team?"

Didn't Jason wish? "You're welcome."

Chapter 18

IT WAS JUST after ten in the morning, and Winona was still in bed, her head on Jason's chest, her heartbeat slowing. He'd woken her with soft kisses and had then made long, slow love to her, carrying her over the edge twice before letting himself go. He was almost too good to be true.

She kissed a brown nipple. "I wish every weekday could start like this. I feel so decadent. Sleeping in, sex, and coffee."

She tried not to remember that he would be leaving soon. He'd said he wanted to stay to see the eagle released into the wild. After that...

He raised his head, confusion on his face. "Where's the coffee?"

"For the moment, it's just in my imagination."

"I can fix that." He kissed the top of her head. "Just stay where you are."

He got up, walked naked toward the kitchen, the twin mounds of his delectable ass shifting as he moved. When he returned five minutes later carrying two full coffee mugs, she got the reverse view, his cock swaying.

He handed her the mug of coffee with milk in it. "Here."

"That is the sexiest thing I've ever seen—you naked and bringing me coffee."

Jason chuckled. "I can do it again if it turns you on."

"It does." She sipped, moaned.

Jason got back into bed beside her, the two of them sitting with their backs against the headboard as they sipped. "I wonder how Hank is feeling this morning."

"Sore, I'm sure, and probably not very happy with himself."

"Did he really blow up his own house?"

"He was trying to extract hash oil from marijuana plants using butane, and the fumes ignited. His house burned to the ground."

Jason shook his head. "That man must have nine lives."

"You were good with him. I think everyone was impressed by what you can do. Megs kept talking about wanting you on the Team."

"That's what she said to me, too."

It was such a normal thing to do—a couple savoring physical contact, sipping coffee together, planning their day. Except they weren't truly a couple.

The thought put a bittersweet ache in Winona's heart. "I need to get to the clinic. It's past time for rounds, and I've got a shipment of food and supplies coming in today. Naomi and little Shota are coming home this afternoon, and I want to welcome them home—and to hold my little nephew again."

"I'm going to give that security company in Denver a call and set up an appointment."

When they had finished their coffee, they showered and made breakfast together. They were almost finished eating when Winona's phone buzzed with a text from the game warden. She scrolled through the message, then jumped to her feet.

"That was Dan, the game warden. He's bringing me an injured bear cub. A driver found it by the side of the road. Dan says it has a broken leg."

"Can I help?"

She hurried to put on her scrubs. "Maybe. You can certainly watch."

"Damn, you look sexy dressed like that."

"In *scrubs*?" She laughed. "You're crazy."

He moved closer, nuzzled her neck. "Maybe I should have my way with you on one of your exam tables."

"Gross! Do you have any idea what's been on those tables?"

"So, that's a no, then?"

She laughed again. "Yes, that's a hard no."

When they arrived at the clinic, Winona got a treatment room ready. Anesthetic. IV kit. Sterile gloves. Sterile surgical kit. Pain meds. "I have no idea what shape our little friend will be in, so I have to be ready for everything."

A few minutes later, Dan arrived, carrying a very unhappy but good-sized nine-month-old cub in a blindfold. "I'm pretty sure her rear right leg is broken."

"Bring her back here." Winona gestured toward the treatment room, stepping out of the warden's way.

The cub bawled, terrified and in pain.

Winona helped the warden settle her on the table, then quickly gave the cub anesthesia through a mask and slipped into a pair of sterile gloves so she could examine it. "There's some ruptured muscle and definitely a fracture.

I'd say she got clipped by a car. I'll need to take X-rays to see how bad it is."

Winona went for her portable X-ray machine, the one she'd held a year's worth of fundraisers to buy, and wheeled it in. She put on a lead apron and asked the two men to wait outside while she took images of the bear's leg.

She studied the images, then walked out into the hallway, where she found Jason and Dan talking. They stopped when they saw her. "The leg is broken, but the fracture is non-displaced. I won't have to do surgery to stabilize it. I'll clean the wound, stitch her up, and put her in a splint."

"That's good news." Dan pointed to Jason with a jerk of his thumb. "I was talking with Agent Chiago about the wolf situation. I was hoping the two of you could head up with a ranger tomorrow and see if you have better luck tracking the animal. We haven't been able to get close."

Jason met Winona's gaze. "I said I'd do it if you have the time."

"I'll have to get someone to cover for me and watch over our newest patient. If I can make that happen, then yes. I'd be happy to help."

"Give me a call when you know." Dan took off.

Winona turned to Jason. "Want to assist me in putting a splint on this little girl?"

"You bet."

—

"TODAY WAS A GOOD DAY." The smile on Winona's face put a hitch in Jason's chest, the last rays of the sun giving her skin a bronze glow. "We saved a bear cub. I got to snuggle Shota and see Naomi."

Jason took her hand, shared his highlight. "I got an appointment for Monday with the security company. We had lunch with your brother and his family, and Chaska didn't punch me."

That made Winona laugh. "He's a good guy—I promise."

"I believe you."

They'd grabbed a pizza from Knockers, and Winona had given him directions to a place above Scarlet Springs that she called Caribou where they could eat and watch the sunset. Now, they sat on the back of his truck, tailgate down, the pizza devoured, the sun dipping behind the high peaks.

"Isn't it beautiful up here?"

He could barely take his gaze off her. "Yeah. Incredible."

It *was* beautiful and peaceful, the air crisp and fresh, the scent of pine on the wind. He couldn't even hear traffic from here or see a single power line or a house or a road. She'd told him there was an old silver mine a little farther on and that Joe and Rain had their home somewhere up here, but, apart from the road, he couldn't see any sign that people had ever lived or labored up here.

"Why did Naomi ask you about baskets?" She'd been changing Shota's diaper and had missed most of the conversation.

"O'odham women are known for weaving beautiful baskets. She wondered if I knew any artists who might want to sell baskets through her store. I told her I'd ask around."

"Your grandmother made them, right?"

"She did. She was a master." Jason pulled out his phone, scrolled through his photos. "These are hers."

Winona leaned closer. "Oh, Jason. They're beautiful! Your grandmother had talent. That one looks just like your tattoo."

Jason scrolled until he came to a photo of his grandmother. "My grandmother had a hard life. Her father married her off when she was fourteen, but her first husband died falling off a horse soon after. To be honest, I think she was relieved. Then she met and married my grandfather. She gave birth to eight children at home, no medical help, no pain relief. They all died before she did."

"That must have been so hard."

"Grief took its toll on her, but she always had a smile for me."

"Grief took a toll on you, too, losing your parents so young."

That was the truth.

"She and my grandfather lived by the old ways—farming, hunting, harvesting food from the desert. She made baskets, and he hunted. After my parents were killed, I was consumed by rage. I lost myself for a while. But they took me in, taught me traditional O'odham skills, taught me our history, our stories. They saved me, stopped me from becoming a statistic."

"They must have loved you very much."

Jason slipped his phone back into his pocket. "My grandfather passed first. My grandmother lasted for almost two years without him. As she lay dying, she made me promise not to abandon my O'odham people. I knew that she wanted me to keep our family name and our culture alive by passing on everything they'd taught me. My sisters took off, so I'm the last one in our line still living in Sells."

"That's why you won't leave the reservation."

"Yeah." The word was bitter in Jason's mouth.

He had made that promise to his grandmother at a time when he couldn't imagine wanting to do otherwise, when he and Elena were together and it had seemed like the path for the rest of his life was laid at his feet. He would never have imagined that the promise might one day come at a cost. But now...

Another twist in the road, another unexpected turn.

For a time, they sat there, neither of them speaking, the mood changed.

Wind in the pines. The hooting of an owl. The distant bugle of a bull elk. The warmth of Winona's hand in his.

"We should go." Winona released his hand and hopped to the ground, her tone of voice light, her gaze averted. "I need to check on the bear cub, and we've got an early morning."

"Right." He stepped to the ground, closed the tailgate, then opened her door.

"Thanks." She started to climb in, then stopped. "If you hadn't made that promise, would you at least consider spending time here with me?"

It hurt even to imagine that scenario, but he understood why she was asking. She wanted to know whether she meant anything to him beyond sex.

"I would. Hell, yes, I would. I care about you, Win. But I *did* make the promise, and nothing can change that."

"It's getting chilly." Making a valiant attempt not to seem upset, she climbed into the passenger seat.

But Jason knew her better than that. He closed her door, walked around the front of the truck to the driver's side, at war with himself, a sense of guilt twisting in his chest. But why should he feel guilty? He'd been honest with her from the beginning. She'd known he couldn't stay.

You knew she'd get hurt if you got involved with her, but you did it anyway.

His next thought stopped him mid-stride.

What you didn't know was that you'd get hurt, too.

Fuck.

He climbed into the driver's seat, started the engine,

and turned up the heat. "Let me know if you're still cold."

Then he headed down the mountain and back into Scarlet.

━━━

FIGHTING A SENSE OF GLOOM, Winona gave the bear cub antibiotics and morphine, then cleaned its enclosure, speaking softly while she worked. "I'm so sorry, little one."

It sniffed, watched her, bawled, in pain and missing its mother.

While the morphine kicked in, she mixed bear feed with seeds and wild chokecherries and thawed venison scraps in a bowl. At this age, the cub had been weaned off its mother's milk and ate bear food—bugs, carcasses, berries, mice, wild honeycomb. When it had healed, Winona would move it to an outdoor enclosure, isolated from other staff, and help it learn to forage so it could be released into the wild next spring.

She gave the bear its food and went to check the other animals. The beaver and the raccoon seemed to be having a conversation, the raccoon trilling and cooing, and the beaver making little humming noises that sounded almost human.

"That's why the Ojibwe call you 'little talking brother,' right?" She was happy with how the beaver's lacerations were healing. She would be able to remove the splint from the raccoon's leg next week. "You'll both be ready to leave me soon, won't you?"

She meant the words one way when she said them, but they resonated in an altogether different way.

Jason would be leaving soon, too.

At least she understood why now. He was the last of his line on the O'odham reservation, the last member of his family to still live in their ancestral land. More than that, he'd made his grandmother a promise on her deathbed.

Winona knew that her non-Native friends in Scarlet probably wouldn't understand why Jason couldn't just forget all of that and move to Scarlet. But Winona respected his reasons. She couldn't ask him to break his word or leave his homeland.

She took off her lab coat, washed her hands, then grabbed her keys. But instead of locking up and walking home, she sank into a chair in the lobby, fighting tears.

I care about you, Win.

She cared about him, too. She cared too much.

She couldn't do this to herself or to Jason. She couldn't cry and ruin the evening for both of them. She couldn't let the anticipation of the loss she'd feel when he left steal what time they had remaining. But, oh, it was hard.

She drew in one slow breath after another until she felt in control of her emotions once more. Jason was here now, and she needed to keep her mind and heart in the moment. If all they had was another week or two, she would make every day—and every night—count.

Then an idea came to her.

She hurried into her private bathroom at the clinic, brushed the pizza taste out of her mouth, then brushed her hair. Remembering what Jason had said about her looking sexy in scrubs, she stripped naked and put on a clean pair. She could tell just by glancing at her reflection that she was braless, but she wasn't sure he would notice.

If he didn't, she would help him out.

She locked up and walked home to find Jason waiting for her, every candle in her house sitting on the coffee table and lit, the lights down low. She took off her parka, dropped it on the chair by the door. "Hey."

"Hey."

It touched her that, while she'd been plotting to surprise him, he'd been busy putting together a surprise for her. "This is nice."

"Our time on the dance floor was cut short last night. I thought we could make up for that now." He picked up her remote and started her sound system, that same slow song by the Timberline Mudbugs spilling out of her speakers.

"Oh! You tracked down the music."

"It wasn't hard. Will you dance with me, Winona?"

She walked into his arms, his spicy scent filling her head, the two of them moving together in time to the music.

He kissed her temple, pressed his forehead to hers. "I'm sorry, Winona. I know this is hard. It's hard for me, too. But I would rather spend time with you and pay for it later than behave myself and go home, never having known you."

"Same." Winona closed her eyes, rested her head against his chest, neither of them speaking again until the song ended. "I've got something for you, too."

"Yeah?"

She stepped back, turned around, and pulled down her scrub bottoms to show him exactly what she *wasn't* wearing. She looked back over her shoulder, saw that his gaze was locked right where she wanted it—on her bare ass.

He moaned. "Oh, Win."

In a blink, he moved up behind her, catching her around her waist with one arm, his free hand caressing her buttocks. Slowly, he marched her toward the wall, his thighs pressing against her. She braced herself, palms splayed against the wall as if she were being frisked, while he tore down her scrub bottoms. Then one big hand got busy between her thighs, the other sliding beneath her top to fondle her bare breasts, his caresses making her ache.

"I love your body." He moaned again, his hands leaving her body just long enough to yank down his zipper and free his erection. "Arch your lower back. Stick your sweet ass out. Spread your legs wider. Just like that."

Anticipation turned her body to liquid, the heat between her thighs almost unbearable. "I want you inside me—*now!*"

He slid his fingers inside her, stroked her. "Like this?"

"I want your cock."

"Ah." Without putting on a condom, he slowly nudged himself into her, their moans mingling as he buried himself to the hilt, nothing between them, their bodies truly joined for the first time. "Like this?"

"*Yes.*"

"You feel *so* good." His voice sounded tight, strained.

He began to move, slowly at first, then faster, his cock stroking her inside just where she needed it, the fingers of his left hand digging into her hip, the right doing incredible things to her clit.

"*Jaaa-son.*" Her thighs trembled, her body spiraling toward climax.

Then he stopped, withdrew.

She moaned in protest. "Nooo."

He chuckled. "Patience."

He turned her to face him and pulled something out of his pocket—a condom. He rolled it down his length, his cock glistening with her wetness. Then he lifted her off her feet, pressed her back against the wall, and buried himself inside her once again.

She wrapped her legs around his waist and wrapped her arms around his neck. There was no holding him back this time. He drove himself into her, hard and fast, carrying her headlong over the edge before joining her in bliss.

Chapter 19

WHILE WINONA DID her morning rounds and brought Dr. Keene up to speed on the bear cub, Jason put his time to good use making breakfast. When Winona returned, he had scrambled eggs and salsa on the table and tortillas warming in the oven.

Winona rewarded him with one of those sweet smiles. "Oh, that smells good. Thanks for doing all this."

After breakfast, they got their gear together, Winona giving him advice.

"Make sure to pack plenty of snacks and water. Bring every warm thing you have. On our way out, I'll grab some frozen beef from the clinic. If we spot the wolf, I want to be able to lure him in with food. I hope we find him today."

They arrived at the Forest Service parking area just before ten and sat in Jason's truck, waiting for the Forest Service Ranger. Twenty minutes. Thirty minutes. Forty-five minutes later, the only people who'd showed up were cross-country skiers and people heading into the mountains with snowshoes.

Winona glanced at Jason's watch. "We could still be sleeping—or doing something else."

Jason took her hand. "Or doing something else."

At last, a Forest Service vehicle pulled into the parking area, and a tall, lanky ranger stepped out. He walked over to them. "Sorry, I'm late. I had a run-in with a couple of wackos on meth in one of our camping areas. I'm Ranger Rob Henriksen."

Jason held out his hand. "Jason Chiago."

"Winona Belcourt."

Henriksen laid out the plan. "We can't leave the animal out there. It's habituated to humans, which puts it in danger. It might not even know how to hunt, and we don't want it to starve. The trouble is finding it. I thought it would make its way back to its owner's camp, but so far, it hasn't shown itself."

Winona nodded. "That's a good guess. The poor thing is probably scared. Wolves have incredible olfactory senses. He can smell all the people who've been there. We might be able to bait and trap him there, but it could take time."

"What about higher up the mountain, where the four-wheeler flipped?" Jason didn't know much about wolves, but it didn't hurt to ask. "That's the last place the wolf saw its owner."

"You're the person who can help us answer that question. If you see fresh sign, we'll have some idea where to set up traps."

"Traps?" Winona looked alarmed. "You're not planning to use leg-hold traps, are you? I was thinking about the big steel cage traps, the kind used to lure problem bears."

Henriksen shook his head. "The only way to get one of those up there is to chopper it in, and the Forest Service won't commit to using a helicopter. That rules out aerial darting, too. I already asked. What other choice do we have?"

The answer was obvious to Jason. "We find fresh sign, track it, tranquilize it, and tone out the Team again."

"I'm not sure about your employer, but the Forest Service isn't going to want me to be tied up with this for the next month."

Jason started to say that it wouldn't take him a month, but Winona spoke first.

"Leg-hold traps can be dangerous. We could injure the animal—or it could injure itself trying to escape. Besides, wolves are notorious for being able to avoid leg-hold traps. You might not capture it."

"I don't like this either." Henriksen shrugged. "It's a risk we have to take."

Jason could see that Winona wasn't happy about it.

Henriksen pulled a tablet out of his pack and pointed to a map on his screen. "Here's the location of the illegal camp, and here's where the four-wheeler flipped and the wolf was last sighted. We head up in my truck, hike to both locations, and set out traps with wolf attractant."

Winona pointed to the screen. "The wolf might go back to the Cimarron. That's where his food came from, and he knows it. Wolves can go without food for several days, but he *will* get hungry. You should contact the Wests and put a trap there, too."

Henriksen nodded. "Good idea. I'll check the traps every day and call you when we catch it. I don't want this boy to get hurt, either."

"I know." Winona drew a breath, clearly not happy with her options. "Once he's trapped, I'll come up with the Team, tranq him, and we'll carry him out. I'll care for him at the clinic if he's injured in the process."

"It's not ideal, but it's better than letting him starve or

get shot by an angry rancher." Henriksen put the tablet back into his pack.

Jason wasn't a wildlife expert. "Don't you risk trapping something else?"

Henriksen shook his head. "The wolf attractant takes care of that problem for the most part. Other animals stay away."

"Even animals that have never smelled a wolf?"

"I guess we'll find out."

Winona shouldered her pack. "We should get going."

"All aboard." Henriksen gestured toward his vehicle.

━━━

WINONA HELD BACK while Jason moved through the site of the camp, cutting for sign. How he could make sense of it was beyond her. So many people had walked through here, the muddy earth a confusion of boot prints. Though the Forest Service had already removed Thomas Graham's structures, belongings, and trash, signs of environmental damage were everywhere—the trunks of felled trees, a pit toilet that had held human excrement, a wide area of mud where there should have been grass and duff.

Jason knelt, touched his fingers to the soil. "The wolf has already been here. These tracks are from early this morning. He was walking around the area where the smokehouse used to be."

Winona glanced at the forest around them, wondering whether the wolf was still nearby. "He's hungry."

"I'll set a trap there." Ranger Henriksen got to work.

He had his job, but Winona had hers. She wanted to find the wolf before it stepped into a trap.

"He went west from here." Jason followed the tracks, and Winona followed him.

They hiked up the mountain, snow crunching beneath their boots.

Owoooo!

Winona stopped, listened. She heard the loneliness and fear in that howl, and her heart broke. "He's searching for his pack. He's all alone."

She needed to find him, to reunite him with his mate and pups.

Jason's gaze was on the snowy ground. "This way."

They'd gone another ten minutes when Henriksen caught up with them. "Did you hear that howl?"

Winona nodded. "He's close, and he's scared."

"We should head in this direction." Henriksen pointed to the northwest. "Up there is where the four-wheeler overturned."

This time, Jason answered him. "That's not where the wolf went."

Henriksen stared at them for a moment. Winona didn't begrudge him. She knew he had a supervisor to please and different priorities.

He relented. "I'm going to call this in and tell them we spotted it. That's not exactly true, but you'll back me up."

"I will." No problem there.

"It will at least buy us time to pursue. But if we don't make visual contact within an hour, we're going back to the original plan. Agreed?"

"Agreed." Winona was genuinely grateful. "Thank you."

They trudged on, stopping once for water and a snack. Then the wind picked up, clouds moving in from the west.

Henriksen reached for his hand mic, asked dispatch for a weather update, got no answer. "I've lost radio contact."

Winona checked her cell phone. "No service."

Owoooo!

Another plaintive howl.

"We're getting closer."

They hiked on, leaving behind a meadow for a thick stand of lodgepole pines.

Jason stopped. "He was just here. He rested."

There at the base of a tree was a depression in the snow. Winona could see not only paw marks, but also dark fur that had been rubbed off by the bark. There were fresh tracks in the snow heading due west now.

Then Winona spotted the animal. "*Stop.* He's still here."

She dropped her backpack, took out a block of frozen beef, cut off a piece. Then she walked between the trees to get a clear line of sight to toss the meat and—

"Win, stop!"

Click. CRACK!

Agony.

Winona screamed, collapsed to the ground, pain shattering her left leg, the shock of it driving her to the brink of unconsciousness.

"Jesus!" Jason was there beside her, but he sounded far away. "It's an old, steel bear trap. Help me get it off her—now!"

"I'll open it. You pull her leg out." That was the ranger.

Fresh pain brought her back as they moved her. "Stop!"

"We have to get this off you." Jason caught her beneath her arms. "You ready?"

Winona heard Henriksen grunt with effort, opened her eyes, saw blood.

"It's stuck!"

"We have to break her free, or she'll bleed out. You can do it, Henriksen."

The ranger tried again. "Got it!"

Jason dragged her backward, pulling her free, the pain of having her leg dragged over the snowy ground making Winona cry out, driving her once more toward darkness.

The trap closed with a sharp *snap*.

Hands touched her leg, the pain terrible.

"She probably has a tib-fib fracture." Henriksen sounded afraid. "She's bleeding pretty badly. I think it severed an artery."

"Do you have a medkit? She needs a tourniquet." That was Jason again.

"Just basic first aid, but there is a tourniquet. No pain meds."

Something landed in the snow beside her. She willed her eyes to open, saw an orange bag with a white cross on it.

"You go for help. I'll do what I can for her."

"I'm going to head back toward the campsite and try to get a radio signal. I'll have to wait there and lead rescuers to you."

"Do it. Go!"

Boots in snow, moving fast.

A zipper being ripped open.

"Win, can you hear me?"

"*Ja... son.*"

"I'm going to tie a tourniquet below your knee. I'm sure it will hurt like hell, but I have to stop the bleeding. You're going into shock."

"My kit." It was so hard to think and harder to speak, her body shaking now. "Ketamine. Seventy-five mgs. My quadriceps."

But her kit was beneath her in her backpack.

"I'll tie the tourniquet first and then get you pain meds." He cut off her pant leg below the knee and then got the tourniquet ready. "I'm so sorry, Win. I saw the chain around the tree the second before you took that last step."

"Not … your … fault."

"I don't want to hurt you."

Her hands clutching at her thigh, Winona gritted her teeth against the pain as he tied the tourniquet. Then she slipped into blessed darkness.

———

HEART SLAMMING, his mouth dry from fear, Jason worked quickly. He secured the tourniquet and checked for a distal pulse to make sure it was tight enough. Then he removed Winona's backpack and took out everything he thought he'd need. Her medical kit. A warm woolen hat. An emergency blanket. An IV kit. A bag of lactated Ringer's. Bandages. Then he spread the emergency blanket on the snow and settled Winona in the middle of it, taking advantage of her unconsciousness to move her. He used his pack to elevate her injured leg, then searched for the ketamine and a syringe.

Seventy-five milligrams.

He jammed the needle into her quadriceps and injected her with the medication, fears rushing through his mind. What if, in her semi-conscious state, she'd gotten the dosage wrong and he killed her? What if help didn't get here fast enough and she lost her leg? What if she bled out?

Damn it! Fuck!

He'd seen it—the big chain tied around the tree—but she'd been beyond his reach, and his shout of warning had come too late.

Shit!

He drew a deep breath and fell back on his training. Because they spent so much time in remote locations, all Shadow Wolves had medic training. He had practiced starting IVs. He willed himself to focus on that and not let his thoughts drift.

He drew one of her arms out of her parka, pushed up her sleeve, found a good vein. In under a minute, he had fluids opened wide. Then he wrapped her in the space blanket, put the hat on her head, and tucked her backpack beneath her head as a pillow.

But there was one more thing he wanted to do while she was unconscious. He found a couple of dead branches close to the ground on some nearby trees and kicked them free from the trunks. Then he used a bandage from Henriksen's medkit to build a kind of splint—just something to hold her leg steady and give it some support.

This was Graham's fault. The bastard!

Jason had seen traps just like this one—illegal thirty-pound steel bear traps with teeth—in the asshole's tent. The son of a bitch had probably strung illegal traplines through the forest, and the wolf had followed them, looking for its master. The animal knew where the traps were hidden—Winona had said wolves were notorious for their ability to avoid traps—and had rested next to one.

Winona moaned as he handled her injured leg, but he steeled himself against his emotions, focused only on the task at hand.

Then he heard it—licking and gnawing.

The wolf.

It was no more than ten feet away from him, lying on its belly, gnawing on the chunk of frozen beef it held between its front paws—the beef that Winona had tried to throw its way.

Damn.

It was huge, with dark gray fur and almost yellow eyes.

Jason's gaze dropped to the blood on his hands, the blood in the snow, the blood on Winona's leg. He had no idea how the hungry animal would respond to the scent of so much blood. Would it attack?

He took his Glock out of the holster, checked to make sure there was a round in the chamber, then slipped it back. Then he reached into Winona's pack and drew out the bag with the frozen beef.

He spoke in a calm voice, broke off another chunk, and tossed it over. "Are you hungry, boy?"

The wolf was startled by his motions and withdrew a few feet before returning and feeding hungrily.

"He's… hungry."

Jason was relieved and surprised to see Winona's eyes open. "How much ketamine did you want me to inject?"

He wanted to double-check.

"Seventy-five milligrams… every thirty minutes. Keep track … how much. Tell the Team."

He glanced at the time. "Twenty minutes until your next injection. Are you getting relief?"

"Enough." There were lines of pain on her face, but her gaze was on the wolf. She spoke to it in her mother tongue, her voice reassuring, both of the animal's ears turned toward her. "He's … beautiful. We should … dart him."

Leave it to Winona to think of the wolf when her own life was in danger.

"How do I do that?"

"The darts… my medkit. They're ready. The dart gun. Strapped to the side of my pack. It's easy."

Jason had qualified as an expert marksman with rifles, so he ought to be able to figure this out. That's what he told himself, anyway.

Without moving Winona, he managed to get the dart gun. He played with it for a moment, examined the action, saw that it was essentially an air gun that used compressed gas to propel the dart, which was, from the look of it, a ballistic syringe.

Okay, he could play.

He loaded a dart into the contraption.

"How long … before they come?"

Jason had been too busy to ask himself that question. He glanced at his watch. "It's only been about twenty minutes. I don't know how far Henriksen has to go to get back into radio contact."

When Henriksen *did* reach dispatch, it would take several minutes to tone out the right people and another hour for the Team to get to the parking area. They'd hiked for three hours to get to this spot.

Jason's heart sank.

They won't make it in time to save her leg.

Not unless they came by helicopter, and even then…

With a tourniquet, she had two hours, and that was it. After that, the tissue damage from lack of blood flow would be too severe. Though he'd originally been trained to release the tourniquet every thirty minutes, that recommendation had changed after too many people had slowly bled to death, one release at a time.

Winona put her hand on his. "Wait. We can't … dart the wolf yet. Too long … until they get here."

Jason's chest constricted to think that she'd been asking about time for the wolf's sake and not her own. "Okay, then. We'll wait."

He set the dart gun aside and got the next syringe of ketamine ready for her.

Chapter 20

JASON INJECTED Winona with another seventy-five milligrams of ketamine, watched the pain on her face ease a little, her suffering tearing at him. "Better?"

She nodded, her eyes drifting shut.

And for a few minutes, she seemed to sleep.

The wolf sat nearby, watching through those golden eyes. It hadn't shown aggression or gotten closer, which was a relief. It also hadn't run off. If it stayed here, he'd be able to dart it, and Winona's suffering wouldn't be for nothing.

He broke off another chunk of meat, tossed it, watched the wolf snap it up with powerful jaws. "You really *are* hungry."

"He wants … to be with people." Winona's eyes were open.

"You think he's lonely?"

"He's … alone and scared. He misses … his pack. He's not used … to being by himself." She spoke to the wolf in Lakota.

As if it understood, it whined and crept a few inches closer, still sitting.

She had such skill with animals—and more than her share of courage. Jason had never been this close to an apex predator, and he couldn't say he felt comfortable with two hundred pounds of hungry carnivore sitting ten feet away.

The minutes ticked by with agonizing slowness. Though it was mid-afternoon, the sun had moved far enough to the west to leave them in shadow, and the temperatures were dropping. The IV of fluids he'd set up had run, the bag empty.

It had been an hour since Jason had applied the tourniquet. In another hour, it would be too late to save Winona's leg. By his estimation, help was still a good two hours away.

Goddamn it.

Winona moaned, her eyes flying open. "Jason?"

"I'm right here." He took her hand, held it tight. "I'm not going anywhere."

Winona drifted in and out, sometimes lucid, other times seeming unaware of her surroundings, speaking in Lakota. Was it dissociation from the drug? Shock? Blood loss?

God, he wished he knew. He'd never felt so helpless.

He found himself humming an O'odham basket song, the music played for his grandmother and other women at basket dances. The sound seemed to comfort Winona, who, for fifteen short minutes, fell asleep.

Moving slowly so as not to alarm the wolf, he checked her leg to make sure there wasn't any bleeding that he'd missed.

The wolf crept closer.

Jason tossed it more meat, but he was running low. He

didn't want to run out before it was time to dart the animal. "That's all for now, boy."

The wolf ate, licked its paws, stared at Winona.

"My leg." Winona's eyes opened. "I'm going to lose it... I know. But I don't ... want to die here."

Jason hoped it was the drug talking, her words cutting through him. He squeezed her hand. "I'm not going to let you die, angel."

"I'm ... so cold."

He dug in her pack, drew out a couple of hand warmers, got the exothermic reaction going, and tucked them inside her parka close to her heart, wrapping the emergency blanket around her once again. "Is that better?"

She nodded. "Thanks."

Hurry the fuck up, Henriksen!

"Jason, I want ... to tell you ... to thank you. I've never ... felt so close to ... or cared about a man more ... than you." A tear slid from the corner of her eye. "You ... You're the best."

"I care about you, too, Win." He kissed her forehead. "You're the most amazing woman I've ever known."

Then the truth hit him with the force of a body blow.

He didn't just care about her.

He *loved* her.

A part of him tried to object. He'd known Win for only a week and a day. He couldn't love her. He was just on the rebound and strung out on great sex.

That's bullshit, and you know it.

Truth was truth.

He loved her. She was like the missing part of him, the soul mate he'd never known he was lacking and had never expected to find. And he had to leave her.

Not yet.

"We'll get you to the hospital, and they'll do all they

can to save your leg. I'll be right there. Henriksen will be back soon. Help is on the way."

God, he hoped he was right.

But Winona was unconscious again.

Five minutes. Ten minutes. This wait was unbearable.

The wolf whined, came closer, still on its belly.

"I'm watching you." Jason prepared another syringe of ketamine.

The wolf's ears went up. It jumped to its feet, growled deep in its throat.

Jason drew his Glock. "Don't do this, little brother."

Rather than attacking, the wolf turned to flee.

"Shit." Jason shoved his Glock back into its holster, grabbed the tranquilizer gun, and raised it, sighting on the wolf, which broke into a run. "Oh, no, you don't. Winona came here for your sake."

Jason pulled the trigger, hit the wolf in its hindquarters.

It yelped, dropped to the snow, nipping at the dart.

And then, in the distance, Jason heard it—the whirring of a helicopter.

A CACOPHONY of voices crashed in on Winona, but the snatches of conversation made no sense, the words just beyond her comprehension.

"Let's get a second IV going... Antibiotics ... Tetanus at the hospital."

"... O positive."

"How long has that tourniquet been on her?"

"... a fever ... "

"When she's safely on the helicopter, we'll deal with the wolf."

"Watch for traps!"

Was that Eric Hawke? Austin? Had the Team come for her?

"Someone bring that trap. Get it the hell off the mountain."

Winona fought to open her eyes. "Jason?"

"He's right here, little sister. So am I." That was Chaska.

Someone took her hand.

"We're moving you to the gurney now, okay, Win?" Chaska again.

"One, two, three."

Gentle hands lifted her, pain making her moan.

"What has she had for pain?"

She tried to speak, but Jason answered. "I've given her three injections of ketamine—seventy-five mgs each time. She's due for another."

"Let's give her seventy-five more and one mg of midazolam."

A prick.

And she was floating.

━━━

JASON HELPED CHASKA, Eric Hawke, Austin Taylor, Jesse Moretti, and Conrad Harrison carry an unconscious Winona to where the helicopter sat, rotors running, the words *Life Flight* painted in white against red. The two paramedics, who were with Life Flight and not the Team, walked alongside them with their gear.

Jason and the other men ducked down and lifted the gurney with its precious cargo into the bird. Then Chaska climbed in and sat beside her, while the others turned back to deal with the tranquilized wolf under Henriksen's direction. They weren't flying down in the chopper.

Jason stood there for a moment, uncertain where he belonged. He wasn't family. No one knew about his relationship with Winona. On paper, he was nothing but an acquaintance.

Fuck that.

He made a split-second decision and followed his heart, jumping into the helicopter, buckling in, and grabbing a set of headphones.

"Are you family?" one paramedic asked.

Chaska answered for him, his gaze locked with Jason's. "Yes."

The helicopter lifted off, nosed into the wind, rotor wash blowing snow.

The paramedics worked on Winona, removing the makeshift splint, checking her vitals, giving her blood and oxygen, and injecting other medications into her IV.

He glanced down, saw the Cimarron, and realized they were flying her away from the mountains. "You're not taking her to Scarlet Springs?"

Chaska shook his head. "We're going to a level-one trauma center in Denver."

"Jason?" Winona's eyes fluttered open, her voice muffled by the oxygen mask.

But Jason was buckled in. "I'm here, Win."

He wasn't sure she could hear him.

The flight lasted twenty minutes, giving them a precious ten minutes until they reached the two-hour mark. The helicopter landed on the roof of the facility, medical staff waiting to take Winona inside. They offloaded the gurney with military efficiency, and Jason followed Chaska as they rushed inside.

A nurse met them with a clipboard and a flurry of questions, some of which Chaska answered. The others were left to Jason—mostly details about what had happened, what time he'd applied the tourniquet, how much pain medicine he'd given her, and other measures he'd taken. Then he found himself sitting in a surgery waiting area with Chaska.

Chaska rested a hand on his shoulder. "You've got Win's blood on your hands."

Jason glanced down. Winona's blood was on his jeans, too, and his parka. "I should wash up."

When Jason returned, Chaska was holding two cups of coffee.

"I thought you might need this. Thanks for saving Winona's life."

Jason took the cup, regret assailing him. If he'd seen the trap just a moment sooner... "I didn't do anything."

"If you'd done nothing, she'd be dead. You put on that tourniquet, splinted her leg, gave her pain meds, started an IV, kept her warm, held her hand."

"I saw the trap just before she stepped on it. I tried to warn her, but it was too late. She was just out of reach." He squeezed his eyes shut against the image of those steel jaws clamping shut—and the memory of her screams.

"You can't blame yourself for that. That's on the bastard who put it there."

"Yeah."

They sat side by side, Jason looking every few minutes at the board, watching Winona's patient number, following her progress. She was in surgery now.

He closed his eyes, sent up a silent prayer.

Creator, save her life and her leg. She did nothing but try to help one of your creatures. Please be with her through the surgery. Save her leg. Amen.

It was more fearful gibbering than a prayer.

Then Chaska came out with it. "What does my sister mean to you?"

How could Jason answer that? "I care about her—more than I've ever cared about any woman."

Jason's answer made Chaska frown. "I heard you're about to get married."

Shit.

After everything that had happened today, Jason couldn't help but laugh, understanding now why Chaska had seemed so angry at the apartment. "I broke up with my fiancée when the DEA busted her for drug trafficking six months ago. She's in prison and out of my life."

"Oh. Shit." Chaska let out a breath. "I'm sorry—but I'm relieved to hear that."

All things considered, Jason was impressed with the man's restraint. He'd thought Jason was attached—and shagging his sister.

Chaska took a sip of coffee and seemed to consider his next words. "If you care about her so much, what's your plan?"

"I'll stay here and help her however I can until I have to go back to Sells." He could see Chaska wasn't going to be satisfied with anything less than the whole truth. "I'm on unpaid administrative leave. I have a disciplinary hearing next month."

He gave Chaska the short version of the story, telling him more than he probably should about the shooting.

"I'd have shot the son of a bitch, too. Does Winona know?"

"She does. She also knows that I won't leave the reservation—and why."

For a moment, a heavy silence stretched between them.

Then Chaska's gaze locked with Jason's. "My sister is a true human being. She has a pure heart. She's generous to everyone—two-legged, four-legged, winged. She doesn't know how to do anything but love. I cherish her more than my own life. I'm asking you as her brother, as someone who loves her—please don't hurt her."

———

ONE HOUR WENT BY. Then two.

Winona's status on the board still hadn't changed.

In surgery.

Then Deputy Marcs walked up to them, distress on her face. "Chaska. Jason. I am so sorry about this. Winona is the last person… *Damn.*"

She blinked tears from her eyes.

Chaska acknowledged her concern with a nod. "Thanks."

"I hate to bother you, Jason, but I need a statement. I've already spoken to Ranger Henriksen. We can go to the cafeteria so that we don't trouble Chaska or—"

"No." Chaska shook his head. "I want to hear it."

Jason recounted the entire story for Deputy Marcs from their decision to pursue the wolf to the moment the helicopter arrived. The terrible irony of what had happened wasn't lost on him. "Winona wanted to find the wolf before it was caught in a leg trap. She was afraid it might be injured. And because of that…"

"It's a damned tragedy." Deputy Marcs put her pen and notepad away. "Winona is one of the kindest people I know. Any word?"

Chaska looked up at the board again. "Not yet."

"I'm supposed to tell you, Chaska, that Joe and Rain are taking dinner to your place tonight so that you don't have to worry about your family. I think Megs and Ahearn are bringing your vehicle down so you can drive back to Scarlet when you're ready."

Chaska didn't seem surprised by any of this. "Thanks for letting me know."

But Jason was impressed. The people of Scarlet really did take care of their own.

"Also, the Forest Service is closing the area around the camp until they've had time to take down any traplines. I've asked the US Marshal Service to speak with the prisoner to get the locations of his traps. Hopefully, the bastard will cooperate. I've got to go and get this report filed. Please know I'm keeping Winona in my prayers."

Chaska shook her hand. "I appreciate all you've done. I know Winona does, too."

Jason held out his hand as well. "Thank you."

Five minutes after Deputy Marcs had left, a group of deputy US marshals—DUSMs—walked down the hallway, McBride among them.

He saw them, stopped, told the others to go on ahead. "Oh, God. Don't tell me it was Winona."

Jason and Chaska nodded.

"Son of a bitch." McBride sat, rubbed his face with his hands. "What happened? I got a call from the Forest County sheriff saying a woman stepped in a trap set by our prisoner and asking me to find out how many more traps he's got out there."

Once again, Jason told the story. Somehow, the weight of it got heavier each time. Seeing the chain. Shouting to warn her. The *snap* of steel jaws. Her screams.

McBride looked like he wanted to punch someone by the time Jason had finished. "I'm going to get the information from Graham about the rest of the traps. I'm also going to ask for an additional charge of assault. He needs to be held accountable."

Jason stared at him. "That's why you're here. He's here —in *this* hospital."

Both he and Chaska stood.

McBride got to his feet as well. "Oh, no. I can't let the two of you into his room."

Jason pushed—hard. "I won't touch him. I just want to give him a piece of my mind before you send him back to Alabama."

But Chaska was more to the point. "I want to look the bastard who almost killed my sister in the eyes."

McBride's gaze dropped to the floor for a moment, and Jason knew he was thinking it through. When he looked up, his jaw was set. "If I take you with me, I need your word you won't lay hands on him. If you do, it's my ass. Understand?"

Jason didn't need the explanation. He knew how things worked. "Got it."

"I understand."

They walked with McBride to the prisoner's room, McBride sharing some of what he knew along the way. "Graham told us he was breeding wolfdogs as a source of income. He hoped to sell them for dog fights and use the cash for ammo, tools, and other supplies he couldn't get from the land or steal."

Jason hadn't thought he could possibly hate Graham more, but that did it. "What a piece of shit."

"He belongs in a cage, not the wolves," Chaska muttered.

They came to a door where two DUSMs stood guard, the rest of McBride's crew milling about, waiting for their boss.

One of the DUSMs looked from Chaska to Jason. "Who are they?"

McBride answered the question truthfully without explaining their connection to this case. "Jason Chiago is with the Shadow Wolves, and Chaska Belcourt did some tracking for us on a fugitive case. They need to talk with the prisoner."

Eyebrows rose. Heads nodded.

"Shadow Wolves. Cool."

McBride opened the door, followed Jason and Chaska inside.

Thomas Paul Graham lay on his back, a morphine pump attached to an IV in one arm, a special pillow beneath his hips. He grinned when he saw them.

Then he recognized Jason, and his grin vanished. "Now, look, I wasn't tryin' to shoot you in the face. I was tryin' to scare you off."

McBride did the talking. "You're facing charges for firing on a federal agent—and a few other felonies besides. Poaching. Use of illegal traps. And now assault with a deadly weapon. A woman stepped into one of your old-time bear traps this afternoon and might lose her leg. We want the location of every trap and snare you've placed on Forest Service land—*now*."

"Not 'til you tell me what you did with my wolves."

"They're fine—all six of them. The Forest Service placed the female with her pups in a sanctuary. The male will join them soon."

"I want proof."

Did this son of a bitch think he was in charge?

Jason walked to the head of the bed, bent down until his face was almost touching Graham's, and let the full force of his rage show. "The woman who was injured means a lot to me. Give the nice marshal the information that he needs, or there won't be a prison cell on earth that can keep you safe from me."

McBride cleared his throat. "Chiago."

Graham's face paled, and he broke. "They're all in a

line up to the ridge heading west. There should be four more."

Then Chaska stepped forward, contempt on his face. "The woman you hurt is my sister. Do you know what we Lakota used to do to our enemies?"

He let the question hang in the air for a moment, let Graham squirm.

"We used to ride up and touch them to show our bravery. But you're pathetic. There's no honor in counting coup on a sick son of a dog like you."

Then he turned and walked away, Jason following him out of the room.

Chapter 21

JASON AND CHASKA WAITED, the minutes like hours. Megs and Ahearn came with sandwiches and the keys to Chaska's truck.

Megs gave them an update. "Everyone in town is praying for her. Joe has already put a donation jar on the bar at Knockers to help cover her medical expenses. We got the wolf safely down. Dr. Keene examined it, fed it, and it's now safely in Shota's pen. The sanctuary folks are coming to get him tomorrow. I know Win will ask."

Chaska hugged Megs. "Thank you."

Megs stepped back, wiped her eyes. "We all love Win. Damned onions."

Finally, four hours and twenty-two minutes after Winona went into surgery, the screen said she had been moved into recovery.

Several minutes later, the surgeon walked into the waiting area, his gaze moving over the room, settling on Jason and Chaska. "Belcourt family?"

As they were the only brown-skinned people present, it was a good guess.

Jason and Chaska stood.

He motioned them toward a private conference room. "Let's talk in here."

Jason's stomach sank. He followed Chaska into the small room, closed the door behind them, and sat at the small table.

Chaska spoke first. "How is my sister?"

The doctor leaned back against the wall, arms crossed over his chest. "She's groggy from the anesthesia. We've given her a nerve block, so she's not in pain. Whoever put that tourniquet on her leg saved her life. One of the teeth on that trap severed her fibular artery. She would have bled out in five minutes. As it was, we had to give her two units of blood."

Jason had to ask. "Is she going to keep her leg?"

"I think so."

But Jason heard only the doubt. "There's still a chance she'll lose it?"

The doctor pulled out a chair and sat. "The break itself was not the worst I've seen. I was able to realign the bones and fix them into place with hardware. There was some tissue damage from the tourniquet, of course, but her blood flow is restored. Our two biggest concerns over the next several weeks are blood clots and infection."

This was all good news.

The surgeon went on. "If she ends up with a serious infection, she could still lose her leg. We've got her on strong IV antibiotics, and we're giving her anti-clotting drugs. I also sprinkled vancomycin powder in the surgical site and around the bone and gave her a tetanus shot. We'll monitor her closely over the next week. There's a very good chance that she'll heal and walk normally. It's the best possible news you could expect at this point after an injury like that."

Jason thought he might actually fucking cry, his throat too tight to talk.

"Thank you for all you did to help her." Chaska shook the surgeon's hand. "When can we see her?"

The surgeon stood. "When she's out of recovery, I'll have a nurse come get you."

Jason swallowed, got to his feet, shook the doctor's hand. "Thank you. Is there a chapel in the hospital?"

"Yes. It's on the first floor. Down the elevator and to your right."

"Thanks."

The chapel turned out to be a small space with pews, kneelers, a pulpit, and a single stained-glass window that depicted a lily. Jason crossed himself and got to his knees, praying silently in a jumble of O'odham and English, pouring out his heart about everything. His fear for Winona. His rage about his sisters and Elena. His uncertainty about his future and whether he would have a job next month. His doubts about the promise he'd made his grandmother. His love for his people.

Thank you, Creator, for bringing Winona safely through the surgery. Thank you for the surgeon and the pilot and the paramedics and the Team. Please drive away infection and help her to keep her leg. I love her. Help me to find my path. I thought I knew what it was, but now ... I don't know where I'm meant to be. Amen.

It was more than he'd said to God in a long time.

When he opened his eyes again, Chaska was sitting in the pew across the aisle from him. "Thank you for saving Winona's life—and for praying for her. I can see that you truly do care about her."

Jason got off his knees, sat in the pew. "Yeah."

"The nurse came out a few minutes ago. She said Winona is asking for you." Chaska met Jason's gaze. "For all of her life until now, she has asked for me. When she was a little girl and had a bad dream or was sick or scared, she called for me, even before our mother died. Now, she's asking for *you*."

Jason heard what Chaska was saying and understood the message beneath it. This was a major shift for him and not altogether easy—the big brother taking a backseat to the lover. It was also a responsibility. "You've always been her rock. She told me how you took care of her after your mother died. She loves you."

"I would do anything for her." Chaska got to his feet. "Are you coming to see her or staying here?"

———

WINONA DRIFTED IN A FOG. "JASON."

"He's right here, little sister."

Warm fingers took hers. "I'm here, Win."

She opened her eyes—it seemed to take a great deal of effort—and found Chaska on her left and Jason on her right. She smiled. "You're both … here."

"Where else would we be?" Jason kissed her hand.

"The doctor said you're going to be okay."

She nodded, then remembered. "The wolf. He was hungry. He—"

"He's safe, angel. I darted him, and the Team got him down."

"He's in Shota's old pen now. Heather is coming to get him tomorrow."

"*Wasté.*" *Good.* A worry that had niggled at her faded.

She drifted in and out after that, sleeping off the anesthesia and doped up on Percocet, her dreams uneasy and strange. She woke when the nurse walked into the room, light from the hallway streaming inside. Chaska had gone

—she vaguely remembered him saying goodbye—but Jason was still there, asleep in a chair.

"It's time to check your vitals and give you more pain meds."

Jason's head jerked up. He got to his feet, walked over to her, took her hand. "How do you feel?"

"It hurts."

His brow furrowed, his thumb stroking the back of her hand. "I bet it does."

"I dreamed that a shark tried to eat my leg, and you fought it off."

He smiled. "Shark wrestling, huh?"

The nurse wrapped a blood pressure cuff around her arm. "From what I hear, that's pretty close to the truth."

While the machine took a reading of Winona's blood pressure, the nurse checked her temperature and then handed her a little paper cup with two pills. "Here's your Percocet."

"Thanks." Winona swallowed them with a gulp of water.

"I'll get you more water and then let you sleep." The nurse left them alone.

"Chaska went home, right?" It was the first time since arriving at the hospital that she'd felt clear-headed enough to have a conversation.

Jason drew the chair up to the bed and sat beside her, taking her hand once again, lines of stress and fatigue on his face. "I think he felt torn between staying here with you and going home to Naomi and the baby. I promised I'd keep him updated."

The nurse walked in with a full pitcher of water and ice and set it on the little table. "Press the call button if you need anything."

"Thank you." Winona waited until the nurse had gone. "You saved my life."

He frowned. "If I'd just been a second faster…"

"Don't blame yourself. I should have watched where I was walking. We all knew there might be traps up there, but I was looking at the wolf, trying to gauge his responses. Did you dart him, or was that the ranger?"

Jason explained what had happened in that last hour, how the wolf had crept closer, and how Jason been afraid the scent of her blood would provoke it. "I kept tossing it chunks of meat. Every once in a while, you would wake up and talk to it in Lakota. It tried to get closer to you. I think it felt safe with you. When the helicopter came, it ran. That's when I darted it."

"Thank you. I was so afraid it would be scared away and starve or get shot."

"I won't lie. Being that close to a predator of that size was … intense."

She couldn't help but laugh. "Was my big, bad Shadow Wolf scared?"

She thought he would laugh too, but his expression crumpled, his eyes filling with the anguish of someone who'd known too much grief.

"I've never been more afraid or felt more helpless in my life. When I saw how heavily you were bleeding… God, Win, I was afraid I'd lose you."

She blinked back tears, reached up, cupped his cheek. "I was afraid, too, and then you told me you wouldn't let me die. You kept me alive. You made me feel safe."

"I'm glad." He gave her a sad smile, turned his head, kissed her palm.

Then something occurred to her that hadn't before, and her heart sank. "I'm going to waste the rest of our time together in the hospital, aren't I?"

He chuckled. "It's not a waste of time to heal. I'll be here every day. I've got almost two weeks before I have to drive back. The hearing is on the ninth of October."

"Twelve days." That was nothing.

It was everything.

"I'll stay in Scarlet as long as I can."

She was starting to get sleepy again, probably from the drugs. "I want you to know that I don't regret any of this— you and me. We've only known each other for a short time, but I…"

What was she about to tell him? That she'd fallen in love with him? Good grief! How would that help either of them?

He was leaving.

He waited, his brow furrowing with concern when she didn't finish her sentence.

"I think the drugs are kicking in. I lost my train of thought."

He kissed her forehead. "You should sleep. I'll be right here."

——

"I WON'T LET YOU FALL." Jason walked beside Winona as she moved down the hallway, trying out her new crutches. "You're doing it."

"I'm not sure how I'm going to get around the clinic like this."

Her nurse walked on her other side. "You're a vet?"

"A wildlife vet."

"Cool. Ever take care of anything like a bear or a cougar?"

"Yes. I've got an injured bear cub now."

"Wow!"

They reached the end of the hallway.

"Do you want to sit and rest for a minute?" the nurse asked.

"I just want to get back to my room." Winona turned and headed the other way.

It seemed to Jason that she was more uncomfortable this morning—and grumpier. The nerve block had worn off long ago, and pain pills were now her only source of relief. She was also worried about the cost of the helicopter flight and her hospital bill.

He walked beside her. "One step at a time."

He and the nurse had just gotten her back into bed when her door opened and Chaska walked in with Grandpa Belcourt, who was dressed in a fine ribbon shirt, an eagle feather in his hair, a leather bundle under one arm.

Winona smiled. "Chaska. Grandpa."

Grandpa glanced around. "This room looks like a flower shop."

A half dozen bouquets sat wherever there was space—on the counter by the sink, on the table beside her bed, on the windowsill. The West family had sent one. Joe and Rain from Knockers had sent another. Lexi and some clinic volunteers had also sent one with a card telling Winona not to worry about the clinic. Zach and Natalie had sent one, too. He couldn't remember who'd sent the others.

"I can wait in the hall." Jason turned to leave the room so Winona could have some private time with her family, but Chaska stopped him.

"Stay with us. Old Man wants to pray."

Grandpa Belcourt unrolled the bundle, drew out a braid of sweetgrass and an eagle feather. He was about to light the sweetgrass when the nurse's aide walked in.

"I'm sorry, sir, there's no smoking … or … uh… no smoke allowed."

Chaska was ready for this. "This is part of our religion. It's how we pray."

The nurse's aide seemed confused. "We have chaplains available if you'd like spiritual support."

Jason wasn't in the mood for this. "This man is an elder and a Lakota spiritual leader. Go read the American Indian Religious Freedom Act, and then come talk to us about hospital rules and chaplains."

The nurse's aide left, red in the face, probably off to fetch the proverbial cavalry.

Chaska met Jason's gaze, approval in his eyes.

Old Man Belcourt lit the grass, blew out the flame, ran the eagle feather through the tendril of smoke, then used the feather to fan the smoke over Winona. He spoke in Lakota before translating his words into English for Jason's sake. "*Tunkashila*, Grandfather, Creator, I give thanks for my granddaughter Winona's rescue and her survival. I ask that you watch over her and help her to heal and walk again."

Tears spilled down Winona's cheeks.

Then he turned to Jason, fanning smoke over him, too, the sweet scent of the grass tickling Jason's nose. "Creator, watch over the man who protected Winona and saved her life, Jason Chiago, this man who moves with the strength of a wolf. Guide him on his way. Keep his feet on the path of a true human being."

Was that the path Jason was on? He had no idea.

Lastly, Grandpa turned to Chaska, fanned smoke over him. "Bless my grandson and help him to be a good father and husband. *Mitakuye Oyasin*. All my relations."

Chaska nodded. "*Aho. Mitakuye Oyasin*"

It was the only Lakota phrase Jason knew. "*Mitakuye Oyasin.*"

The prayer was over by the time the nurse arrived. "I'm sorry. She's new and doesn't understand. We allow indigenous spiritual practices at this hospital, provided patients aren't placed in danger. I'm really sorry for the misunderstanding."

"Thank you for teaching her." Grandpa rolled the feather and sweetgrass back into their sacred bundle. "And thank you for taking good care of my granddaughter."

"You're welcome. I apologize once again." The nurse left them in peace.

Grandpa Belcourt sat next to the bed and asked to hear the whole story from Winona and Jason. He listened thoughtfully, as if every word mattered, nodding his head every so often, his expression grave. When Jason finished with the helicopter's arrival and his darting the wolf, there was silence.

After a moment, Old Man spoke. "It's hard to know why such things happen. But I believe Creator meant for you to be there, Chiago. Otherwise, my granddaughter would have died, and the wolf would still be alone. We should talk more about these things."

Chaska grinned. "What Old Man is saying is that he's pouring water for an *inipi*—a sweat lodge ceremony—and he wants you to be there."

There was only one answer Jason could give to an invitation like this. "Of course, I'll be there. I would be honored."

"Kat James is coming by this evening to stay with Winona."

"Kat's coming?" Winona perked up.

Chaska nodded. "Gabe is joining us for the lodge. You

know what he went through. He'll have some powerful prayers for you."

Jason saw in Winona's eyes how much that meant to her. "Gabe is a good man."

Old Man got to his feet. "You can help me tend the fire, Chiago."

Chaska grinned, gave Jason a friendly jab on the shoulder. "I'll pick you up at about three this afternoon, brother."

"I'll be there."

Chapter 22

WHILE GRANDPA BELCOURT cleaned the sweat lodge and prepared it for the ceremony, Jason threw more logs on the fire, the stones that would heat the lodge beneath the blaze. So far, the old man had barely spoken to him, but Jason knew the whole point of his being here was so that they could have a private conversation.

"*Chanupa*. That's our word for the pipe. It's *wakan* —sacred."

Jason repeated the word. "*Chanupa*."

Grandpa chuckled and set leather pouches of tobacco, sage, cedar, an old drum, an eagle-bone whistle, and his sacred bundle on the small, earthen mound that served as an altar between the fire and the sweat lodge door.

The lodge, a low structure with canvas and blankets fastened to a frame of willows, was built up the mountain-side above the old wolf pen in a small clearing that over-looked Scarlet. Two tipis—one for men and one for women—stood on the edge of the clearing, giving people a place to change before and after the ceremony.

Grandpa sat on a nearby bench. "You're a hard worker. Tell this old man about your family, your people."

Here we go.

While Jason tended the fire, he gave Grandpa Belcourt his life story, holding nothing back. His parents' murders. His brief descent into drinking and drugs. His life with his grandparents and learning the O'odham *himdag*. His job with the Wolves. His grandmother's death. The promise he'd made. Elena's arrest. His upcoming hearing.

As he'd done at the hospital, the old man listened intently, never interrupting, not even to ask questions. When Jason finished, Old Man nodded. "You have already walked a long, hard road with many twists and turns—just like the maze on your arm."

Jason glanced at his tattoo. "You know the meaning of the Man in the Maze?"

Grandpa chuckled. "We old people share stories at the pow wow."

That made Jason laugh. "Right."

"This promise you made your grandmother—what words did you say to her?"

Jason thought about it, trying to remember the exact words. "I promised never to leave the O'odham people."

Grandpa nodded. "A promise is a sacred thing. So is the love of one's half-side."

"Half-side?" Jason hadn't heard that expression before.

"Naomi is Chaska's half-side, and he is hers. Two people meet and find they were always looking for one another. They are two halves of one whole."

Jason felt the truth of those words to his bones. "If both things are sacred, Grandfather, how can a man choose between them?"

"You must pray on this today, for it's clear to these old eyes that my granddaughter loves you and you love her.

She called for you, not her brother. You are her safe haven now. Remember that Creator doesn't lead us to dead ends. We do that to ourselves. Creator gives us choices."

Jason bit back his frustration. If there was a compromise here, Jason didn't see it. Winona wanted to live near her family, and Jason couldn't blame her. He could see how close they were. But he'd made a promise.

"Tell me about the rest of your family."

Jason tossed more wood on the fire. "I have three older sisters scattered around the country and seven nieces and nephews. I never see them. My sisters left me in Sells and never came back. They married non-Natives, and they're not raising their children in the O'odham way."

"This makes you angry."

"Yes." It was the truth. "They abandoned me. I was still a boy when they left."

"How about in Sells or over on the Mexican side—aunties and uncles?"

"Not any longer. They've all passed. I am the last of my family still on the land."

Grandpa seemed to consider this. "It could be that it's time for you to break free of your anger toward your sisters so you can consider your path in a new light. Be certain you're not making decisions out of resentment toward them. These matters deserve careful thought."

Break free of his anger? How would that change anything? And why did Grandpa think Jason would make decisions based on resentment toward his sisters?

Grandpa Belcourt was as cryptic as Jason's grandfather had been.

The sun was close to setting now, and the others had arrived—Chaska, Gabe, and Doug, Naomi's father, who would be driving back to Pine Ridge with Star and their kids in the morning.

Jason left the fire, walked to the men's tipi with the others to change.

Chaska pulled off his shirt, exposing the Sun Dance scars on his chest. "Have you been to an *inipi* before?"

"One of my fellow Wolves is Lakota, so, yes, I've been to a few." Jason stripped naked, put on his swim trunks, and wrapped a towel around his hips.

"I was hoping you'd say this was your first." Gabe picked up his towel. "Old Man Belcourt goes easy on newbies."

Grandpa chuckled, dozens of Sun Dance scars on his chest and back. "Are you complaining that my lodges are too hot?"

"Too hot? No. Never."

The others laughed.

They walked together to the lodge, Chaska removing his wedding band, setting it on the altar, Doug and Gabe doing the same. If the *inipi* was hot enough, metal could burn. Gabe also removed his prosthetic leg and left it on the altar.

Then, one by one, they dropped to their knees and crawled into the lodge, Old Man first and then Jason, followed by Gabe and then Doug. Chaska remained outside to assist by handling the hot stones, using a steel shovel to pass them into the pit at the center of the lodge. Then, at last, Chaska entered, sitting to the right of the lodge door.

Sage. Cedar. Sweet grass. Smoke. Heat.

Then the door went down, the darkness total.

Jason willed himself to relax into the rhythm of the *inipi*.

The hiss of steam on hot stones. Scalding heat. The cry of an eagle-bone whistle. The beating of Old Man's drum. Voices raised in song.

Jason didn't know the songs, so he turned his thoughts inward, thanking Creator for saving Winona's life and Naomi's, asking God to heal Winona's leg and Naomi's body, praying for the Source of Life to protect the two women and baby Shota. But beneath it all flowed a single persistent plea, straight from his heart.

Help me, Father. My path leads me away from Winona, but I love her. Help me to find the answer.

━━

WINONA WAS in the middle of another walk on her crutches when Kat stepped out of the elevator. She smiled when she saw Winona and hurried over to her.

"You're up and walking already. You're doing so well."

The nurse agreed. "Isn't she?"

"I don't feel like I'm doing well."

Kat walked beside her. "It's hard, but I know you'll get there."

Winona reminded herself that Kat had been through this. She had watched Gabe recover from the amputation of his leg below the knee, an injury he'd sustained saving Kat's life. Gabe had cut a climbing rope, surrendering himself to death rather than pulling Kat over the edge with him. He'd fallen more than three hundred feet, landing in deep snow, which had saved his life. But he'd hit his leg on the cliff wall on the way down, damaging it beyond repair.

"One step at a time," the nurse said.

When Winona was back in her bed and had taken her next dose of pain pills, Kat drew up the chair and sat beside her. Kat already knew what had happened, so Winona didn't need to repeat the story. For a time, they kept the conversation light, talking about Kat's kids, her job at the newspaper, and the Cimarron, which Kat had visited many times because one of her coworkers was Nate's sister-in-law.

It was Winona who changed the direction of their conversation. "The doctor says he's pretty sure I'm going to keep my leg."

"I'm so glad. Gabe and I have been praying for you. But if the worst happens, you know we'll be there for you. Gabe knows what it's like. That's why he's at the *inipi*."

"That means so much to me. Thanks." Then Winona remembered. "He's not engaged."

"Who's not engaged?"

"Jason. He's not engaged. His fiancée was arrested for drug smuggling six months ago and is in prison. He broke up with her the day she was arrested. I don't think it's easy for him to discuss. He felt betrayed."

"Of course, he did. Poor Jason." Kat let out a breath. "I never did like Elena. I'm sorry he went through that, but I'm also relieved. I'd heard that the two of you had grown close. I was worried."

Winona told Kat how she and Jason had ended up at the Cimarron, with Jason cutting sign, helping Jack and Nate resolve the mystery of the wolf. "It was inspiring to watch him work. I was so impressed. I felt so guilty being attracted to him. But when I found out he was single, I suddenly felt nervous around him."

Kat laughed. "I would have loved to see your face when you learned the truth. I'm married, and I love Gabe. I love him and find him incredibly sexy. But I still have eyes. Jason is *hot*."

"You're right about that." Winona told Kat how Jason had comforted her after a nightmare, how he'd loved watching her feed the eagle, how he'd made her feel safe when she thought she might die on that mountainside.

And then her emotions overflowed, tears filling her

eyes. "I love him, Kat. My heart tells me he's my half-side, but he's leaving."

"Oh, Win."

"He made a death-bed promise to his grandmother not to leave his O'odham people. If I want to be with him, I would have to close my clinic, move to Sells, and live far away from my family. I can't imagine watching little Shota grow up through photographs and text messages or not living next door to my brother and Naomi or being far away when Grandpa…"

She couldn't finish that last thought.

"Does Jason feel the same about you?"

"I'm not sure. I know he cares about me. He said so, and he's proven that. But he's also made it clear that he won't leave Arizona."

"I'm sorry. That's hard."

"How did you and Gabe work it out?"

"You really can't compare our situation to yours. I was working at the paper in Denver when we met. No one had to give up anything or move for us to be together. We visit Kaibito for a couple of months every year to see my grandma and teach our kids about their Diné heritage. I gave birth to my two older children there. But when Grandma Alice passes, I'm not sure we'll be able to maintain that connection."

Winona and Jason's circumstances were completely different. She lived here. He lived in Sells. Neither of them had a career that enabled them to take long vacations to visit the other. She'd only met him because he'd been placed on administrative leave.

Kat took her hand. "Life has a way of working these things out. That probably sounds hopelessly optimistic, but I believe it's true."

Winona wasn't so sure.

"When Gabe cut that rope, I watched him fall. I knew he was gone. My heart truly seemed to break. I lay there shouting for him for maybe an hour. I don't know for sure. I was injured and hypothermic. My memory is foggy."

"I can't imagine how horrible that was."

"When I was in the helicopter on my way to the hospital, the rescuers got word that Gabe was seriously injured but alive. He'd fallen more than three hundred feet, and he was still alive. It felt like a miracle. After that, no obstacle we've faced has seemed insurmountable."

Winona could understand that. "What he did was incredibly brave and unselfish."

"He loved me. He was willing to die to save me."

Winona remembered Jason taking her hand and warning her when they first encountered Graham. He'd shielded her body with his when they'd hurried inside the cabin from the hot tub at the Cimarron. He'd fought to save her life and had done all he could to comfort her after she stepped into the bear trap.

Maybe he *did* love her.

"You need to focus on getting better. Try not to waste your strength worrying about what comes next." Kat smiled. "If Jason truly is your half-side, then nothing will keep you apart for long."

━━━

JASON DROVE through heavy traffic on I-25 toward the hospital, Grandpa Belcourt's words still running through his mind.

A promise is a sacred thing. So is the love of one's half-side.

It could be that it's time for you to break free of your anger toward your sisters so you can consider your path in a new light. Be certain you're not making decisions out of resentment toward them.

Still, Jason was no closer to having an answer.

He'd spent these past five days driving back and forth between the hospital and the clinic, working with the installers to get Winona's security system in place, checking in with Dr. Keene and Lexi about the animals at the clinic, and doing his best to keep Winona's spirits up. But today, after six days in the hospital, Win was coming home.

He parked at the hospital and made his way upstairs to her room, where he found her ready to go. "Someone is eager to get out of here."

"That someone is me." She sat in the chair, dressed in a white T-shirt and a purple broomstick skirt he'd brought from home, her leg elevated, her belongings in a plastic hospital bag on the bed. "I'm just waiting for my discharge papers."

He walked over to her, kissed her, then pulled up another chair to wait with her. "Lexi says hello. That woman could command an army. She gets things done. She had Megs cleaning up fox poop this morning."

Until Winona's incisions had healed, she was still vulnerable to infection, so Lexi had made a schedule covering the next six weeks. She had even called the university and asked for an intern or vet to give Dr. Keene a break.

"Megs?" Winona laughed. "I wish I had seen that."

"I knew you'd say that." Jason pulled out his cell phone, opened his photo library, and turned the phone so that Winona could see.

She smiled at the image of a glowering Megs with the poop scooper. "Wow. I'm touched. Everyone has been so helpful and kind."

"The people of Scarlet love you. I've seen that for myself." Jason couldn't wait for her to see the welcome the town had set up for her.

Even more incredible was the financial support the town had shown. Joe's donation jar at Knockers had brought in enough to pay for Winona's rescue flight and her hospital bills. She didn't know it yet, but she wasn't going to owe a dime. That wasn't Jason's news to share, so it would have to wait until later.

He brought her up to date on the security system. "You'll be able to see on your phone who's at the doors. If anyone breaks in through a window or a door, it will notify both you and the Scarlet PD. You can leave the clinic's front door unlocked during business hours or, if you're alone, set it up so that you have to buzz people in."

"And how much is this costing the clinic?"

"Nada. I couldn't even get the man to show me the invoice."

"Why are the Wests doing this? They already gave the clinic a huge donation."

"They're good people." That's what everyone had told him, and it had turned out to be true. "I think they feel partly responsible for your being injured."

"That's nuts."

The nurse walked in with papers and a smile. "Let's get you out of here."

She went over the discharge instructions with both of them. No baths, but showers were okay provided she kept the incisions dry. Leave the dressing on the incisions for another week. No weight on her injured leg until she was given the okay. A prescription for pain meds. Call her doctor immediately if she got a fever higher than 101 or if her leg became more painful or swollen or there was redness.

"I've got it all printed out for you. You can pick up your prescription at the pharmacy downstairs. And here's your ride now."

An aide pushed a wheelchair up to the door. "It's not a limo, but it will do."

Jason helped Winona into the wheelchair and set her belongings and the discharge papers on her lap. "I've got your crutches."

Fifteen minutes later, Jason was helping Win into the passenger seat of his truck. "Watch your leg."

He stowed her crutches behind the seat, covertly sending a text message to Chaska telling him they were on their way. Then he climbed into the driver's seat. "Next stop, Scarlet Springs."

"Oh, thank goodness!"

They talked for the entire hour-long drive, Jason more at home in her presence than he'd felt with a woman before.

A promise is a sacred thing. So is the love of one's half-side.

Soon they left the city behind, drove through Boulder and up into the canyon, passing the spot where Hank drove off the highway and getting closer to town.

Jason tried not to give anything away, but he couldn't get the smile off his face.

Then, there it was—the town limit sign for Scarlet.

He slowed, gave her every chance to spot it on her own.

"It looks like most of the snow has melt… What?! Oh! Do you see that?"

*Scarlet Springs Town Limit, Pop. 1,469, Elevation 8,936
Home of Wolf Whisperer Winona Belcourt*

"I do." He chuckled, slowing even more.

It was only a temporary change written on paper and taped to the sign, but it was the thought that counted. And the thought was sincere.

They left the canyon behind and headed into town, Winona's head turning this way and that, taking in all the balloons and cardboard and paper signs stuck in the windows of homes and businesses and at the ends of driveways.

We love you, Winona!

Winona is our hero!

Heal well, Winona!

"I don't understand. All I did was step in a stupid trap and hurt myself."

"You were almost killed while trying to save an innocent animal."

She looked over at him, tears spilling down her cheeks. "You knew, didn't you?"

"Of course, but I couldn't spoil the surprise." He drove through the roundabout, waving to Bear as they passed.

"Jason Chiago. Winona Belcourt! My friend Winona is home!"

Then Jason turned the corner and parked in front of Winona's house, where her family and a few Team members stood, waiting for her—Chaska, Naomi with the baby, Old Man, Megs, Ahearn, and Sasha.

Jason got out, opened her door, and carefully lifted her into his arms. "Welcome home, angel."

Chapter 23

ON THE BRINK, Winona's fingers clenched in Jason's hair, his head between her thighs, his lips and tongue driving her crazy, his fingers thrusting deep inside her. "*Jason!*"

It felt so good, so unbelievably good.

She hovered on the edge of an orgasm, savoring every second of it, the intensity of the pleasure overwhelming. "Yes. Oh, God!"

Then she shattered, climax washing through her in a shimmering rush, making her cry out. He was relentless, staying with her until the tremors had passed, his clever mouth and fingers coaxing every bit of pleasure from her that they could. Then he kissed his way up her body, tasting her nipples, her throat, her lips, bringing her back.

She opened her eyes, drew his mouth to hers, kissed him. "Help me turn over."

They'd practiced over the past two days and had gotten pretty good at managing sex despite her injured leg. It was all a matter of positioning and persistence, and Jason was very creative.

She lifted her injured leg off the stack of pillows, Jason

supporting her ankle as she rolled onto her right side. He moved the pillow stack and helped her gently lower her leg once more. When she was comfortable again, he slid into bed behind her, his palms cupping and caressing her bare buttocks.

"I love your ass." He slipped his fingers between her thighs, stroked her clit, reviving the lust he'd just slaked. "You are *so* wet."

Then he rolled a condom onto his erection and nudged himself inside her, the thick, hard feel of him making her moan.

He thrust slowly, his lips and teeth on her bare shoulder, one hand reaching around to fondle her breasts, his fingers teasing and plucking her puckered nipples, sending jolts of pleasure to her womb.

In this position, she could do nothing but surrender. The helplessness of it turned her on, but only because she trusted Jason entirely. She'd never been able to give herself so completely to a man before, and, oh, the reward was sweet.

In… Out…

Each achingly slow thrust sent a surge of pleasure through her belly, heightening her arousal, driving her need for him. And she *did* need him. She needed him to put out the fire he'd started, to satisfy the growing ache inside her.

In… Out…

She reached back, rested one hand on his hip, her other hand curled into a fist against her pillow. His powerful body moved against hers, his hands still busy with her breasts. She whimpered in frustration, wondering why he hadn't touched her clit. He knew she couldn't come like this. Oh, but it felt so good.

In… Out…

Slowly, slowly the tension inside her grew, thrust upon thrust, pleasure drawing tighter in her belly, her need for release becoming desperate, his cock stretching her, filling her, stroking that sensitive place inside her.

Climax snuck up on her like the slow rising of a tide, the intensity of it growing as it moved through her, making her cry out, the torrent lifting her higher and higher, until she thought she might drown in bliss.

Then his control snapped, and he pounded into her from behind, the hand that had teased her nipples now caressing her clit. She found herself rushing headlong to an amazing third climax. This time, he came with her, groaning against her nape, finishing with three hard thrusts, his body shaking.

For a time, they lay there breathless, Winona's mind blissfully empty, Jason's heart thrumming against her back, one big hand caressing her thigh.

Gradually, the world around them returned.

"Good morning."

"Good morning." He sat up. "I'll make breakfast."

Winona made her way to the bathroom to brush her teeth and comb the tangles from her hair. She slipped into her bathrobe and went to the kitchen, where Jason was busy at the stove.

"I could get used to this—you making me breakfast every morning in your underwear."

He *did* have the finest ass in the entire world.

He chuckled. "I wouldn't mind that."

Over cheese omelets, breakfast potatoes, and coffee, they talked about the day.

"We should have dinner at Knockers tonight."

"What's with you and Knockers?" She would rather stay home with him.

They'd spent the past two days holed up in her house,

Winona doing her best to savor the time she had left with him. Already, a week had gone by, the days slipping like sand through her fingers. It was Sunday, and he would be leaving early on Thursday to make it back in time for the hearing on Friday.

Four days. Four days was all Winona had left with him. After that…

"Hey, I like the beer—and I thought I'd give the climbing wall a try."

"Really?" The thought of him rock climbing—well, it didn't turn her off. "Okay then. You're on."

They talked about other things he might want to do before he left town. Visit Rocky Mountain National Park. Get a tour of Team HQ, affectionately referred to as The Cave. Visit Naomi's shop, Tanagila's, to see the jewelry she made.

Winona held her coffee mug. "Are you afraid?"

"About the hearing?" He leaned back in his chair, picked up his mug, sipped. "Nah. I broke the rules. I killed a man on the wrong side of the border, and I endangered myself. If they terminate me, I will have earned it."

She had to ask. "Is there any chance you'll go to prison?"

Jason shook his head. "No. This isn't a criminal proceeding. The man I killed was caught red-handed smuggling drugs into the country and had just shot a federal agent. I only fired after he pointed his rifle at me."

"Thank God." She let out a breath, relieved. "I'd hate to have to figure out how to bake you a cake with a file in it. I'm not very good with cakes."

Jason's head fell back, and he laughed.

JASON PARKED in a spot Rain had reserved for Winona and helped Winona climb down from his truck.

"They saved me a parking space?"

"I knew it would be harder for you to walk a long distance, so I called ahead."

"That's so sweet."

Yeah, angel? Just wait.

They walked to the front door, which Jason held open for her, conversation, laughter, and music spilling into the cool October air.

Rain saw them first. "Make a path, please. Let Winona through."

People saw Winona on her crutches and stepped aside.

Rain hugged her. "I'm so glad you came through this. Are you going to the Team table, or do you want a table close by?"

"We'll sit at the Team table." Winona smiled. "Jason is going to try climbing tonight."

Rain looked surprised—and pleased. "I'll head back with you."

Rain cleared a path for Winona, Jason following behind. People waved and called out to her as she passed, heads turning her way.

Winona moved steadily toward the back. "It's busy for a Sunday night."

"Is it?" Rain gave Jason a wink. "I suppose it is."

Jason wasn't surprised to see the Team table full. He recognized most of the faces now. Chaska and Naomi were there, the baby in Naomi's arms. Old Man Belcourt sat next to them. He acknowledged Jason with a nod.

His words still hadn't left Jason's mind.

Megs had saved Winona and Jason a couple of seats on the end of the table where it would be easier for her to maneuver.

Jason helped her stow her crutches out of the way. "Are you good?"

This *was* a lot for someone who'd just gotten out of the hospital.

Win smiled. "Yeah. Thanks."

Rain handed Jason a menu. "By the way, Win, your money is no good here tonight. That goes for you, too, Chiago. Heroes eat for free at our house."

Everyone on the Team wanted to hear how Winona was doing, but the place was packed, and Win almost had to shout.

Megs turned to a table of particularly rowdy men. "Hey, pipe down, would you? We're trying to have a conversation here!"

Clearly touched by people's concern, Winona answered their questions and then said what he knew she'd wanted to say for a week now. "Thank you all for rescuing me— and for saving the wolf. I never thought I'd need a rescue. I wouldn't have my leg if you hadn't gotten there so quickly, and I wouldn't be alive if it weren't for Jason. You're the best, and I'm proud to work with you."

Cheers. Raised bottles.

"We *are* good." Megs smiled to herself and drank.

Then the band fell silent, and Joe took the stage, a woman with strawberry-blond braids standing beside him in overalls.

"If I could have everyone's attention for a moment, Libby, our talented brew master, wants to tell you about her latest creation." Joe stepped aside.

Winona blew out a relieved breath. "Whew. For a moment, I thought he was going to say something about me."

Jason tried not to grin.

The woman in the overalls—Libby—took the mic. "I

hope everyone is having a great night. I've got a new double cream stout for you. This one has a mix of eleven different malts with undertones of chocolate and just a hint of sage and pine. I've named it Wolf Whisperer Double Cream Stout in honor of our own Winona Belcourt."

Cheers. Wolf howls. Applause.

Winona looked utterly taken aback. "Thanks, but I don't even drink."

Laughter.

Then Joe took back the microphone. "For those of you who don't know, Winona is a wildlife vet. She runs a sanctuary for wild animals here in town. She was trying to rescue an abandoned wolf when she stepped into an illegal bear trap. She almost lost her leg and her life. But we're happy to welcome her back to Knockers tonight."

Cheers. Applause.

Some people even got to their feet.

Winona glanced around, eyes wide, surprise on her face. She met Jason's gaze. "I don't deserve this."

"Yes, you do." He kissed her forehead. "Listen."

Joe was still talking. "Now, this leaves Winona with some big hospital bills—"

"They didn't!"

"—so we've been collecting donations at the bar and are happy to present Winona with a check for eighteen-thousand nine-hundred dollars to cover her helicopter flight and medical expenses."

Jason smiled. "They did."

Tears spilled down Winona's cheeks. "But all I did was step in a stupid trap!"

"She's just home from the hospital, so we won't ask her for a speech. Thank you, Winona, for your service to this community and the animals that share the mountains with us. This town wouldn't be the same without you. And a big thank you to Jason Chiago for tracking the wolf and saving Winona's life. You might not be a resident of Scarlet Springs, but you're one of us now."

Cheers and applause

It was Jason's turn to be surprised.

Megs laughed, probably because of the expression on his face. "You thought you'd get away without Joe mentioning you. That's cute."

It was more than that. What surprised Jason the most was how Joe's gratitude and the warmth of the people's reaction had made him feel that he, an O'odham man, had a place in their crazy little town.

Then the Timberline Mudbugs retook the stage. "We're dedicating the next song to you, Winona. We know you'll be back up here, dancing the two-step soon."

As Joe made his way toward their table, the band broke into a bluegrass version of *Werewolves of London*, half the pub howling along.

Winona looked accusingly at Jason and then Chaska. "You knew, didn't you?"

Chaska nodded. "Joe may have mentioned something."

Jason admitted it. "I knew, but I wasn't going to ruin the surprise."

"That's why you kept insisting we come to Knockers."

Then Joe and Rain were there, standing beside them.

Joe handed Win an envelope. "We're all so glad you're going to be okay. If you need anything else, Chaska has promised to let us know."

Rain leaned down, kissed Winona's cheek. "You didn't think we'd let you deal with this by yourself, did you?"

Winona gave them a wobbly smile, tears on her cheeks. "Thank you."

And Jason knew he could never ask Winona to leave this community where so many people loved her.

Chaska stood, motioned to Jason. "I heard you wanted to try climbing. Let's put you in a harness and get vertical."

Winona watched as her brother gave Jason an introductory lesson, showing him how to tie a figure-eight retrace, teaching him the etiquette, explaining how to read the routes on the climbing wall. Then she watched with everyone else as he climbed to the top of the wall on the first try.

Cheers rose from the table.

"Way to go, Chiago!"

Megs sat in Jason's vacant chair. "He moves well."

Megs had no idea.

"He reminds me of my brother. Chaska took a few lessons—and that was it."

Megs placed her hand over Winona's. "He'll be back, Win."

Her words cut through Winona's façade to the ache in her heart, left her fighting not to cry. "How can you be sure?"

"I've spent my entire damned life in the testosterone-soaked world of men. I can tell a good one from an asshole in a minute flat. He's a good one—and he's hopelessly in love with you."

Winona hoped Megs was right.

⸻

IF WINONA COULD HAVE HELD her breath to stop time from passing, she would have. She and Jason spent much of their time over the next few days in bed together. When they weren't making love, they were sharing meals, talking and laughing together, and going for drives in the mountains. It would have been the best staycation ever—if it weren't about to end.

Winona did her best to memorize every detail of his body, his scent, the timbre of his voice, the velvet feel of his skin, his taste. She also took lots of photos of him and selfies of the two of them together. Jason learning to belay. Jason shirtless at the breakfast table. Jason stretched out and asleep on the sofa. The two of them watching the sunset from the parking lot at Moose Lake.

On Monday morning, he got a tour of The Cave. Megs and Ahearn explained how the Team had started with the death of a climbing buddy. They told him where the organization got its funding, how it bought and maintained its specialized equipment, how it operated.

Jason seemed especially impressed by the gear that Chaska had engineered for Team use—and the fact that he'd refused to file patents on any of it. "Chaska is a good man. I doubt many others would make that same choice."

"We're lucky."

Then Jason told them how his only experience with climbers before coming to Scarlet was with people who violated tribal sovereignty to climb on sacred land. "I'm glad there's more to the world of rock climbing than that."

Megs nodded. "I know the type. I'm sorry you've had to deal with them. Sadly, every group has its assholes."

That was the truth.

That afternoon, Jason drove to the wolf sanctuary, Winona giving directions from the passenger seat. She wanted to see how the rescued wolf, wolfdog, and pups were doing, and she wanted Jason to meet Shota.

The animals they had rescued were doing well. The pups had grown. The wolf had just been neutered, and the wolfdog and her pups would also soon be sterilized. Animals that couldn't survive in the wild couldn't be allowed to reproduce.

Winona petted the pups through the fence, while the

mother sulked several feet away. "Aren't you all sweet? They look healthy. Hey, Mama, it's okay."

Jason knelt beside Win. "Hey, guys. Good to see you again."

"I think the mother was abused," Heather said. "She's shy and afraid, but we'll get her through it. She's already putting on weight and being more physically active."

Winona couldn't abide people who abused animals.

Then Heather led them to Shota's enclosure.

The moment Shota saw Winona, he ran to greet her.

Heather unlocked the enclosure and let Winona and Jason enter. "I wouldn't let anyone else do this."

Jason hesitated. "Are we sure this is a good idea?"

"I'll be with you."

"Right. The wolf whisperer."

Shota ran to Winona, so excited to see her that he almost knocked her over.

She spoke to him in Lakota at first, scratching behind his ears and keeping an eye out for Aput, who might feel threatened. "Shota, I want you to meet someone."

Her arm around Shota's neck, she motioned Jason to come forward. "Just walk slowly but confidently. Now, hold out your hand."

Jason did as she asked, and Shota sniffed his hand. When it was clear Shota didn't consider Jason a danger, Winona told Jason he could pet the wolf.

Jason ran his hand over Shota's back, wonder on his face. "My God, I never thought I'd do this. Hey, buddy. You have a little boy named after you now."

They visited for almost a half-hour, and then Aput made an appearance.

"Time to go," Heather said.

"I'll see you again, my friend." But there was an ache in Winona's chest that wouldn't go away.

She had given up Shota, and now she had to give up the man she loved.

———

ON TUESDAY AFTERNOON, Naomi felt strong enough to show Jason her shop, Win and Chaska coming along with the baby. "This case is all my work, but everything else in the store comes from Native artists and artisans around the country. My website gives them national exposure. Most of them have seen a big increase in income."

Jason picked up a sterling silver bracelet with an inlaid image of a monarch butterfly. "The detail here is incredible. You made this?"

Naomi smiled, but it was Chaska who answered, pride in his voice. "She did. My wife is a true artist."

Jason set the piece back in the case. "So, this is your day job and not the camp."

"The camp is just my way of trying to give back to the Lakota community."

It was then Jason spotted it—the silver pendant of a wolf track. When Win was distracted by the baby, he let Naomi know he wanted to buy it as a gift for Winona. It would be something she could touch and hold when he was gone.

Then all too soon, it was Wednesday.

After their usual routine—sex, showers, breakfast—they met with Erin, Colorado Parks and Wildlife's raptor rehabilitation specialist. Erin captured the bird, put a hood on it, and carefully placed it into a large dog crate before loading it into the bed of her truck. "Today is freedom day for you. You are one lucky eagle."

With Winona in the passenger seat, Jason followed the CPW truck up to Pinnacles, an area of ragged cliffs that was ideal habitat for golden eagles. "How does it make you feel when an animal you saved goes back to the wild?"

"It's the greatest feeling." Winona's face lit up. "It's why I do this job. I thank Creator every time. Wait until you see it fly."

Erin drove to the edge of an open meadow, lifted the crate out of the back of her truck, and carried it into the field. There, she waited while Jason helped Winona down from his vehicle and the two of them slowly but steadily made their way to her.

"Winona, would you like to do the honors?" Erin asked.

Winona looked up at Jason. "Jason should do it."

Jason was surprised. "I would love to. Thanks."

He did what Erin and Winona told him to do, opening the door to the crate, lifting the hood from the bird's head, and getting the hell out of the way.

Nothing happened.

"What if it doesn't leave the crate?" he whispered to Winona.

"It will. Patience."

The bird hopped out, took a step, looked around at its surroundings. Then it spread its massive wings and took to the sky, Jason's heart soaring with it.

He let out a breath, in awe of what he'd just witnessed. "God, Win. Look what you've done."

"Make good choices!" Erin called after the eagle, the three of them watching until it had disappeared in the distance.

By the time they were back at Winona's place, it was snowing. Jason started a fire in her wood stove, the two of them cuddling on the sofa, scrolling through the photos on their phones, letting the fire warm them.

"Look! We got photo-bombed by a raven at the lake."

"I love this one." Jason turned the phone so that she could see. "What were you thinking about?"

It was a photo of her at an overlook, the wind in her hair, an expression of what could only be called longing on her face.

Winona's answer put a knot in his chest. "I was wishing I could make that moment last forever."

But they both knew nothing lasted forever.

They kept dinner simple—spaghetti with sauce from a jar and salad—and then Jason packed his duffel bag.

Jason chastised himself for the sadness that had stolen over him. He should be grateful for the past three weeks. He hadn't seen Winona coming, and she'd given him the best time of his life. Besides, they still had tonight.

While he packed out in the living room, she was busy hobbling back and forth to her bedroom, brushing her teeth, combing her hair. When he walked back into the bedroom, she was lying naked like a seductress on the bed, lit candles everywhere.

And you're leaving?

He pulled his T-shirt over his head. "You are beautiful."

They made love after that, their gazes locked as they gave each other pleasure. Afterward, they lay together in a tangle of limbs, Winona's head on his chest.

Out of nowhere, Winona laughed.

"What?"

"I would never have imagined when I ran into you with the cups and the creamer that you and I would end up as lovers. I was *so* embarrassed. I'd just made a fool of myself in front of the hottest guy I'd ever seen—and a Shadow Wolf, too."

He chuckled. "I spent the rest of that day thinking about you."

"You did?"

"Don't act so surprised. Why do you think I agreed to go up to the Cimarron in the first place? I just wanted more time with you."

She sat up, reached beneath her pillow, pulled out a small gift box. "This is for you—a way for you to remember me."

"For me?" He sat up, opened it, stared. In the box sat an exquisite bolo tie clip, a wolf's head made of inlaid semi-precious stones. "A wolf for a Shadow Wolf from the Wolf Whisperer of Scarlet? It's beautiful, Win. Thank you."

"It's one of Naomi's pieces."

"I can tell. I'll wear it with pride." He tucked it carefully back in its box and set it on the nightstand. Then he cupped her face between his palms. "I won't need anything to help me remember you."

Then he made love to her again, drawing it out, making their pleasure last, until the two of them were sated and fell asleep in each other's arms.

Chapter 24

JASON GOT UP BEFORE DAWN, tiptoeing so as not to wake Winona. He skipped the shower, washed his face, brushed his teeth, and made coffee. Then he ate a quick bowl of cereal, cleaned his dishes, and got the gift he'd bought for Win out of his duffel.

He walked into the bedroom and stood there, watching her sleep, memorizing every detail of her sweet face. She looked so peaceful that he hated to wake her. "Winona, angel, it's time for me to go."

This felt wrong. Leaving her felt *wrong*.

She stirred, opened her eyes. "Jason?"

"Hey. I need to hit the road."

It was a fifteen-hour drive to Sells.

She sat up. "I'll make you coffee."

"I already did that. You can stay in bed." He sat beside her. "This is for you."

She looked at him, surprised. "Thanks."

She opened it, drew out the silver pendant on its silver chain. The wolf track was cut out of polished sterling

267

silver, abalone shell beneath it, giving it a shimmer. "It's beautiful. Is it from Naomi's store?"

He nodded. "It's a wolf track from a humble Wolf tracker for the beautiful Wolf Whisperer of Scarlet. Let me put it on you."

She turned, lifted her hair out of the way, while he fastened the clasp.

He kissed her nape. "Let me see."

She ran her fingers over the pendant. "Thank you."

"It looks good on you." There was one other thing. "It will be hard to manage on your own here. You should call Chaska and Naomi. Now that Doug and Star are gone, they have room. You can stay with them for a while."

"They've got Shota, and Naomi isn't healed yet. I don't want to bother them."

"I'm sure they wouldn't be bothered. Promise me you'll think about it."

"I will think about it."

He started to rise, but she stopped him.

"I don't know when I'll see you again. I don't know how to be without you now. But I do know one thing."

"What's that?"

She touched a hand to his cheek. "*Tecihila.* I love you, Jason."

Her words put an ache in his chest. "I love you, too, Win. *Te amo con todo mi corazón.*" *I love you with all of my heart.*

"Say it in O'odham."

He kissed the tip of her nose. "We don't have a word for 'love' in O'odham. We try to show our love through actions."

"You've done that." Her smile couldn't quite hide the anguish in her eyes.

This was hell.

Reluctantly, he stood. "Stay in bed. Stay warm."

"I'll walk you to the door." Winona reached for her crutches, stood, followed him to her front door, where his duffel waited. She disarmed the security system. "Do you want to pack a lunch or something, take an apple, some carrot sticks?"

"I'll be fine." He drew her into his arms, held her close, savoring the feel of her. "I don't want to go, Win. You feel like a part of me in a way that no woman ever has."

"I'm going to miss you so much." She held him tight, finally breaking down, her body shaking as she wept.

He held her for a time, then drew back, tilted her face up to his, kissed her tears away. "Don't give up on us, angel. We'll work this out somehow."

She nodded, smiled through her tears. "Text me along the way. Let me know when you're home again. Good luck tomorrow. I'll pray for you."

"I will." He willed himself to let her go. "Goodbye, angel. *Tom ñei.*"

She smiled again, laughed. "There is no word for 'goodbye' in Lakota."

Jason laughed, too. "Then let's just say, 'until I see you again.' Stay safe. I'll let you know when I'm home."

He must have been stronger than he knew—or incredibly stupid. In the next moment, he did the impossible. He turned away from her, shouldered his duffel, and walked out into the cold, snowy morning.

———

WINONA WATCHED Jason's truck disappear down the street as he made his way toward the highway, her heart feeling like it had been ripped in two. When he was gone, she shut the door, made her way back to her bed, and sobbed into her pillow. But there was only so long a person could cry.

She made herself get up, take a shower, brush her teeth. Then she went into the kitchen to make breakfast. It wasn't easy to do when she needed both hands on her crutches to move around.

A knock.

"Chaska?"

He stood at her back door, concern on his face.

She made her way over to him, checked to make sure the security system was still disarmed, and opened the door. "Hey."

Chaska stomped the snow off his feet and walked inside. "How are you holding up? I was out shoveling and saw his truck drive away."

Winona shook her head, tears filling her eyes. "I miss him so much already."

Chaska drew her into his arms and held her, comforting her like he'd done a thousand times before. "He loves you, Win. It will work out."

"That's what Jason said."

"Come. Sit." Chaska pulled out a chair for her, poured himself some coffee, and sat across from her. "Do you remember when Naomi went to live on the reservation with Doug and Star? She and I were apart for what felt like an eternity, and now we have a new baby boy."

"I remember."

"It was hell. I knew she needed to live with her family, to learn about her heritage. But living without her was hard."

"How did you get through it?"

"One day at a time." Chaska stood. "Here's what we're going to do. You're on medical leave. It can't be easy to manage alone with crutches. Naomi and I are on parental leave. You're going to pack a few things. Then we'll lock up your house, and you'll stay with us for now. You can keep Naomi company, listen to Old Man's stories, and cuddle Shota when Naomi needs to rest."

"I won't get in the way?"

"You're my sister, Winona. You're *never* in the way."

"Thanks." She sniffed back her tears. "I would like that. That's what Jason wanted me to do, too."

"He's a smart man."

While Chaska packed up perishable food and carried it to his place, she threw clothes on the bed and gathered her toiletries. By the time Chaska came back, she was more or less ready to go. He got out one of her bags, helped her pack, then carried the bag outside. "I brought my truck. It's slick out there. I don't want you falling."

He helped Winona into his vehicle, drove around the corner, and walked beside her, carrying her bag, as she slowly made her way to the front door.

Grandpa was there, waiting. He held the door open for her. "Come in out of the cold and have some breakfast with your family. Coffee is on the stove."

JASON WAITED outside the hearing room for the decision, his Wolf brothers with him—at least the ones who weren't on duty. Even Ren, who hadn't yet returned to duty, was there. They'd come to show their support and offer their testimony on his behalf about his work as a Shadow Wolf.

"You're one of the best. There's no way they're going to terminate you, man." Ren rested a hand on Jason's shoulder. "This is just a formality. When you pulled that trigger, it was either kill or be killed."

"We'll see." Jason had expected to be nervous, but he

wasn't. Some part of him had already accepted that this was his last day in uniform.

His mind was fixed on the future—and Winona.

She had sent him a text message wishing him luck. It had included a photo of her blowing him a kiss, her hair tousled from sleep.

If he got fired, he'd pack up, head to Scarlet, and sort out his life from there.

"You seem worried, brother." Ellio cracked open a can of soda. "But you know we'll stand with you, no matter what happens."

"It's not that. I'm not worried."

"Then what is it?" Dale asked.

Jason knew he shouldn't tell them. They were his brothers, which meant that they could be true pains in the ass. But some part of him couldn't hold back. "I met someone in Colorado, a Lakota woman. She's special."

That shut them up—for a moment.

Six sets of eyes stared at him, blinked.

Then they all spoke at once.

"You got pictures? I want to see."

"Yo, man, I knew you'd get over Elena."

"You think she's the one?"

"You in love again, bruh?"

Jason shook his head. "I shouldn't have mentioned it."

"Come on. Just show us a photo. You took photos, right?"

Jason knew they wouldn't give up. He took his phone out of his pocket, scrolled to his favorite photo, and held it up for them.

Ren leaned closer. "Whoa. She's … hot."

Ellio grabbed his phone. "Does she have a sister?"

Milo took the phone next and began to scroll through Jason's other photos. "She is fine. What's her name?"

Jason took back his phone, locked it. "Winona."

He was saved from further idiocy when the door opened, and he was called back inside. He drew a breath, got to his feet, and went to face his fate, the Pack following him inside and taking their seats, while Jason remained standing.

Cal Milford, their division director, sat, hands folded over Jason's file, looking grim. Jason's supervisor, Resident Agent-in-Charge Mick Nez, sat beside Milford, his expression giving nothing away.

It was Milford who spoke. "Agent Chiago, we've carefully reviewed the details of this incident, along with your service record. Crossing the border while on duty and in uniform was a clear violation of our regulations and resulted in considerable and avoidable risk to your life. Further, this infraction caused conflict with our neighbor and ally, the United Mexican States."

Yeah, this was it, his last minutes as a Shadow Wolf.

Milford went on. "However, there are several mitigating factors that we took into consideration. In light of years of meritorious service, this committee has decided that you be reinstated to the Shadow Wolves at your current paygrade."

Jason stood there for a moment, stunned, the Pack cheering behind him.

Nez stood, a broad grin on his face. "It's good to have you back, Chiago."

"Thank you, sir." Jason knew he ought to be smiling like everyone. Instead, he felt … disappointed.

You honestly thought it would be this easy, that they'd fire you, and you'd have an excuse to pack up and go back to Scarlet?

Now he would have to make a choice—keep a deathbed promise to the grandmother who had raised him or claim happiness with the woman he loved.

Remember that Creator doesn't lead us to dead ends. We do that to ourselves. Creator gives us choices.

Sometimes Jason *hated* it when elders were right.

Ren slapped him on the back. "Come on back to my place. Have a beer and join us for supper. Teresa is making *cemait* and stew for dinner. You look like a man who needs to talk."

———

JASON TOSSED BACK his fourth and final shot of whisky. "Then her grandfather held a sweat lodge to pray for her and Naomi, her sister-in-law."

"The one who had the baby."

Jason nodded. "He said, 'A promise is a sacred thing. So is the love of one's half-side.' Then he said it was time for me to break free from my anger toward my sisters so my resentment toward them wouldn't color my decision."

"He sounds like a wise man."

"What does that even mean? How does the fact that my sisters left their people and their culture behind influence my decision?"

"Maybe they hurt you, and you're just determined to show them that you're not like them."

Well, that made too much sense.

"Have you prayed about it?"

"What do you think? Of course, I have." Jason knew he'd had a bit too much to drink, but that was no excuse for snapping at Ren. "Sorry, man."

"Don't worry about it." Ren took a sip of his beer. "Help me understand. Your grandma made you promise not to abandon your O'odham people, and you think that means you can't leave Sells to go live with your Lakota hottie. Am I right?"

"Yeah."

"How does living in another place mean you abandon the O'odham?"

What was Ren's problem? What didn't he understand?

Jason spoke like he was talking to a child. "I wouldn't be here, on the reservation."

Ren laughed. "Being O'odham isn't about where you are. It's who you are. You're an O'odham man through and through. If you leave, you won't be abandoning us. You'll be taking us with you. We're inside you. We'll always be a part of you."

"That's just semant... seman... just word games." Jason wished there was more whisky in his glass. "What about the O'odham kids I coach in basketball? What about the Pack? What about passing on our *himdag* to the next generation?"

Then Teresa stepped out of the kitchen, corn flour on her hands. "You're like a brother to us, Chiago. You know that. You've always had Ren's back. So listen to your sister's advice. You met the woman you believe is your soul mate, and you're going to throw away your happiness and hers to keep a promise."

"It's a promise made on my grandma's death bed."

"Yeah, I got that part. Look at your arm. Does the Man in the Maze stay where he started? Does he just stand there, looking confused like you do right now?"

"Um..." Jason was actually drunk enough to look at his tattoo.

"Life isn't about standing still or staying in one place. It's a journey. Your grandmother knew that. I don't think she meant you to promise that you wouldn't leave the rez. She wanted you to promise to hold onto our ways. Besides, what would she want for you now? She would want the grandson she loved to be happy."

Jason struggled to think this through.

But Teresa wasn't finished. "Ren is right. You can't abandon your people by moving away. Who gives a damn what your sisters did? That's their choice, their journey. As long as you hold true to our beliefs, to our values, you'll carry us with you wherever you go—and pass what you know on to your children. And why do you have to be here *or* there? Can't you go back and forth? Isn't that what roads are for?"

Teresa threw up her hands and walked back to the kitchen, muttering to herself and leaving Jason to stare after her.

Ren cleared his throat. "Brother, I think you've just been told."

———

WINONA WOKE to a buzz from her cell phone. She rolled over, picked it up, read Jason's text message.

Good morning, angel.

Along with the text was a photo of him sitting in his pickup at a gas station, either at dawn or dusk.

Her heart swelled to see him. She saved it to her photo app and replied with a selfie she'd taken with the bear cub yesterday.

Good morning, my love.

This was her new morning routine. Every day began and ended with a text message from Jason, most of them accompanied by selfies or beautiful pictures of the desert or wildlife—roadrunners, a desert tortoise, an elf owl peeking out of a giant saguaro. He also sent emails when he could, and, on his days off, they chatted on the phone or online, sometimes for hours. And still, it wasn't enough.

Jason had been gone for a little more than five weeks now, but it seemed like an eternity since she'd watched him drive away. She missed his face, the sound of his voice, his touch, his scent. She missed sharing meals and unhurried conversations. She missed falling asleep beside him and waking up in his arms.

She missed the sex, too, of course. God, yes, she missed that.

Worse than missing him was the niggling fear that he'd get back into his routine in Sells, surrounded by his Pack and his people, and lose interest in her.

Grandpa had told her to give Jason space. "Let him find his path back to you."

But it was hard to live every day not knowing when they'd be together again.

Jason had told her he was working on their situation. When she'd asked what he meant, he'd said he didn't want to get her hopes up and had kept it to himself.

Long-distance relationships sucked.

Winona sat up, reached for her boot, and slipped her Frankenleg inside. She'd been off crutches and walking for a little more than a week now. Though each step had been painful at first, she was grateful to still have her leg and be more mobile.

She walked to the bathroom and brushed and braided her hair. It was a Saturday, but she wanted to get her rounds at the clinic done early so she could help Naomi at the shop. Shota was almost two months old now and went to work every day with his mother. But when Naomi needed to breastfeed him or work on jewelry or even eat her lunch, someone needed to take care of the baby or cover the sales floor and the register.

Her phone buzzed again.

How is your morning going?

She typed a reply.

It would be better if you were here.

Still in her bathrobe, she started toward the kitchen to make breakfast when her phone buzzed again.

Then open your door and let me in.

"What?" His message made no sense, so she read it aloud. "Open your door and let me ... Oh, God!"

She hurried to the door and looked outside. "Jason!"

He stood there, handsome as sin, huddled against the cold in a denim jacket, a smile on his face.

She punched in the code to deactivate her security system and opened the door.

He stepped inside and drew her hard against him. "God, Win, I've missed you."

She held on tight. "I can't believe you're really here. Am I dreaming?"

He stepped inside, closed the door behind him. "If you are, then we're both having the same dream."

He lowered his lips to hers and kissed her, deep and slow.

Five weeks of longing flared into sexual need in a heartbeat.

"I want you, Jason."

He scooped her into his arms, carried her into the

bedroom, then set her down beside the bed and began to undress. Winona let her robe fall to the floor and removed her boot, then lay back on her bed, feasting on the sight of him.

He stretched out above her and kissed her, the two of them rolling in a tangle of limbs, hands moving hungrily over soft skin, seeking to arouse and please. After so many days apart, there was no need for seduction or finesse.

Jason ripped open a condom packet with his teeth, rolled it onto his erection—and then he was inside her, his hips a piston as he drove himself into her. She came hard and fast, Jason moaning her name as he joined her.

They hadn't yet caught their breath before they started laughing.

Then it hit her. "Did you drive all night?"

He drew her close. "I left Sells yesterday after supper. I was going to leave this morning, but I just couldn't wait."

"How long can you stay?" She wanted to know upfront so she could steel herself.

He grinned. "That's the thing. I was hoping to stay forever."

"You want to stay... *forever*?" Her pulse skipped. "What about your promise?"

Jason's fingers caressed her shoulder. "At the *inipi*, Old Man said something that stayed with me."

Winona couldn't help but smile. "He's good at that."

"He said, 'A promise is a sacred thing. So is the love of one's half-side.' At the time, it seemed impossible to reconcile those two things. But when I left you, it felt … *wrong*. I got back to Sells, and everything was the same—except that nothing was the same. I realized I would never again feel whole without you."

Winona understood. "I felt the same way—as if part of

me was missing. But I don't understand. You said you would never leave your people."

"I didn't leave them. I brought them with me. They're here." He placed her hand over his heart. "They're with me no matter where I go. I'll keep in touch, visit when I can, and do my best to be a voice for them in the outside world."

"What about the Shadow Wolves? What about the Pack?"

"I resigned last Friday. The Wolves understand."

She swallowed, her throat tight. "You gave up a job you loved and moved away from your brothers—for me?"

"I had to make a choice. I chose you."

"Are you going to ask Sheriff Pella for the job he offered you?"

"You're looking at the newest Deputy US Marshal for the Colorado territory."

"What?!" Winona sat up, stunned.

"That's what I've been working on all this time. Staying with a federal agency enabled me to keep my salary and pension. McBride came through for me. He helped broker a deal that gives me time off for ceremonies and enables me to track for other agencies in the state as the need arises. If Megs wants me on the Team, I'm in."

Winona struggled to keep up. "It's like having all my wishes come true at once."

Jason sat up, and took her hand. "I probably should have called and talked with you about it, but I didn't want to disappoint you if things fell through. I just signed the final contract yesterday. Then I packed my shit into my truck and drove here."

"Thank you." Her heart melted to think he'd been in such a rush to be with her again. "It's the best surprise ever."

"I love you, Winona, and I want to spend the rest of my life with you. I want to be the one you reach for at night. I want to be the one who holds you when you're sad or scared or sick. I want to be the father of your children."

Tears filled her eyes. "Jason."

"I know this is all pretty sudden, so if you're not ready to live together, I can find my own place here in—"

She pressed her fingers to his lips, tears of happiness on her cheeks, her heart soaring with the eagles. "Welcome home, half-side."

Epilogue

July 10

WINONA SAT on a bench beside Kat, sheltered by the new sunshade, the two of them watching while Jason, Chaska, Gabe, and the camp counselors guided a rowdy group of O'odham children through the recently rebuilt ropes course. Naomi snapped photographs for the kids to take home, little Shota in a carrier on her back.

Winona watched while Kat's oldest showed the other kids how it was done, fearlessly crossing the high rope, a smile on her little face. "Alissa takes after her father when it comes to climbing, doesn't she?"

"You have no idea." Kat shook her head, her two younger children playing nearby. "She is absolutely fearless at the climbing gym. Last week, she climbed our chimney. I went looking for her and found her sitting on the roof, her legs dangling over the side. I ran for Gabe to help her climb down, but by the time we returned, she was already down."

Winona laughed. "I'd have had a heart attack."

Kat laughed. "I told Gabe he needs to build a climbing gym for the kids in our basement—with lots of padding on the floor."

It was the last day of the first camp session this summer and the first session set aside exclusively for Tohono O'odham kids. Jason and Naomi had worked hard to set this up, building the curriculum around O'odham *himdag* with storytelling, basket weaving, tracking, gardening, and traditional games. Jason knew some of these kids and their parents personally, and it meant the world to him to give something special to his community.

He and Naomi had also set up agreements with O'odham artists—basket weavers, potters, and others—to sell their goods at Tanagila's. Winona had made several weekend trips to Sells with Jason to sign agreements and select stock. It had opened a new income stream for O'odham artists who otherwise had to rely on tourist traffic and the casino to sell their work.

Over at the ropes course, the children lined up for their turns, some of them excited and others clearly afraid, Jason speaking to them in O'odham, while the counselors, Chaska, and Gabe spoke English, doing their best to build the children's confidence. That was the entire point of the ropes course.

The first brave kiddo crossed, a bright smile on his face when he reached the other side to cheers from his fellow campers. Jason cheered, too, helping him to the ground and detaching him from the rope. Winona couldn't understand what he said, of course, but she could see the pride on the little boy's face.

Kat smiled. "He's going to be a wonderful father. Is he excited?"

"He's thrilled. He puts his hand on my belly and talks to the baby every morning when he wakes up."

"How are you feeling?"

"Much better." Winona was starting her second trimester, and the nausea that had plagued her all day for three months was almost gone. "Your advice helped. I nibbled crackers all day and slept a *lot*."

Kat rested her hand on Winona's, sympathy in her gaze. "It's not easy bringing new life into the world."

Another boy crossed the ropes to cheers, but the next child in line began to cry. Jason took her hand, drew her aside, speaking quietly to her while another child went in her place. Soon, she was smiling again.

"It's been almost exactly a year since the fire." Kat glanced around them. "Look at this place now."

A year ago, the wildfire had burned through here, turning the camp to ash and almost taking Chaska, Grandpa, and Gabe from them. It had been devastating for Naomi and everyone in Scarlet Springs. But so much hard work, so many volunteer hours and donations, and so much love had gone into rebuilding Camp Mato Sapa.

Ten new freshly painted cabins dotted the landscape, all of them solar-powered. The ropes course had been rebuilt. A new tipi stood near the fire circle at the center of the camp, and on the other side of the fire circle stood an O'odham wickiup. With Chaska's help, Jason had even built a stone maze so the O'odham kids could have the real-life experience of walking one—getting lost, hitting dead ends, recovering, changing direction.

God, she loved him.

Kat glanced around. "It will be a lot of work getting this place ready for your wedding. Are you nervous?"

Winona glanced down at the diamond solitaire engagement ring Jason had given her when he'd proposed on her birthday in February. "Nervous and excited both."

As soon as the children had boarded the bus and

headed toward the airport, the cleaning crew would clean the cabins for wedding guests, and the party tent with its dance floor would replace this sunshade. It wasn't going to be a big wedding—just friends and family. But there was still a lot to do.

"Are his sisters coming?"

"He didn't invite them, not after they ignored his invitation for the kids to come to camp. One, the oldest, said she wanted her kids raised with mainstream culture."

"That must have felt like a smack in the face."

"Yeah, he was hurt. He had a long conversation with Grandpa and Chaska about it one night. He had to face that his sisters have chosen their own path. If he can connect with his nieces and nephews later, he will."

"I'm sorry." After a few minutes of silence, Kat changed the subject. "Is your dress finished?"

"Yes, and I love it. I can't wait until Jason sees it."

Winona had initially wanted to wear her grandmother's doeskin dress with its beautiful antique quillwork, but Grandpa said it was stained. Also, the thought of wearing doeskin in summer heat didn't hold much appeal. So, she'd tried to find a gown that contained elements of Lakota culture. She'd searched for Native wedding gowns, but she'd found only dresses that looked like they belonged at Woodstock or on the set of a Spaghetti Western. She'd felt consigned to getting a more conventional white dress—until Naomi had connected her with a Lakota woman who made bespoke clothing and was an expert with beadwork.

The result was one of a kind. Sleeveless and made with white silk tulle and guipure lace, its bodice was decorated with Lakota beadwork in purple, green, blue, black, and white that matched the long, quilled earrings she would wear. Strands of white beads attached to the bodice would drape across her upper arms.

"He's not going to be able to take his eyes off you."

The line had dwindled, which was Winona and Kat's signal to help the cooks get lunch on the buffet line. Hungry seven- to twelve-year-olds were a tough bunch.

Kat stood, went to pick up her youngest. "Noelle Yanaha! Have you been eating dirt? You silly girl. Come, Kai. It's time for lunch."

Winona got to her feet, her hand resting on her belly. Six months to go before she'd be able to hold her little one.

———

JASON FUMBLED with his bolo tie as he tried to use the clip Winona had given him. He'd done this a thousand times but was suddenly all thumbs.

"Let me." Chaska took the tie clip, examined it. "Naomi made this."

"It was a gift from Win when I left Scarlet."

Chaska got the tie in place and slipped on the tie clip, then straightened Jason's collar. "You look good, man."

"Thanks." Jason reached for his jacket.

Chaska helped him into it, then smoothed one of Jason's lapels. "I wasn't sure about you at first. Yeah, I knew you were a Shadow Wolf, but there are lots of big, bad men with impressive resumés who don't treat women well. I thought you were engaged and sleeping with my sister. I was wrong. You've been good for Winona. I've never seen her so happy."

"I will do my best to be the man she deserves."

"I know you will." Chaska rested his hands on Jason's shoulders, met his gaze. "You're a good man. I am proud to call you *brother*."

Those words meant more to Jason than Chaska could

know. "You've been Winona's rock since she was a little girl. Thank you for taking good care of her."

The door opened, and Old Man walked in, wearing a white shirt and a bright red quilled vest with yellow designs that had been handed down from his grandfather. In his hands was his Medicine Wheel hair-tie with the bald eagle feather. "Chaska, can you help an old man? This arthritis in my fingers is givin' me trouble. I can't look sloppy at my granddaughter's wedding."

Grandpa was officiating the ceremony.

Chaska took the small ornament and fixed it into his grandfather's hair, adjusting the feathers. "You're good."

From below came the sound of Ren's voice followed by men's laughter. Ren, Gabe, and Zach were standing with Jason today. They'd gotten to know one another pretty well last night at the lodge that Old Man had held for him.

Old Man glanced in the mirror, then looked Jason over, nodding approvingly. "You're lookin' sharp. You're a true warrior. You're gonna be a good half-side to my Winona and a good father to her children."

Funny he should say that… "Thank you."

Grandpa didn't yet know that Winona was pregnant. Winona had only shared that with Naomi and Kat. She'd wanted to keep the baby secret until she was out of her first trimester, when risk of a miscarriage was highest. Jason had been fine with that decision, but for entirely different reasons. He didn't want anyone in Scarlet believing that he was marrying Winona only because a condom had broken.

"I'll get my sacred elements, and then it's time to get up to the camp, eh?"

Ren met them at the bottom of the stairs, drew Jason into an embrace. "Man, you sure clean up pretty. I'm used to seein' you in dusty camo."

Jason hugged him back. "I could say the same about you."

Gabe shook his hand. "Congratulations. Kat and I are so happy for you both."

McBride gave him a bear hug. "I'm so damned happy for the two of you. I knew something was up between you from the start. I asked, and you denied it."

Jason couldn't help but laugh. "Yeah, yeah. I remember."

They climbed into McBride's SUV and made the short drive up to the camp.

Camp Mato Sapa had been transformed. An elegant party tent stood in place of the sunshade. Chairs sat in rows before a table that would act as an altar and hold Old Man Belcourt's sacred elements, large bouquets of bright flowers on either side. Caterers bustled in and out of the Mess Hall. Guests took their seats in the party tent, while uninvited guests sat on the ground or held tailgate parties.

Winona had warned him this would happen. "When Lexi and Austin got married, the whole town came, even those not on the guest list."

Hank, who had just finished his six-month jail sentence, was sitting under the tree with a friend. "That's the man who tracked me the night I drove into the creek."

Inside the tent, the West clan sat together. The Team took up a couple of rows, Kenzie and Conrad holding their new baby boy, Bruce, and Erik and Vicki with their month-old daughter, Molly. Doug and Star and their kids had come from Pine Ridge and were dressed in their finest. Joe and Rain sat with their little girl and Bear, who wore a neat, white shirt rather than buckskin. Ellio, Milo, and Dale had driven up with Ren and sat off to one side.

Jason waved to them, grateful to have some of his Pack brothers back together.

"Don't you look pretty?" Megs said.

"You, too, Megs. A skirt? I've never seen you in a skirt before."

It was denim, but for Megs, it might as well be formal attire.

Megs spread her legs. "It's culottes."

Jason hadn't expected that. "I see."

Ahearn laughed, shook his head. "I can't take her anywhere."

Jason found himself needing space, just a bit of quiet before the ceremony. He walked over to the maze he and Chaska had built, and it hit him. At the age of thirty-eight, he was marrying a woman he loved more than life.

Somehow, he'd found the path to the center.

———

WINONA STOOD in one of the camp cabins where she'd gotten dressed, barely aware of the photographer snapping photos. She drew a breath, then turned to face the mirror. Staring back at her was a Lakota bride, her dark hair pulled away from her face and spilling down her back, quill earrings hanging to her shoulders, her heritage worn proudly on the colorful beaded bodice of a gown with skirts of white silk tulle.

Naomi arranged Winona's skirts and stepped back. "Oh, Win, you look beautiful. Chaska and I are so happy for you."

Kat handed Winona her bouquet of white roses, blue penstemon, lavender, and sage. "Jason is going to be blown away."

Lexi dabbed her eyes. "I'm so happy for you, Win."

Winona glanced around at them, her closest friends.

"Thanks for everything you've done through the years, and thanks for being here today. You're the best."

They looked beautiful, too, the three of them wearing the same gown as Winona but in lavender tulle and without the beadwork. Lexi's had been altered to accommodate her six-month pregnant belly. She and Austin had decided to have another baby after the fire and were expecting a little boy.

Star walked in. "I just have to hug the bride before the cer… Oh, Win! That dress. It's … *stunning*. Look at that beadwork."

"Thank you, Star." She gave Star a careful hug. "I'm so glad you, Doug, and the kids could be here."

"We wouldn't miss it for anything."

Then Chaska stepped inside. "I think we're…"

He stopped, stared, an expression on his face she'd never seen. "Look at you, little sister. Jason is a lucky man. Would the rest of you mind if I had a moment? I think it's time for us to head toward the tent anyway."

Star, Naomi, Kat, and Lexi left Winona with her brother.

For a moment, there was silence. Then they both spoke at once.

"I…"

"I…"

Chaska laughed. "It's your wedding day. You go first."

Winona didn't want to cry and mess up her makeup, but this was important. Her throat tight, she did her best to share what was in her heart. "Thank you for all you've done for me. You took care of me. You made me so many peanut butter and jelly sandwiches. You kept me safe. You chased away the nightmares after Mom died. No sister could hope for a better big brother. You will always be the first boy I loved."

Chaska's brow furrowed, an almost sad look in his eyes. "You will always be the little girl I cherished, the one who looked at me with her big brown eyes and made me want to take on the world just to see her safe and happy. I am so proud of you, Winona. I'm proud of the human being you've become."

Winona's heart seemed to swell until it was almost too big for her chest. But it was time to tell him. "Can I share one last secret with my big brother?"

"Of course."

"I'm three months pregnant."

Chaska gaped at her, then let out a wild howl, lifting her off her feet and spinning her around. "Congratulations! Shota is going to have a little cousin. This is the *best* news. Wait until Old Man finds out."

He set her carefully down. "How are you feeling? What does Jason think?"

Winona smiled, her brother's reaction pretty much what she'd expected. "I was really sick for a while, but I'm fine now. Jason is excited. He's taken good care of me."

"I'm so happy for you both." He pressed a kiss to her temple. "Naomi had a hard time with nausea for a while, too. But you're feeling better?"

"I'm twelve weeks as of yesterday, and the past week hasn't been bad."

"I'm glad to hear it." He glanced at his watch. "We need to go. Your man is waiting. I think all of Scarlet turned up. They're sitting on the ground around the party tent and picnicking in the backs of their pickups."

Winona laughed. "I warned Jason that would happen."

Chaska walked with Winona out of the cabin and toward the side entrance at the rear of the party tent, where her bridesmaids fussed with her gown. And then the music started—Bach's *Air on the G String*.

Lexi turned and gave Winona one last smile before starting down the aisle, Kat following a few moments later.

Naomi glanced back at them. "I love you both."

Then it was just Chaska and Winona.

Winona's pulse quickened as they entered the tent and started up the walk up to the altar together. Looking impossibly handsome, Jason stood with his groomsmen at the front, Grandpa beside them, all of her friends and loved ones rising to their feet.

Later, Winona wouldn't remember the tears that spilled down her face or her nervousness as she walked up the aisle. All she would remember was the love shining in Jason's eyes as they vowed to care for one another all the days of their lives.

WINONA LEANED BACK AGAINST JASON, his arms around her, the two of them watching the clouds drift in front of the stars, her heart so full of happiness it seemed to overflow. Music, conversation, and laughter spilled out of the party tent, the scent of ponderosa pine carried on a cool summer breeze.

It had been a perfect day.

Jason nuzzled her ear. "I can't wait to get you to our hotel so I can strip that gorgeous dress off you and have *married* sex."

Winona liked that idea. "We should say goodbye to our guests and drive Grandpa home. He must be tired."

They had an early morning flight to Mazatlán, so they had booked a suite next to the airport. Jason wanted to share his other homeland with her, so they were honeymooning in Mexico.

"Where is Old Man?"

"He and Jack have been talking all evening. They're new best friends or something." Winona supposed it wasn't that much of a surprise. For two men from completely different worlds, they had a lot in common. "They've been sitting in the exact same spot since we finished dinner."

"Yeah. I see them now." Jason chuckled. "They're still talking."

"Did you see the look on Grandpa's face when we told him I was pregnant?"

"I did." Jason's hand moved to caress her belly through the silk of her dress. "That entire wrinkled-apple face of his turned into one big smile, and that laugh…"

"One minute, he was telling me he was ready to make the journey now that I was settled. The next, he said he had to stick around because he had young people to teach."

"Your grandfather is one of a kind."

"He's what traditionals would call a true Lakota."

"Let's see if he's ready to go." Jason threaded his fingers through hers, and they started back toward the party tent.

Winona saw they were near the maze. "I've never actually walked it, you know. Is it as hard as the kids say?"

"Give it a try."

"Now?"

"Why not?"

Winona found the entrance and set off, trying to find the center. The stone walls were high enough that she couldn't see dead ends until they were before her. Jason watched, laughing, as she retraced her steps several times, twice going all the way back to the beginning. "Another dead end?"

Jason went to stand at the entrance. "Come here. I'll help you."

This time, she walked with him as he guided her at last to the center.

"Woohoo! Journey's end. That *was* hard. I can see how your old ones found the maze to be a metaphor for life's journey—all the twists and turns, not being able to see what lies ahead until you're there. And here we are—the two of us—at the start of our journey together, with a baby coming."

Jason looked into her eyes, his expression now serious. "When you walked down the aisle today, one thing became clear for me."

"What's that?"

"Wherever life takes us from here, Win, *you* are my center."

Then he drew her close and kissed her.

WE HOPE you enjoyed this story. Read on for a special note from the author.

Author's Note

Jason and Winona's story was born out of the fifteen years of my journalism career spent reporting on Native issues. As a journalist, I made a conscious choice to give the voice I had to others, focusing on women in prison and Native peoples. I learned all I could about the challenges these two groups face and did my best to share their struggles with my readership.

From the start, I had two rules for myself when it came to covering Native issues. The first was not to go to any reservation without first being *asked* to come. I did not want to be the stereotypical white journalist who asks questions about the wrong things of the wrong people in the wrong way—and then gets the answers wrong in print.

My second rule was to never go to any ceremony without being invited. I refused to impose myself on people practicing their own beliefs or to make demands of their time. I was an outsider, and I knew it. My job was to report, not to invade.

Then one afternoon, I got a call from a woman in Denver who'd heard from her husband, a Sun Dancer, that the elders wanted me to report on the harassment of Sun Dancers by federal agents.

I dropped everything, hopped in my car, and made the twelve-hour drive over rutted, unpaved roads with a map drawn on a napkin to the Sun Dance site. I had to go off-road to get around a federal van that was blocking access to the site. I covered the story as best I could and, in the process, witnessed an authentic Sun Dance that was being run by a hereditary Lakota Sun Dance chief.

I was one of very few non-Natives there. I ate mutton stew, did my reporting, and volunteered in the first-aid tent, giving elders foot massages. At night, I slept in a tent under a piñon pine, waking every morning around sunrise to the sound of the drums. I was invited to join in the cere-mony, standing under the arbor, smoking the *chanupa* for the first time, learning songs and some of the language. Time became irrelevant. The welcome I experienced was profound.

I did my best to cover the story accurately. As a result, word got around. I got calls from Native people around the country facing problems they wanted me to cover. This effort took me as far north as the Cheyenne River Reserva-tion, where I reported on the Si Tanka riders in the coldest weather I've ever experienced (-60F with wind chill) and as far south as Navajoland in Arizona.

I met Hopi, Cherokee, Diné, Canadian Cree, Quechua, Inuit, and Lakota/Dakota people. I listened to the stories of Native leaders of all kinds—tribal presidents, spiritual leaders, and community activists. I learned from all of them.

In 2005, I found myself in an inipi ceremony with Native spiritual leaders and NASA scientists. Who was pouring water at that inipi? The Sun Dance chief from that first Sun Dance I'd attended. He became a friend, though we have since lost touch.

Over time, I was asked by three spiritual leaders from three different Nations—Hopi, Diné, and Lakota—to act as a bridge between the white and Native worlds. That is a serious request, and it's one that I still try to honor, even though I'm no longer working in journalism. The world needs more bridges and fewer walls.

I have tried to share what I know in a way that is respectful of Lakota and Tohono O'odham traditions, while being mindful of their values. I have deliberately obscured or left out elements of ceremony due to their sacred nature. I have also done my best to avoid stereotypes and "tokenism," bringing to life a contemporary Native couple—plus relatives—who might live down the street in Anytown, USA. Any mistakes I've made concerning customs and language are my own.

I offer this story with respect and gratitude and in the hope that this broken wheel of our land can be healed, bringing us together as one.

Mitakuye Oyasin. All my relations.

Pamela Clare
April 21, 2021

A portion of the proceeds of this book are going to Friends of Pine Ridge Reservation. I encourage you to visit their website and give generously.

Thank You

Thanks for reading *Breaking Free*. I hope you enjoyed Jason and Winona's story. Follow me on Facebook or on Twitter @Pamela_Clare. Join my reader's group on Facebook to be a part of a never-ending conversation with other Pamela Clare fans and get inside information about my books and about life in Colorado's mountains. You can also sign up to my mailing list at my website to keep current with all my releases and to be a part of special newsletter giveaways.

Also by Pamela Clare

Contemporary Romance:

Colorado High Country Series

Barely Breathing (Book 1)

Slow Burn (Book 2)

Falling Hard (Book 3)

Tempting Fate (Book 4)

Close to Heaven (Book 5)

Holding On (Book 6)

Chasing Fire (Book 7)

Romantic Suspense:

I-Team Series

Extreme Exposure (Book 1)

Heaven Can't Wait (Book 1.5)

Hard Evidence (Book 2)

Unlawful Contact (Book 3)

Naked Edge (Book 4)

Breaking Point (Book 5)

Skin Deep: An I-Team After Hours Novella (Book 5.5)

First Strike: The Prequel to Striking Distance (Book 5.9)

Striking Distance (Book 6)

Soul Deep: An I-Team After Hours Novella (Book 6.5)

About the Author

USA Today best-selling author Pamela Clare began her writing career as a columnist and investigative reporter and eventually became the first woman editor-in-chief of two different newspapers. Along the way, she and her team won numerous state and national honors, including the National Journalism Award for Public Service. In 2011, Clare was awarded the Keeper of the Flame Lifetime Achievement Award for her body of work. A single mother with two sons, she writes historical romance and contemporary romantic suspense at the foot of the beautiful Rocky Mountains. Visit her website and join her mailing list to never miss a new release!

www.pamelaclare.com

Made in the USA
Middletown, DE
14 July 2023

35043162R00187